Green Grow

the

W0008015

Shamrock

By

Amy Carter

CREMER PRESS

First Published in Great Britain in 2000 by
Amy Carter
PO Box 52
Clitheroe, Lancs
UK BB7 4GP

Email: aseaswim@aol.com
Web: http://amysbooks.freeyellow.com

ISBN 1 898722 24 2

AMY CARTER

Amy Carter, was born in Radcliffe, Lancashire, and was an only child until aged fifteen, when her sister was born. Her mother was a cotton mill weaver of Irish descent, who wrote a novel at the age of eighteen, and later some delightful poetry.

Amy and her husband have been together for nearly forty years. Both were previously divorced, and both have had eight children, five from their own union.

Apart from Lancashire, they have lived in Devonshire and Southern Ireland. When living in Ireland, Amy learned the truth, after seeing photographic evidence, of the dreadful persecution formerly perpetrated against Irish Catholics.

These facts, never taught in English schools, together with her Irish ancestry, inspired her to write '**GREEN GROW THE SHAMROCK**'.

CONTENTS

CHAPTER 1 .... No place like home

CHAPTER 2 .... Abide with me

CHAPTER 3 .... Days of Desperation

CHAPTER 4 .... Come back to Eireann

CHAPTER 5 .... The living and the dead

CHAPTER 6 .... As the years roll on

I dedicate this book to my loved ones Karl, Rebekah and Robert, for their invaluable assistance and encouragement.

CHAPTER 1
NO PLACE LIKE HOME

Kathleen O Sullivan lay wide-eyed on her bed
listening to the dawn chorus. This first day of July 1880
promised to be one she would never forget.

Her shapely young body, newly blossomed into
womanhood, rebelled against the heat, clothed as she was in a
long-sleeved flannelette nightgown. She shared a loft
bedroom of the small farm cottage with her younger sisters.
Three-year old Molly slept beside her, whilst ten year old
Eileen, and Sheelagh aged eight, lay together fast asleep at the
other side of the room. James, their thirteen-year-old brother
shared the other loft bedroom with her parents.

Her father, Daniel O Sullivan, a man of his word, had
promised to take James and herself to see the sea for the first
time in their lives. Kathleen was looking forward with joyful
anticipation to the long journey, twenty miles it would be,
over the mountains from their home village of Kilgarvan to
Bantry Bay, that glorious part of God's earth in the remote
South West corner of Ireland. Kathleen had never been more
than six miles away from her home, and she was so excited as
she thought of seeing her Grandmother O Sullivan for the first
time since her grand-daddy had died seven years ago. It was
then that her grandmother had gone to live with her widowed
sister at Ballylickey on the shores of Bantry Bay.

Gently lifting herself into a sitting position, careful
lest she should disturb Molly, she leaned over and deftly lifted
a lock of hair from her sister's forehead. "Will my children be
beautiful like Molly?" she mused. "I'll be sixteen in October,

1

I wonder if I'll be married when I'm eighteen like my mammy was?"

The shrill cry of the first cock crowing disturbed her meditations. Getting out of bed she stood up and removed the offensive nightgown, glad to be rid of it. Quickly she reached for the new brown cotton dress she had so painstakingly and skilfully made herself. It had a plain bodice, a neckline that was not too high, like her other dress, short puff sleeves and a long full skirt. She was justly proud of her needlework.

Quietly she crossed the room, passed through the door to the small landing, then descended the wooden steps with nimble bare feet to the kitchen below. Unlike the divided loft, the ground floor of the cottage was all one room. The back door was near to the bottom of the steps; the front door directly opposite. The two small windows allowed very little light to penetrate beyond the thick stone walls. An open fireplace, with an arched chimneybreast, almost filled one side of the room, and blocks of peat and logs were piled high at each side of the hearth.

As Kathleen came down the steps her first thought was for the nine bonhams lying with the sow. Were they all alive? Yes they were! "You've been a good mammy not lying on any of your babies in the night," she commended the sow with a sigh of relief.

Because the weather was so hot, the top half of the back door had been left open all night, she picked up a pail and milking stool and pushed open the bottom half. Walking outdoors all her senses drank in the beauty of the familiar scene. The rock-strewn rugged Kerry mountains, silhouetted against the advancing golden sunlight, rose up like brown, green and grey sentinels into the cloudless blue sky, and formed the lush green valley through which flowed the clear sparkling waters of the river Roughty. A white mist, lying low across the valley, induced in the early morning stillness a sense of unreality. Delighting in the softness beneath her feet of the dew-laden shamrock with tiny bright green leaves, she walked to the small field where a black and white cow stared at her with a solemn long face.

"You can't be sad today Dolly," she murmured to the cow mischievously, as she placed the pail beneath its udders.

The beast shook her head to remove the fly pests from around her eyes.

"No Dolly, you mustn't be sad today," Kathleen repeated, as she positioned the stool and started milking.

She began to think of the things she was going to take for the journey, the oatcakes she mustn't forget those, and the bastable bread, and some for grandma, and the crochet mat she had made. It seemed impossible to believe that she was going to stay the night at Ballylickey, it would be the first time in her life that she had slept away from home. She stared at the milk rising in the pail whilst resting her head against the belly of the cow, in her happiness she stroked her forehead affectionately along Dolly's warm soft hide.

Kathleen watched as James came out of the cottage to fetch some water from the well. He was a handsome boy with dark curly hair, who worked hard on the farm, being keen to learn all the skills his father was able to teach. He walked over to the donkey and car to examine the harness, as if wondering whether it would stand the strain of the long hard journey?

"I do hope daddy will be happier today," Kathleen thought. Times are so hard and he has been worrying so much lately.

She finished the milking and lifting the pail returned to her exuberant mood, kissing the cow on the side of the neck, "Thanks be to God for the beautiful milk Dolly, might see you tomorrow," she announced, laughing to herself as she walked back to the cottage.

Encountering James by the door she inquired "Is mammy awake?"

"Yes," he replied as he knelt down on the grass by a bowl of water preparing to wash himself.

"Mammy said you must wear your best trousers, you can't go looking all raggy; they'll run you out of Bantry town. I wish she was going with us!"

"Don't you be worrying about me," her mother said as she emerged through the doorway; "and you must remember to wear your bonnet my girl and you your cap James, the sun will get at your head and make you sick if you don't."

In spite of her thirty-four years and the hard life she led, Bridie O Sullivan had not lost the charm of youth. Her thick dark brown hair fell in natural waves and ringlets about her face, her green eyes, high rounded cheekbones and slightly tilted nose, were features that marked her as a classic beauty of the Celtic race. Her eldest child Kathleen was formed in her image and likeness; mother and daughter shared the same zest for life and a love of nature, which their frugal living could not take away.

"Are you taking some water with you Kathleen?" she asked.

"No we don't need to, daddy said there'll be plenty up in the mountains, the thunderstorm we had the other day has swelled the rivers."

As Daniel came down from the loft James asked, "How long will it take us to get there, Daddy?" a question he had asked many times during the past few weeks.

"Well, 'tis twenty miles, so if we travel at four miles an hour how long will it take?"

"Oh!" the boy studied, "err?"

"Come on now lad, you should know the answer to that one."

"Five hours," Kathleen said.

"Why did you tell me, I knew the answer all the time," James scolded his sister.

"Come on now, you'll never get there at all if you don't stop all this talking, the bread and wholemeal cake is here sliced ready." Their mother indicated a bundle she had tied up in a piece of cloth, then she almost tripped over a bonham that squealed and ran out through the back door.

"What time is it with your black marble clock Mammy?" James asked as he bent his curly head to kiss her goodbye.

"Tis a quarter to six. Have you got your cap? Tell grandma I pray to the saints for her."

Daniel held Bridie in his arms, kissing her forehead. "We'll be back tomorrow, take good care, say goodbye to the girls."

He was tall and lean, his blue eyes and handsome weather-beaten face expressed a gentle, kind and understanding nature, which in no way detracted from his manliness. Bridie and he quiet and undemonstrative, were deeply in love. Separation, even for only one night was for them a very rare occurrence.

They moved outside to where James had harnessed the donkey, placing in the car the few bundles and a small bag of potatoes for Daniel's mother. The sides of the car consisted of box-shaped strips of wood, almost three feet deep, the back and front flaps were pegged into place and could be let down for loading. A loose board placed across the car formed a seat. On it was a sackcloth straw-filled cushion; it would hold the three of them. The wooden wheels had been soaked in water for two days, so they would not contract due to the hot weather and allow the iron rims to come off.

"Can I drive daddy?" James asked.

"Yes you can, till we start to climb."

The barefoot boy climbed up and sat in the middle of the seat and took hold of the reins, back straight, head held high, he proudly waited to start.

"Goodbye Mammy," Kathleen hugged her mother

tightly.

"Goodbye now, 'tis a good time you'll be having, don't tire the ass. Bring me back some shells from the shore of the sea."

Kathleen climbed up to take her place beside her brother; she looked very lovely in a bonnet of stiffened cotton made by her mother in the same brown material as her dress.

"Come on Billy," James urged "gid up me boy. Goodbye Mammy."

The three of them waved back as they began the journey. No one spoke until they had reached Kilgarvan, half a mile from their home, and had turned southwards away from the village at the start of the straight and long boreen, leading towards the Sheehy Mountains. The iron-rimmed wheels screeched and grated whenever they came into contact with the stones, which were sunk down into the beaten earth. James coaxed the donkey into a trot.

"Mammy said you mustn't tire him, he'll never pull us up that big hill." Kathleen spoke apprehensively, indicating the gradual slope in the distance ahead, the rock face of a mountain rising sheer to the right of the road.

"Tis all right Kathleen," her father assured her, "Billy has four good legs, we'll let him make good time while he can."

The lane was banked high on each side with shrubs and wild flowers, sweet scented honeysuckle, hawthorns, wild deep red fuchsia and purple foxgloves.

Half an hour later they were moving slowly and steadily up the narrow mountain road, gazing down on the vast and sweepingly splendid scene, some three hundred feet below. The panorama of the rich green boulder-strewn valley, dotted with white stone cottages and a few sheep and cattle, gradually fell away to their left as they continued to ascend.

"There is a tunnel, Daddy isn't there?" James asked.

"Yes, it's nearly at the top of this road. I've only

been here twice before."

"Look how high we have to go yet, how did they manage to build a road so high up in the mountain Daddy?" the boy marvelled.

"The famine relief workers built it for the government, they were paid four pence a day to help them to buy food, but many of them died. The work was very hard and they didn't have enough to eat."

James's curiosity got the better of him, "Tell us about the famine daddy."

"It was terrible! I was only six years old in black '47, but I remember it very well. Thousands of people from all over Ireland died. All the potatoes went bad and they smelled awful. We ought to walk now to give Billy a rest," he said changing the subject.

They climbed out of the bumpy car, glad to stretch their limbs and to relieve the pressure on their buttocks. They walked on in front of the donkey with James holding the reins.

"I think it will be about a quarter past eight now,"Daniel said as he studied the angle of the sun. "We're making good time!"

After they had passed through the rock tunnel James had been so anxious to see, they rounded a corner.

"Oh look daddy," the children shouted both together, as they came upon a cascade of sparkling clear water tumbling down the side of the rock face.

Kathleen was the first to cup her hands to drink from the deliciously cool mountain stream. She splashed her face and took a deep breath filling her lungs with the fresh mountain air. "Let Billy drink," she said as the ass moved forward.

They all screamed with laughter as his loud braying echoed across the valley, he lifted his head, his big fat tongue and lips coming into action to gulp down the water.

"Daddy looks so happy now," thought Kathleen "I wish he could be like this all the time."

They stayed to rest, sitting on the low stone parapet enjoying the wonderful view over a thousand feet above the valley, with Carran Mountain rising high at the other side. They were fascinated as they watched the waterfall cascading down under the path, then rushing on down to the valley far below. Resuming the journey and taking turns to ride in the car they stopped to look at a deserted cottage with its two small out buildings.

"Who lived here daddy, where have they gone?" The children wandered around, wondering what they would see.

"Come away now," Daniel called to them, "those people probably died in the famine."

"How awful," Kathleen shuddered, "please God we never have to starve."

Reaching the highest point of the narrow trail they began the descent to the valley and the road, which would lead them to the hamlet of Ballylickey by the shore of Bantry Bay.

Totally captivated by the beauty and the grandeur of her surroundings, Kathleen felt literally on top of the world. What if she could fly like the herons they were watching, down the big long valley, down to her grandma and the great blue sea beyond! Only another ten miles and they would arrive.

The widow Mary O Sullivan and her sister Maggie busied themselves in the tiny cottage on the bank of the Coomhala River. Daniel's letter had said July 1st, and this was the day. Every ten minutes or so Mary would go to the

8

door, followed by her black and white collie dog. Standing with her hand shading her eyes from the sun, she would gaze along the road towards the mountains. Her eyes still sharp in spite of her age, looked for some sign of her eldest son and her two grandchildren.

At last her vigil was rewarded and her old heart leapt in her breast. The donkey trotted at a fast pace towards her, and Kathleen and James waved excitedly. Daniel pulled on the reins to halt the donkey; jumping down from the car he enfolded his precious mother in his arms. She was speechless with joy, and after hugging the children she walked into the cottage with her son, their arms around each other.

Having enjoyed the rest and a good feast of stirabout, made from fine yellow meal and buttermilk, Kathleen and James mounted the donkey car again. Their grandmother gave them instructions as to how to get to Bantry town. Billy trotted along the coast road at James's bidding. The view across the magnificently beautiful bay, surrounded by the green hills and mountains, far exceeded Kathleen's wildest expectations.

Arriving at Bantry town they tethered Billy to a post in Wolfe Tone Square. Having a whole penny each to spend, they felt rich and important as they inspected the wares in the New Street shops. They bought two cream buns each for two farthings and tucked the six farthings change safely away. They would spend them later.

Walking up Bridge Street to where the road crossed over a tumbling wide stream, they climbed up to the top of the town. They walked around the hospital and the convent and looked out from this commanding vantage point towards the sparkling blue sea beyond, then settled down on the grass to admire the wonderful view. Kathleen removed her bonnet.

James bullied her until she put it back on, "Mother said you'll be sick if you don't wear it."

Wondering about Billy, they decided to hurry back

down the steep streets to the square below. Finding him grazing peacefully, they left him again and walked to the beach where they paddled their dusty hot feet in the cool salt water.

Kathleen noticed a small graveyard by the edge of the shore and she read the names on the tombstones. Her own name O Sullivan was there along with O Brien, McCarthy, O Shea, O Leary, O Mahony and O Hea. "When I die James, will you bury me here, she sighed!

James laughed at her seriousness, "You're not going to die silly. Come on, I'll race you back to the square."

They rode back to Ballylickey and again they went down to the shore, ran along the golden sands, climbed over the rocks, collected sea-shells for their mother and examined the funny seaweed in their hands.

"If only I could stay here much longer," Kathleen said wishfully.

That night as she lay on a straw mattress on the floor in a corner of her great Aunt's cottage, her skin burning from the heat of the day's sun, she listened, half asleep, to snatches of the quiet conversation between her father and his mother.

"You don't think they'll really take it?" she heard her grandmother say.

"Yes I do. They're collecting all the small ones together. What can I do Mammy?" her father whispered.

Kathleen heard the question but did not understand the meaning behind it, and her mind being filled with the happiness of the day, she soon fell soundly asleep.

As the battering ram swung with thunderous force against the thick stone wall of the cottage the crowd gave out a raucous roar of fury and disdain.

In the foul smelling suffocating interior the occupants of the ill-fated dwelling trembled and cowered, they were about to be evicted from their home.

Kathleen stood in the middle of the room her eyes closed tightly, clenched fists pressed over her ears. Her father and James stood by her, both of them shaking with fear and anger. Her mother crouched on the floor clutching Molly to her breast, Eileen and Sheelagh knelt at each side of her, the four dark heads bent together.

"Don't be frightened now, don't be frightened, don't be feared," their mother sobbed, she herself trembling more than ever as the deafening bedlam increased.

The day they had dreaded had arrived. They were being forced to leave the pitifully small farm where, for the past seventeen years, Daniel and his wife had scratched a meagre living from the soil. Lord Cecil Rothmere, a wealthy English aristocrat, had always exacted an extortionate rent, now he wanted the farm for himself, plead as they might he had no thought for mercy.

The sledgehammer thudding continued relentlessly against the wall. The crowd of angry villagers jeered at the police and the red coat soldiers who surrounded the cottage. Fourteen Irish ruffians, known as the emergency men, had erected a tripod of poles from which they had slung, by a thick rope, a large wooden battering ram to break down the wall. The crowd roared their disapproval each time they wielded the object of devastation.

The elaborate ostentation and unnecessary force used to remove these simple, defenceless people from their humble abode was hypocrisy in the extreme. It was indeed an attempt to make the innocent appear guilty of some crime, a fabricated effort to justify the abominable act.

"Once more now lads," yelled the landlord's agent above the din, "we'll get the bastards out."

Daniel had been determined to resist were it even only as a token. He knew that thousands of other Irish peasants had shared the same fate, now it was happening to himself and his loved ones. He had boarded up the two tiny windows and the narrow doors in the early hours of the morning, his family being imprisoned in the shelter they so earnestly wanted to keep.

The dust from the crumbled stone started to choke them, the children began to howl as the bailiff's henchman climbed through the hole they had made. Others followed him - villainous cowardly ruffians who were highly paid to execute the dastardly deed.

The only candle in the cottage had fizzled out an hour ago, now the dust particles were silhouetted as the light from the warm October sun came streaming through the gaping, ugly, hole in the wall.

"Daddy the stools, don't let them take the stools," James cried as he lunged forward attempting to rescue the precious furniture, that one of the invaders had picked up to throw outside.

The man succeeded in slinging it out, pushing the boy down on to the rubble and cursing him loudly. The furniture had been used to barricade the doors, now the family sought to protect vehemently their few possessions, which had suddenly become so important to them all. The doors were broken down and trampled underfoot. The crowd continued to curse and jeer.

Quickly Bridie was on her feet desperately trying to help her husband to salvage what they could. "Kathleen take the skillet!" she called. "Eileen fetch the kish and blankets. Don't forget the blankets!"

As they all rushed around in total chaotic confusion Daniel and Bridie struggled to get the table out through the narrow front doorway.

"It won't go through" sobbed Bridie.

"Yes it will, oh yes it will!" Daniel in his frustration and bitterness raised his booted foot and smashed off one of the legs.

"Now it'll go through, won't it?" He shouted venting all his spleen on the table as he forced it, now minus one leg, through the doorway, sending it flying as far as his strength would allow.

Then he stepped outside his home for the last time, with Bridie following close behind. Standing near to the doorway with his back to the wall he looked up for a short while across the green valley to the blue sky beyond. Heaving a great sigh, his head fell forward burying his face into Bridie's thick dark hair. He began to weep. Uncontrollable sobs shook his tall manly frame as all the pent-up emotion and dire helplessness overcame him.

To have his home and the land on which he had toiled for so long torn away from him so cruelly. To know that the future held no hope, no way to feed and shelter, or to provide for those he loved. Where could they go, what could they do, how could they face tonight, tomorrow, and every other day after that?

The angry villagers of Kilgarvan, who knew him so well, became silent. They began to turn away with tearful eyes, unable to look upon his grief. His persecutors stomped around, obviously embarrassed at the sight of the weeping man. The bailiff strutted his horse pretending not to have seen him; he gave orders for the dismantling of the apexed poles.

The captain of the Welsh Fusiliers marched his men off, with the police following close behind. Their infamous work finished, many of them were away to the nearest alehouse. The priest, Father Murphy left the scene, head bent as if intent on some urgent errand.

Kathleen stood outside the cottage where she was born, the heavy iron skillet cooking pot hanging from her hand. The memory of her father's weeping would be indelibly imprinted on her heart and mind for as long as she lived. Throughout the day she had hoped and prayed for a miracle to save their home, never really believing they would be put out. She stood head bowed, trying to avoid looking at her father and the chaos surrounding her beloved home.

This year of 1880, like the one before it had been a good one for the English landed gentry and the absentee landlords. Throughout Ireland thousands of small farms and properties had been taken over, the families mercilessly evicted and left with nowhere to go. Whether they had paid the high rent, it mattered not; one class only ruled, and that was not the very much under-privileged and pitifully poor, to which the O Sullivan family and the majority of villagers belonged. Land inherited from their ancestors, had now been taken from them by their Imperial masters.

Kathleen raised her head at the sound of hammering; watching as though stupefied as one of the men nailed planks of wood across the cottage doorway. Should there be any attempt by the family to go back inside, it would constitute an act of 'breaking and entering'.

The sun was fast disappearing behind the mountains, leaving the family to face the cold autumn night without a roof over their heads. Daniel's brother, Seamus and his red-haired wife, Maureen, had stayed with their loved ones to do whatever they could to help. Suppressing their chagrin and hatred for the persecutors, the two of them started to load the donkey car with the oddments and the few items of furniture; broken or not, what did it matter?

Taking Kathleen's arm, Maureen gently led her niece to where the rest of the family now stood, away from the cottage. Their faces were completely devoid of all expression, and each had head and shoulders bowed, numbed

14

with shock; all were filled with despair and disbelief.

The dark-haired handsome Seamus, almost identical in appearance to his nephew James, looked around bewildered, not really knowing whether he had finished loading the car or not. James walked towards him and taking hold of the reins began to lead the donkey away. It was a signal for the pathetic group to leave.

Daniel lifted the little child Molly to his shoulder, and reaching out blindly for the hand of his wife, began to follow behind the donkey and car. The children whimpered but no one spoke as they slowly made their way along the boreen to the village. Small groups of people stood in doorways watching them silently as they approached and passed by, on their way to the cottage in the street where Seamus and Maureen lived with their three little ones.

Seamus broke the silence, "Come in lad," looking at his now homeless older brother and choking on the words. "You're welcome to what we have."

Leaving all their worldly goods piled up outside, Daniel and his family sadly entered the tiny two-roomed cottage.

Immediately inside the front and only door, a steep wooden open staircase rose to join a gap in the bedroom floor. The bedroom had a polished apexed wooden ceiling fixed under a slated roof; there were two small windows back and front in the thick stone walls, and a small fireplace. A large iron bedstead with a straw-mattress and two straw-mattresses on the floor, each covered with grey blankets, were the only bedroom furnishings. The downstairs room also had small windows back and front, but had a larger fireplace than the room upstairs, with bars across to hold the cooking pots. The furniture consisted of two wooden chairs and a table, with another mattress laid on the floor underneath the stairs. Bits of straw were strewn around the cold stone floor. There was no running water or any sanitation facilities.

A white calico curtain hung against the front window, and Seamus lit the oil lamp on the window ledge. Mattresses were lifted from off the donkey car and placed on the stone floor wherever they would fit, and a cot was made up under the table for little Molly. The family would sleep here tonight, that would soften the blow just a little – tomorrow would be another story – sufficient unto the day is the evil thereof!

Daniel awoke, as he usually did, at first cockcrow. His head was aching and finding himself in strange surroundings, for a moment he wondered where he was. Then a dreadful fearfulness gripped at his heart as he recalled the events of the previous day. It was his custom to thank his Lord each morning as he welcomed each new day, but now his thoughts were racked with confusion and anguish. Lulled into insensitivity by the ale he had drunk the night before in the company of his friends, as he attempted to drown his sorrows, and try to forget the cruelty and the injustice, he now faced the inevitable rude awakening.

Slowly, holding his head, he pulled himself up from his bed on the floor, and staggering to the door he went outside to urinate. In the cold light of dawn he could barely see Billy the donkey tethered to a post at the other side of the street where the grass was thicker. He shivered and quickly went back inside carefully striding over his sleeping children. He could not help but smile to himself as he listened to his brother snoring upstairs, the old iron bedstead creaking loudly each time he and his wife turned over.

Lying down again beside his wife, Daniel tried to gather his thoughts. He remembered that Mary McCarthy had offered to care for Eileen and Sheelagh, she was Bridie's childless lifelong friend, and he knew she would look after them well. Maybe Seamus and Maureen would let Kathleen stay with them, he could not bear to think of his beautiful girl, of whom he was so proud, having to suffer without a home.

How long will it be before we have another place he wondered? "We'll go to England to my brother Dennis as soon as we can, we must write a letter to tell him what has happened, that's what we'll do," he determined.

Two hours later Patrick O Donoghue came to tell them the men were starting to build a 'sod cabin' on a piece of vacant land close to the village. An area of ground equal to the size of the cabin was being dug to a depth of two or three feet until the subsoil was reached. Then the loose earth would be piled up around to form a mound, leaving a narrow gap for the door. On top of this was to be placed a wall of turf sods, grass side down, built to a pointed apex at each side. Straight timbers and trees were to be laid across from wall to wall to form a roof and these overlaid with long strips of turf overlapping, grass side down. A hole would be left in the roof above a hearth stone to allow smoke from the fire to escape. A very small window in the wall at the back would let in the light. This dismal dark dank hole in the ground would be 'Home Sweet Home'.

The November rain poured down incessantly and the bitter cold wind blew, lashing the water through the cabin doorway and forming puddles on the beaten earth floor. Try as she might, Bridie could not get a good fire going to keep herself and little Molly warm. The peat had become damp and would not burn up, it just smouldered and the smoke swirled around instead of rising up and out through the hole in the roof. It was getting dark outside and darker inside. Unable to see clearly Bridie laid aside her crochet work and lit the lamp on the table in the middle of the cabin.

In the increased light she became more conscious of the black rats running around close to the wall. Sometimes their beady eyes shone and she watched fascinated as one of them sat up on its hind legs apparently cleaning itself. "Daniel where are you?" she whispered, "please come home."

"Daddy coming mammy, daddy catch fish," said Molly sitting up on the trestle bed.

As she did so her father and brother came sliding down on the mud through the doorway, both of them soaked to the skin. Shivering and shaking, they both went over to the smouldering fire.

"Look Mammy" said James holding up a large dead trout, the blood congealed in its gaping mouth.

"Oh you caught one!" exclaimed his mother recoiling at the sight.

"What's happened to the fire?" Daniel asked trying to kindle some life into the damp embers.

"Why are your trousers so wet? Take them off both of you," Bridie scolded. "You're going to get your death of cold."

"James slipped down the banking, I tried to pull him back and we both fell into the river," Daniel explained. "That water was terrible cold, it fair took our breath away."

"We've got some good news for you Mam," James chirped in.

"Oh have we got another place?" Bridie gasped taking hold of Daniel's arm, her face shining with expectation.

"No it isn't that," Daniel replied looking down at her with a wistful expression. "It's Kathleen, she's going to work for Squire Townsend at the big house. She'll be working in the kitchen and they will pay her one whole shilling every Saturday, and she says she is going to give it to us."

"Oh God be praised, that is good news! A nice warm bed to sleep in she'll have, and good food to eat. How did she manage to get the job?"

"Squire's wife heard about us being evicted and she

wanted to help. You see not all the English are bad, some of them have good hearts." Daniel replied.

"Where are my trousers mammy?"

"In the box, I'll get them for you."

As James walked over to his straw mattress, raised up on planks of wood, one of the rats gave a piercing scream.

"Leave it lad."

"I'm not touching it," the frightened boy called back at his father, at the same time jumping up and kneeling on the bed his head hanging down dejectedly. He was cold and miserable; water dripped from the black sodden roof onto his bed, and the air was full of the smell of the soaking soil, vegetation and smouldering peat.

As he took off his wet clothes his mother came over to him, and seeing the look on his face, she put her arms around him. There was a long cold night ahead with nothing to do but watch the flickering fire and the flames making weird shadow patterns on the black walls, and to listen to the wind howling and whistling outside.

Daniel took hold of the trout on the table and began to chop off the head and the tail. Having done so, he went outside to bring in the old iron bowl full of rainwater, which he poured into the skillet. He then placed the fish in the water, hanging the skillet above the fire suspended on an iron bar, supported by bricks at each side of the hearthstone.

"That'll be good to eat for supper," Bridie said, "I'm so hungry. When will Kathleen be moving to the Squire's house?"

"On Sunday after mass," Daniel replied. "Did you know that Michael O Shea is going to America soon, and Betsy Houlihan might be going too? There'll be nobody left in Ireland soon, everybody's going abroad. We must all go to Seamus's tomorrow, Kathleen's going to write to my brother Dennis in England."

The next day was Friday and the fine bright crisp

morning was all the more appreciated after the gales of the previous day. Daniel and Bridie made their way with James and Molly to Seamus's.

As they entered, Kathleen rushed to embrace her mother. "Oh Mammy I'm going to work," she said smiling. Then she covered her face with her hands.

"What's the matter child?" her mother inquired anxiously.

"I'm frightened mammy." she sobbed. "I won't know what to do at the Squires, I'll be doing everything wrong."

"Don't worry, you'll be all right, they won't expect you to do everything at once, will they Daniel?" she asked, seeking assurance.

"No of course not," Daniel reassured them both. 'Tis nothing to be feared of." Kathleen you should be glad you're going."

"I am, but it's the china cups and glass things they have, I'm so frightened I'll drop them."

"Well you'll just have to be extra careful won't you?" her father retorted, with an impatience not at all like his usual self. "Did you get the paper and the envelope for the letter?" he asked, as he broke into a fit of coughing.

"Your daddy and James fell into the river yesterday, they were both soaked to the skin, and your daddy hasn't been feeling very well," Bridie spoke gently to her daughter.

"You don't want to be catching cold now do you?" her sister-in-law Maureen said joining in.

"Now don't you worry Maureen, we're all right," Daniel assured her. "Kathleen is going to write the letter to Dennis. Have you got the address?"

"Yes it's here in the jug. There it is now," she passed the scrap of paper to Kathleen. "Tell your Uncle Dennis that we want to come as well won't you, as soon as he can find a job for your Uncle Seamus and a place for us to live."

"Yes I will, I've got a pencil and paper here, what do

you want me to write Daddy?"

"Put Dear Uncle Dennis... 'Err" he paused looking with a blank expression at his daughter. "Err just tell him about us havin' no home."

Kathleen began to write laboriously whilst all the family made various suggestions as to what should be written down. The letter, when she had finished it read as follows:

Dear Uncle Dennis,

Daddy and mammy are very unhappy because we have been evicted from the farm. They are living in a sod cabin and they want to move to England. Can you please find a place for us to live and a place for Uncle Seamus and Auntie Maureen, and some work for daddy and Uncle Seamus on the railway?

We are very glad about your wife who is now our Auntie Nellie and we hope you are happy.

I am going to work at the big house for Mrs. Townsend.

Please write back soon.

Your loving niece,
Kathleen O Sullivan.

The next forty-eight hours passed so slowly and apprehensively for Kathleen. She was scared and excited at the same time. Finally, the moment when she stood outside the massive solid oak door of the Squire's house arrived. Trembling, she pulled the bell cord and the echoing clang startled her. A maid opened the door, a young woman aged about twenty. She had a long narrow face and rather prominent teeth.

"Come in." she instructed. "Wait here please, I'll tell the mistress you're here."

Kathleen stood in the hallway holding her cloth bag

awkwardly in her hand. She was totally unprepared for what now surrounded her - mirrors and polished wooden floors, decorated vases filled with plants and flowers, and sheep skin rugs all creamy white, so soft and clean looking. A big clock ticked away, its bright brass pendulum swinging to and fro. There were pictures on the walls, shining crystal chandeliers suspended from the high ceiling, and beautiful floral curtains. Indeed there were so many things that Kathleen had never seen the like of before, nor ever could have imagined, in this hallway.

She waited, not knowing whether she should stand on the polished wood floor, or on the sheepskin rug. Then the lady came. She wore a dress so beautiful that Kathleen stared. It was pale green and made from soft material that she later learned was velvet.

"Good afternoon Miss O'Sullivan. I hope you will be happy here at Muxnaw Lodge. How are your mother and father?"

"Oh very well thank you ma'am," Kathleen replied.

The woman's clean silky brown hair and soft creamy skin fascinated her. She guessed that she must be about as old as her mother.

"Come into the sitting room and meet Mr. Townsend." She turned and opened the double doors into a large and very beautiful room, decorated in blue and gold with floral curtains and cushions.

"Charles dear, this is the O Sullivan girl I told you about, you know, the family who were evicted, she's come to work in the kitchen."

The handsome man with dark hair and a big moustache, who was reading a newspaper, turned his head and looked over the back of his chair towards Kathleen.

"Oh very good darling. I'm sure she'll be useful to you. Mm quite a nice little thing isn't she?" he remarked as he briefly eyed Kathleen; then nodding to his wife, turned back to reading his paper.

Charlotte Townsend walked over to the side of the large black marble fireplace and pulled the sash cord. The maid who had opened the front door, appeared as if by magic in the room.

"Take Miss O Sullivan, err what's your first name?" she enquired turning to the girl.

"Kathleen ma'am."

"Oh yes, Mary take Kathleen to her room, see that she has something to eat, and show her the kitchen. You begin work at six o'clock tomorrow morning Kathleen. Mrs. O Reilly, the cook, will show you what to do. Go now with Mary will you."

Kathleen worked very hard for the next five weeks leading up to the Christmas festivities. Although making many mistakes she enjoyed learning, and especially did she delight in the regular meals, eating foods she had not previously known existed. She was overjoyed to have her very own tiny room, with its soft warm feather bed and clean white sheets to sleep on. Mrs. O Reilly was very kind.

On Christmas Day the work in the kitchen was continuous from six o'clock in the morning to two in the afternoon. She had just sat down to have her meal, exhausted but happy.

Mary came running down into the kitchen and giving her a queer look, she said, "You have to come upstairs Kathleen, Father Murphy wants to see you."

The big tall black-robed elderly priest was standing in the hall. "You must not worry child, it is all for the best, he has gone to his reward."

"What was the man talking about – who – what – No not my daddy! What does he mean? MY DADDY DEAD, OH NO NOT DADDY!" Kathleen heard the words the priest said and the grief overwhelmed her. How could she be so happy one minute and so desperately grieved the next?"

Her father had died of pneumonia, a direct result of the eviction from their home. It was a bitter pill for Kathleen to swallow - her first taste of the death of a dear loved one, but not her last.

Holy Mary and Jesus please don't take my mammy. Please don't take my mammy and little Molly, I can't live without them. Please, you have my daddy himself, and James, and now you're taking my mammy too!" Kathleen prayed and pleaded softly in bitterness and desperation as she sat high up on the lonely hillside above Kilgarvan village. She wanted to cry out at the injustice of it all. Everything around her contrasted so sharply with her grief, the sheep munched the grass, the birds tweeted incessantly, just as if no bad thing was happening. Her whole world was collapsing, yet the life of nature continued on so peacefully.

The hot August-sun burned into her head and bare arms; the short grass was thick and soft under her toes. She wiped her tears with her long skirt, hating the sickly smell still clinging to it from the many hours she had spent nursing her loved ones. She was dazed from lack of sleep yet sleep eluded her. The heartache and suffering was too unbearable to allow her young mind any rest. How could she live without her mother who meant life itself to her?

Wearily lifting herself from the ground, she began the slow descent of the steep green hillside, the stony Kerry Mountains towering in the background. Thinking and remembering the many happy times she had romped with her family, as she passed each boulder, she bent to let the cool water of the mountain stream trickle over her hand. She could see down in the valley the home where they had been so happy together. As the memories flooded back, she made no attempt to stem the flow of tears that ran down into her mouth.

When James had died at the end of February, eight weeks after her father's death from the terrible cold, Kathleen had thought her cup of sorrow was full to the brim. Her mother and Molly had moved after James's funeral to a one-roomed hovel at the corner of the Kenmare road. Five weeks ago they had started to be ill with the fever. Doctor Twomey said it was the bad water that they had been drinking. Now their skin was yellow like the gorse flowers, and for many days they had been too weak to get up to use the bucket. The smell, in the heat, was sickeningly foul.

Kathleen had left the hovel two hours ago when her Aunt Maureen and Maraid O Shea had come to help with the nursing, now she must return to continue her vigil. A strong nausea and dizziness overcame her, am I getting the sickness too she thought bitterly? She soon reasoned that the heat of the sun beating down on her head was the more likely cause.

In the quiet afternoon stillness, she came nearer to the village, and glimpsed her Uncle Seamus running along the street. She gasped and quickened her steps knowing instinctively that he was hurrying to fetch the priest for the sacrament of the last rites. A few minutes later, in the road outside the stone built hovel, she fell into the arms of her Aunt Maureen. The two women clung tightly to each other in their grief, standing together sobbing for what seemed an eternity, as each one struggled to gain composure and comfort the other.

Between the sobs, Maureen conveyed the news that her niece knew all to well she would hear. "Your mammy went – peacefully – Molly's going too – Father Murphy…" her words tailed off, she could say no more.

Seeing that Kathleen looked as though she was going to faint, Maureen led her home. She carefully guided

Kathleen over the two hundred yards to her own cottage. Maureen's children were standing bewildered on the doorstep, aware that something dreadful had happened, yet not fully able to comprehend the enormity of the tragedy. Five-year old Oonagh ran to her mother burying her face in her skirt.

Kathleen stumbled through the doorway to the mattress under the stairs, where she fell down exhausted. Her head throbbed and her stomach was sick with grief. The heat and weariness were just too much. Her cousins, Peggy and little Thomas, stared down at her in dismay.

Entering the cottage a few minutes later, Seamus noticed his wife's tear stained face and he took her into his arms, the tears welled again into her eyes. "Hush lass," he soothed, kissing her cheeks and forehead, "don't cry anymore. It won't bring them back."

"Please Seamus, can we go soon, I can't stand it here any longer, please can we go to England?"

"Yes my love, I promise we'll go soon, I'll write to Dennis to see if we can go before the winter comes. Oh God it's so hot, I wish there was something cold to drink, I'm fierce thirsty."

The couple turned to see the young woman, Maraid O Shea, standing in the open cottage doorway. Without speaking she held out her hands towards Thomas and Oonagh. Each child took hold of a proffered hand. She beckoned to Peggy with a slight of her head, then nodding knowingly to their mother she took the three of them away to her own home.

Kathleen had fallen into a deep sleep, born of exhaustion. For the next few hours the cottage was quiet with the kind of silence appropriate to a house where deep sorrow reigns in everyone's heart.

It was almost seven o'clock when Seamus looked out through the small window across the narrow street, to see the tall slim figure of Mary McCarthy holding the hands of his two orphaned nieces, Eileen and Sheelagh. They came over the cobbles and stood in the open doorway.

Mary wiped the sweat from her brow with the back of her forearm. "Where is Kathleen?" she asked.

Maureen nodded to where her niece was sleeping.

Mary moved towards Kathleen looking down at her pitifully she said softly, "Poor girl," poor girl."

Turning back to Seamus and Maureen and nodding towards Eileen and Sheelagh, she spoke almost in a whisper "I've told them their Mammy's gone to Jesus."

Ever since her close friend Bridie O Sullivan had been evicted, Mary had cared for Eileen and Sheelagh, now what was to become of them? She and her husband Michael were planning to go to America. Mary now looked upon Seamus as being the legal guardian of the two girls, whom she had grown to love as she would have done her own, had she been blessed with any.

Deciding there and then to take the bull by the horns, she voiced the question uppermost in her mind. "Seamus, "Michael and me are going to America, and we want to know if we can take Eileen and Sheelagh with us? I promise before God, we'll love them and look after them just like our own, my Michael will work for them I promise, poor bairns."

Seamus rose from his chair and standing facing Eileen and Sheelagh, he placed his hands on their shoulders, looking down at them he spoke slowly and deliberately. "Your mammy and daddy and James and Molly have passed away to heaven. Kathleen," he looked over to their sleeping sister, "is going to Preston with your Aunt Maureen and me. Now you," he paused as though the solemnity of the occasion was too much for him, "will you, both of you, go across the sea with Mary and Michael McCarthy to America and take them as your new mammy and daddy?"

Mary opened her mouth to speak but Seamus lifted his hand, raising his voice he commanded "Quiet, let them decide. Do you want to go with Mary McCarthy?" He looked at the woman, defying her to speak whilst he insisted on an answer from his nieces. Eleven-year old Eileen slowly nodded in assent and her sister followed suit.

Mary grasped them both by the shoulders pulling them close to her breast. "Oh the Lord bless you Seamus O Sullivan I'll love them just like my own I promise, I will just so. Come on now girls, we must go tell himself that he's now your new father, so he'll know for sure who it is he has to be lookin' after."

The three of them walked out into the street, almost into the path of a horse drawn landau pulling up sharply outside the cottage. A woman wearing a blue satin dress and a large matching picture hat leaned slightly from the carriage seat.

Speaking to Mary McCarthy in a high-toned aristocratic English voice she inquired, "Kathleen O'Sullivan, is she here?" she gestured towards the cottage with her folded parasol, "I want to see her."

"Oh Ma'am," Mary McCarthy stuttered, turning quickly to go back inside and bumping right into Seamus.

He came rushing out to see the visitor he knew to be Charlotte Townsend, "Err, I'm Seamus O Sullivan Ma'am, Kathleen's uncle." He stood looking up at her, despising himself for his subservience and his obvious admiration for the beauty and richness of the woman. "Can I help you Ma'am?"

"Yes your niece, she is here, is she not?"

"Yes she's inside asleep, she's sick."

"Sick man, what do you mean?"

"No Ma'am, not that kind of sick, just tired, her mother and sister have passed on with the fever," he explained defensively.

"Yes I know, I came to see if I could help? Will you tell her when she awakes that Squire Townsend has offered to pay for the funeral on her behalf, and he will also provide the necessary refreshment for the wake. Will you please send up to the lodge?"

"Oh thank you Ma'am, that's very kind Ma'am," Seamus mumbled touching his forelock.

"And will you tell Kathleen that she need not come back to work until after the funeral."

She turned to the coachman, "That is all driver thank you." He whipped the horse and the carriage moved off into the hot August evening as quickly as it had appeared.

Seamus walked slowly back into the cottage. "Did you hear what she said?" he inquired of his wife.

"Yes I did, that is something to be thankful for," she replied. She watched as he sat down beside the table dropping his head into his hands." He probably wants to get away from this place of poverty and death as much as I do, she thought. At this moment Maureen was even more conscious of what she strongly suspected was happening inside her body for the fifth time in her life. She had been afraid to tell her husband but now she felt a strong compulsion to 'confess'. She moved towards him, placing her hand lightly on the back of his bowed head, he looked up at her without speaking, his dark eyebrows raised in inquiry.

"Seamus," she paused, then speaking quickly she watched for his reaction, "there's another baby coming."

His head went down again and he gave a long low whistle. He remained with his head lowered for what seemed to Maureen an age, as she stood waiting beside him, then he reached out pulling her down to sit on his knee. Lovingly he rested his curly dark head against her shoulder, then looking up at her he smiled broadly.

"What's so funny?" she asked with relief.

"He's going to be an Englishman, when will it be, not before October is it?"

"Don't be silly, how can it be, 'tis not till the spring

time, and how do you know it's going to be a boy?"

"I don't know what it will be but I bet it'll be another carrot head like you."

"Why will it?" Maureen smiled at his expression.

"Well Peggy is dark like me, Oonagh's a carrot head, and little Thomas is another dark one, so now it's your turn again."

"What about the baby who died?" she reminded him.

"Oh I don't know, but I bet you I'm right."

They had both been only nineteen when their first child, Peggy was born, now they felt like an old married couple at twenty-eight.

"Isn't it funny how people come and go," he said. "Bridie and Molly dyin' and now you tellin' me that there's a new one comin', tis too much for a body to understand." Then turning to look at Kathleen who was still fast asleep, he asked, "Do you think she really wants to come with us to Preston?"

"Yes I'm sure she does but I don't know what she's going to say when she knows about Eileen and Sheelagh going to America. All of them in her family will be gone then and she'll be all by herself, except for us," she added. "Poor thing, all of them gone," she repeated unbelievingly.

Kathleen thought the wake would never end. "Why can't we all go home to sleep, it will be morning soon and time to go to Killarney for the train."

The men and women were talking over old times, they were drinking and singing, the flutists were playing and there was dancing and laughing. These people were everything she held dear, she would probably never see them again, probably never see Kilgarvan again. "I must think about the things Mrs. O Reilly told me, I mustn't be afraid, maybe I will be able to come back to Ireland some day just like she did."

When she had been told about her two young sisters going to America she was deeply shocked. How could they arrange it all without asking me, she fretted? She still found it very hard to reconcile herself to being separated from them, everyone kept telling her that it was for the best, but how that could possibly be she did not know.

"Come on Kathleen, 'tis your last dance in Kilgarvan," Freddie O Donoghue pulled her up and whirled her around.

She loved the dancing and the music, diddlely, diddlely, diddlely diddlely. On and on the fiddles played faster and faster, everyone clapping to the music.

Wooing and shouting, "Oh 'tis a grand dancer ye are Kathleen O Sullivan, you'll soon be showing them English a step or two, ye will an' all."

Finally the crowd of villagers were leaving the hall, staggering home to their beds, full of merriment and good cheer.

"Goodnight Seamus O Sullivan, don't you be sick on that boat out from Dublin, don't you be letting down the Irish! Goodnight Maureen, goodnight Kathleen, God bless ye."

Kathleen fell asleep at twenty past three, her last thoughts before nodding off were mixed feelings of sorrow, excitement and fearful anticipation, as she pondered on the question, "Where will I be going to sleep tonight?"

At 10.25 a.m. on Wednesday, 5th October 1881, the bay horse, pulling a box car driven by young Tom O Connor stopped outside Seamus O Sullivan's cottage. The time to say goodbye had finally arrived; the rain poured down as if the heavens had opened to weep at their departure. A dozen sleepy relatives and friends gathered around, silently and sadly watching as the small amount of luggage was loaded onto the car.

Standing in the doorway, Kathleen held on tightly to Eileen and Sheelagh, holding them both together in her arms, and kissing each one in turn. "Be good girls for Michael and Mary," she sobbed. "Write to me from America, don't forget number ten Stanley Terrace, Preston. Here I've written it down for you," she pushed a piece of paper into Eileen's hand.

The two girls nodded and kissed her, their tears mingling with the raindrops. Kathleen stepped up into the car, trying to smile bravely through her tears. As the horse began slowly to pull them away, tearing at their heartstrings, they waved and shouted to their beloved ones, whom they knew very well they might never ever set eyes on, or even speak to again.

"Goodbye Eileen, goodbye Sheelagh, goodbye Mary and Michael McCarthy. God bless you all."

The tears rolled down and the cries and shouts of "Don't forget to write" reached a crescendo as they came to a bend in the street near the small church yard, where their other beloved ones lay sleeping in death.

The horse's pace quickened steadily as it moved along the rutted roadway, and soon the little group standing by the cottage were out of sight. Seamus, Maureen, their three children and their niece all settled down on the narrow wooden seats. Being much too overcome with emotion to speak to each other, they watched what little they could see through the mist and rain, of the familiar landscape as it disappeared into the distance.

Maureen had insisted that they each carried a grey blanket as insurance against the cold, and she busied herself wrapping them around each of her children. Seamus held open their one and only umbrella, trying his best to shelter all his family underneath.

They had to sit on the luggage or place the bags under their feet, as there was no room in the small car to do otherwise. Kathleen had a brown canvas bag wherein she had carefully packed the most treasured thing she possessed, her mother's small black marble clock. She had packed two flannelette nightgowns and two shawls, (Mrs. O Reilly had given her a lovely brown one), a pair of long black woollen stockings, with one pair of black garters decorated with pink rosebuds. The bag also held three pocket handkerchiefs, one snood, one liberty bodice, one white petticoat, one pair of bloomers, some ribbons, a crochet hook and cottons, a black woollen skirt, a white cotton blouse and her brown cotton dress.

She was wearing a lovely grey woollen, high necked dress with a tight fitting waist that had been given to her by Charlotte Townsend, with her blessing, she had been so sorry for her beautiful kitchen maid, who had suffered so much. The dress was to say the least, very elegant, and Kathleen felt like a queen. She also wore a grey woollen, full-length shawl and her brown bonnet. Because she had been compelled to wear high laced-up boots at Muxnaw Lodge, she was much happier than her relatives who were chaffing at the necessity of having to wear anything at all on their feet.

It would take almost two hours to travel the fourteen miles to Killarney, where the train was due to leave for Dublin at twenty past one. Time had been allowed for Maureen to say goodbye to her elderly parents and some of her brothers and sisters who lived at Glenflesk, a small hamlet they would pass on the way.

"When will we get to Preston?" Peggy asked looking up at her father.

"Preston!" he said, "we've hardly started yet. 'Tis tomorrow it will be before we'll be gettin' to Preston."

"Will we be on the ship all night?" she asked again with childlike wonder.

"Yes you know we will," her mother replied, "we've explained it all to you so many times."

"I just wanted you to tell me again mammy," then asking, "Will we go to sleep?"

"We'll try, so we will" Maureen answered with trepidation, wondering herself what it would be like to sleep on a big ship.

Kathleen was trying to imagine what Preston and the big cities would be like, she had seen pictures of London at her school, "Perhaps Preston will be like Kenmare on market day," she thought.

As they approached Glenflesk, Maureen's excitement, in anticipation of her reunion with her loved ones, became obvious. They crossed the river Roughty at Loo Bridge and joined the main Cork to Killarney road. The road surface improved and Tom O Connor whipped the horse into a canter. Maureen soon recognized the fields and the bog where she had helped her family to cut the peat before she had married Seamus.

"It's here Tom," Seamus announced as they approached a house on the right.

Maureen had written to her family so they should be expecting her. Tom pulled on the reins and the horse came to a halt outside the Fitzpatrick house. Maureen's father, John, was still a busy tailor in spite of his sixty-eight years. Two of his sons worked with him and the women folk helped as well.

They all alighted from the car and walked along the narrow garden path to the house. The rain had slackened off and the sun was doing its best to shine through the clouds.

There were no less than thirty-six of Maureen's relatives who had gathered to say goodbye. Two large jars of poteen had been opened which was an illegal drink, looking like gin but tasting nicer and sweeter, so Seamus informed them. They all drank, laughed and talked for almost half an hour, until Tom tapped Seamus on the shoulder telling him it was time to resume the journey along the quiet road to Killarney town. Once again there were kisses and good-byes and more tears, and then they were away to catch the train.

Forty minutes later they were riding down the hill to Killarney and under the railway bridge. They turned left, opposite the Friary Church, then left again passing the Great Southern Hotel and alighting outside the station, which was a siding, where the trains shunted in and then out again to rejoin the main line.

Kathleen and the children had never seen a train before. As they walked on to the station platform the big clock showed ten minutes to one. The rain had stopped and the warm October sun helped to dry their damp clothing.

"That's the ladies waiting room," Kathleen nudged Maureen, "do you want to go?"

"Oh the WC, do we have to?" Maureen whispered.

"Yes if you want to go, I do," Kathleen replied.

"Yes I do too but you'll have to show me, I don't know what to do. Come on children," she said then hesitated, "can Thomas come?"

"Yes he's only little."

"Do we have to put a half penny in?" Maureen asked. They all giggled, whilst she delved into her dolly bag for the coins. "I'll take Thomas with me, you go in the other one with the girls."

Taking a halfpenny from Maureen, Kathleen dropped it in the slot and pushed the brass knob to one side. The heavy door opened and in she went with Peggy and Oonagh.

"You have to use the paper as well," Kathleen whispered to Peggy.

"Do we have to pull the chain?" Oonagh asked. Where does the water come from, can I do it?"

"No you can't reach, I'll do it, come on hurry up now."

Kathleen pulled the chain and the girls watched fascinated as the water swirled around the lavatory bowl. Unlike Kathleen, who was familiar with the one at Muxnaw

Lodge, it was their first encounter with any type of water closet. How strange the ways of modern townspeople appeared to be to them, and how difficult to get accustomed to.

Rejoining Seamus on the platform, they waited alongside the other passengers until the iron monster, puffing out steam, smoke and flames, shunted into the station.

Thomas jumped up and down squealing "Mummy, daddy, train, train."

The adults grasped hold of their children pulling them back, fearful lest they should suddenly disappear beneath the enormous iron wheels.

"Get the bags, don't forget anything!" Seamus shouted above the din of the engine letting off its steam.

They boarded the train and were able to have a compartment to themselves. Seamus lifted the luggage onto the racks and they settled down on the brown leather seats. Kathleen remained standing in order to straighten her hair and admire her reflection in the mirror. Smiling at each other they watched and listened.

The railway porter, wearing a peak cap, shouted, "Dublin train, all passengers aboard, all aboard for Dublin."

They felt like the landed gentry, to be sitting in such style, all dressed as they were in their Sunday best clothes.
"What will Preston be like Mammy?" Peggy asked.

"I don't know, we'll have to wait and see. It will be dark when we get to Dublin won't it Seamus?"

"Yes, we won't be in Dublin City till about eight o'clock tonight, 'tis a long journey, two hundred miles, and then another one hundred miles across the Irish Sea. We then have to travel on another train from Liverpool to Preston."

They heard a shrill whistle, then everyone laughed as Kathleen over-balanced when the train unexpectedly lurched forward. Thomas was shrieking with laughter and excitement, for he was such a happy child.

They all dozed fitfully throughout the journey, becoming wide-awake with interest in the other passengers, and place names they saw as the train halted at stations along the route. By the time they arrived at Kildare the train was full. Their expectation increased knowing that each turn of the rhythmic, singing wheels brought them closer to the famous city of Dublin, and the big ship that was to carry them, as so many of their countrymen who had gone before, over to England across the Irish sea.

CHAPTER 2
ABIDE WITH ME

Hundreds of weary travellers stood waiting patiently at the quayside ready to embark on the British and Irish Steam Packet Ship, *'S.S. Connaught'*. The weather was very calm, not too cold, but damp, drizzly and misty.

"You don't need to worry," Kathleen assured Peggy and herself at the same time. "I don't think we'll be sick, the sea isn't rough. Poor Thomas, he's so tired, he's fallen asleep on your daddy's shoulder."

For the past few hours Seamus had taken charge of Thomas whilst Oonagh clung to Maureen leaving Kathleen to care for Peggy.

For quite some time Kathleen had been aware of a smartly dressed, studious looking young man standing behind them, who was only half interested in his newspaper, whilst carefully watching her. She felt shy and awkward, wanting him to take notice of her and at the same time being afraid to respond to his admiring glances.

Suddenly, she cried out as her Aunt Maureen collapsed in a heap on the cold wet stone cobbles, causing quite a stir amongst the crowd. Seamus was beside himself, trying to hold the sleeping Thomas, console Oonagh and attend to his wife who, in her pregnant state, had fainted from exhaustion.

"Can I help?" the young man asked, coming forward and quickly bending down as he raised Maureen's head from the ground, holding it in the palm of his hand. "Stand back please!" he called to the people who had gathered round, "let the lady have some air." He took a bottle of smelling salts, offered by a woman, removing the cap, he held the bottle under Maureen's nose.

"How much longer do we have to wait before we can get on the ship?" Kathleen voiced her anxious thoughts aloud to no one in particular.

"She's coming round now, she'll be all right," the young man said.

Oonagh began to cry quietly, wondering what was going to happen next.

Maureen started to sit up pulling Oonagh towards her, "It's all right love, mammy's all right," she spoke soothingly

"Would you like to sit on my bag," the young man offered, as he returned the smelling salts to the woman.

"Oh thank you," Maureen answered, "you are very kind, I'm afraid I can't stand up any longer."

Just as she was attempting to sit down on the suitcase, there was a cheerful murmur from the crowd as they realized the gangplank was at last being lowered. In contrast to where they were standing, the ship was brightly lit by many lanterns, which swayed as the boat rocked gently on the water.

Officers and seamen were now busy ushering the passengers into line. "Tickets please, careful now madam, mind how you go."

The O Sullivans began to move slowly towards the ship with the young man, Kathleen supported Maureen, whilst simultaneously watching and holding on to the children. It was by no means an easy task for them to board, carrying the blankets and their luggage. As they queued they could hear the coal being poured into the bunkers. After what seemed an interminable time, their feet were finally planted firmly on the deck.

"Steerage passengers astern," the officer shouted, pointing the way for them to go.

At last they were seated under cover on large wooden polished seats. Thomas and Oonagh were wrapped in their blankets and were able to lie down. The bags were pushed back under the seats, and as soon as they were settled down the young man rushed away saying he would be back soon.

The time was now 10.45, the night air was getting colder, Kathleen shivered drawing her blanket and shawl closer around her shoulders, and also trying her best to see that Peggy and the still sleeping Thomas, were also kept warm. She wondered where the young man was? She had hardly spoken to him, and he had been so kind. She thought she had heard him telling her uncle that he came from Dunlaoghaire, and that he was going to Cheshire.

"Can we go to look at the sea over the side of the ship, Daddy?" Peggy asked, still very wide-awake and enjoying every minute of what was to her, a great adventure.

"No, it's too dark and you'll get lost, be quiet, your mammy's trying to go to sleep."

The engines started to vibrate down below, and the ship began to move slowly and almost imperceptibly, away from the quay. Hot tears welled in Kathleen's eyes as she thought of Kilgarvan. She thought of her Mammy and Daddy, James and little Molly. Would she ever see Eileen and Sheelagh again? They would soon be on a big ship too, going far way to America at the other side of the world. She was deep in thought when the young man came back carrying a big enamel jug, full of steaming hot coffee and two enamel mugs.

"Would you like some coffee?" he asked beaming at them all.

"Oh you are good to us," said Maureen, who had been dozing. She sat up straight, brightening visibly at the idea of a much welcomed and unexpected hot drink.

"Thank you," said Seamus, "we've never had coffee, it smells very good."

"Oh haven't you?" the young man was surprised. "I like it very much. Err, please call me Francis, my name is

Duffy, Francis James Duffy."

"Good to know you Francis, thank you for everything." Seamus continued, "Give Francis some oatcake Maureen. Here you are, there's some in this bag. I'm Seamus O Sullivan, this is Maureen my wife, these are our children and this is my niece Kathleen."

"Pleased to meet you," Francis nodded and shook hands all around.

Everyone laughed with relief when the formalities were over, they then relaxed in each other's company. Francis managed to manoeuvre himself to a seat next to Kathleen. They all sat together eating and sharing the coffee from the two enamel mugs. The sea was as calm as a duck pond, and as the night wore on, Seamus, Maureen and the children soon fell fast asleep. Kathleen and Francis stayed wide-awake, they were much too enamoured with each other to allow drooping eyelids to obscure them from each other's enraptured gaze. The enforced quietness of their conversation made it seem more intimate and romantic.

"The coffee was lovely," whispered Kathleen.

Francis nodded his agreement, "Yes it was. I have to take the jug and the mugs back, will you come with me?"

"Yes," she replied without hesitation, her eyes shining at the idea of walking off with a strange young man unchaperoned.

They quietly picked up the jug and mugs, and careful not to disturb anyone, they crept towards the nearest door.

As the door closed behind them Kathleen queried,"Do you know the way?"

"Yes, come on, it's down these steps on the deck below. Be careful these steps are steep," he held his hand out for hers. Fortunately, her dress was only ankle length so she was able to see the steps as she walked down.

After returning the crockery he asked, "Would you like to look around the ship?"

41

"Are we allowed?"

"Yes of course, look there's the bar, would you like a drink?"

Kathleen giggled with excitement, nodded and smiled, whilst he, still holding her hand guided her into the lounge bar where they found two comfortable seats.

"What would you like?" He stood looking down at her.

"Err – I don't know," she responded.

The steward came up to them, "Would madam like a glass of wine?" he inquired smilingly.

"Oh yes please," Kathleen beamed.

"And a pint of Guinness please," Francis added.

"How old are you Kathleen?" he ventured as the steward moved away.

"I'll be seventeen on the eleventh. How old are you?"

"Twenty-one, I'll be twenty-two on 9th February. "He called you madam."

"Who?"

"The steward, and we're in the first class bar."

"I've never had wine," she stated as she watched the passenger's attendant approaching with the tray.

Francis paid for the drinks then enquired, "Do you like it?"

"Mm!" she answered sipping the wine and smiling demurely. Her bonnet, which she had been wearing for more than twelve hours, began to irritate her so she untied the ribbons and removed it. Her lovely long dark hair fell around her face and she blushed at his look of obvious admiration.

"You are beautiful."

"Am I?"

"Yes, your eyes are green."

"Are they, yours are brown." They sat contentedly holding hands. The lounge was half full and the other passengers, especially the men, watched enviously.

"What time is it?" she asked.

He took out a silver pocket watch, "Quarter past one" he replied. "Are you tired?"

"Not really, can we stay in here it's nice and warm?"

"We'll stay as long as we can. Where did you say you are going to in England?"

"Preston in Lancashire."

"Do you know anyone there?"

"Yes my uncle, Dennis O Sullivan, but I don't remember him, he left Ireland when I was a baby."

"Does he work in a cotton mill?"

"A cotton mill?"

"Yes your Uncle Dennis?"

"Err no, he works at the railway booking office, he married the station master's sister, and he's very good at numbers," she said proudly.

"Arithmetic you mean, yes he must be."

"Are you going to Cheshire?"

"Yes, how did you know?"

"I heard you telling my Uncle Seamus."

"My Uncle John works for Lord Stanley of Alderley, I'm hoping to get a job as a librarian on the estate."

"Oh you must be very clever."

Dismissing her remark he continued, "My uncle's cousin was an Irish Member of Parliament, and he came to know Lord Stanley through his friendship with the writer Thomas Carlyle, that's how my Uncle John became the lodge keeper on the estate."

"I worked in a big house at Kilgarvan."

"Did you? Are your parents still there?"

"No, my mother and father died, and my brother and sister."

"I am sorry. My mother died too when I was born, and my father married again. My mother's sister, Aunt Mary brought me up in Dunlaoghaire."

"My sisters are going to America."

"How many sisters do you have?"

"Two, Eileen and Sheelagh, they're younger than I am."

The two young people continued to talk until after three o'clock, declaring their undying love for each other and promising to write when they arrived at their destination.

"Maybe I'll be married before I'm eighteen after all," Kathleen mused, as she dozed with her head resting against his manly shoulder.

The voyage passed all too quickly for the new sweethearts. The grey dawn was breaking behind the clock tower on the Royal Liver building as the *S.S. Connaught* steamed up the River Mersey. The time was now 6.30 a.m., and the ship was due to dock at seven.

Most of the passengers were astir, preparing to disembark. The O Sullivans and their friend were leaning against the deck rail watching the vague outline of the coast of North Wales in the distance. A cool breeze blew across the water, the small tugs bobbed around, their hooters sounding loud and clear. Lanterns burned on the anchored sailing ships and the sound of the clinking masts echoed across the wide river.

"Mammy look at the stars," Oonagh pointed towards the land.

Everyone laughed, "They're not stars Oonagh," her father corrected, "they are lamp lights on the streets. Don't they stretch out a long way?"

Seamus and the children could hardly believe their eyes.

Kathleen noticed her aunt was looking at Francis's hand over hers on the rail. She withdrew hers quickly, apologizing to him with her eyes. He smiled at her to let her know he understood.

When the ship docked, the quayside was a hive of activity, for the majority of the hard working Liverpudlians had been up before dawn. All were very conscious of their important role in this gateway to the empire. Francis held Kathleen's arm as they walked together down the gangplank. They moved away from the ship with the crowds, wondering which way they should go. Everyone struggled with the luggage and Thomas kept crying.

"He's hungry," Maureen apologized.

The time came for them to say goodbye to Francis who had to travel south to Alderley.

"Goodbye Francis," Maureen held out her hand.

"Goodbye Mrs. O Sullivan."

"God bless you," said Seamus shaking his hand energetically.

"Goodbye," Francis said then turned to Kathleen.

"Take good care of yourself, I'll write to you soon." He squeezed her hand and her spine tingled. "Goodbye Kathleen."

"Goodbye Francis, don't forget to write." She watched his back disappearing into the crowd and she waved her hand. Turning to speak to Maureen her heart leapt with fear as she found herself alone in the crowd.

They were separated by only a few yards and she heard her aunt's voice calling in panic. "Kathleen where are you?"

She followed the sound and they both clasped hands with relief.

"Keep close together now, don't get lost." Seamus felt like panicking; for a country lad to find himself in this teeming city was a frightening experience. The voices were a strange babble as he could scarcely tell what the people were saying. Were they speaking English, or had they landed in some foreign country by mistake? he wondered.

Then, all at once Seamus saw him, standing there

with his big black hat like an angel sent from heaven. He remembered his brother Dennis's words in the letter, "If you have any trouble, ask a policeman."

"Can you tell us sir, we're looking for a train to go to Preston, Lancashire?"

The constable smiled as he listened carefully to the accent of the Kerryman. "Go this way now," he pointed across the big wide road, "walk along Chapel Street, third turning on the left, Exchange Station. Glasgow train sir, number three platform."

Somehow they managed to negotiate their way through dozens of horses and carts and carriages without injury, striding over the dung on the ground. Scores of people were walking along, with big wooden shoes on their feet that clanked over the cobblestones. The noise was unbelievably loud.

Thomas and Oonagh screamed and cried as their parents dragged them along. Peggy's face was as white as a sheet and she held on to Kathleen's hand with a vice-like grip.

The noise on the station itself, when they finally arrived was no less terrifying.

"Tickets please," the man stopped them. The crowd behind waited whilst Seamus fumbled in his pockets and located the pieces of cardboard.

Seeing their plight, a tall broad-shouldered porter, with a big red face shining out from under his uniform cap, came towards them. "Can I help you sir? Carry your bags miss, which train do you want, Preston? Right, follow me, she's out at 7.40, not much time. This way ma'am."

The porter helped them to find a compartment on the big, long Glasgow train, then assisted whilst they loaded the bags on to the racks and under the seat.

They thanked him profusely saying, "God bless you," with feeling and deepest gratitude, then settled down for the journey.

Leaving the city behind they were soon speeding across the flat countryside towards Ormskirk. There was another passenger in the corner reading the *'News Chronicle'*. He was a middle aged, well-dressed man who kept looking at them over his horn-rimmed glasses and newspaper, as though they had just crawled out of an old curiosity shop.

Kathleen placed her hand anxiously over her mouth.

"What's the matter?" Seamus asked.

"How do we know when we get to Preston?" came the reply.

Seamus thought before he answered impatiently, "It says it on the station, doesn't it?"

The man shook his newspaper, and looking round it grudgingly informed them, "I'll be getting off at Preston. I'll tell you when we get there."

"Thank you," muttered Seamus, touching his forelock.

Their tiredness and the unfriendly man discouraged further conversation. The family sat for the rest of the forty-mile journey watching the strange land passing by.

When they alighted at Preston station, Seamus recognized his brother standing on the platform, like an oasis in the desert. He was a tall, stout man, in his late forties, with dark receding hair, and a handlebar moustache.

"Dennis! Uncle Dennis!" they all rushed forward into his arms.

He tried to embrace them all at once; overcome with emotion he found it hard to speak. It was fifteen years since he had said goodbye to his family in Kilgarvan. Now at long last he was united with kin of his own. Seamus shed tears of relief and joy at the sight of his oldest brother.

A small buxom woman with a round pink face looked on. She had wavy sandy hair.

"Are you Auntie Nellie?" Kathleen asked.

"Yes love, and you must be Kathleen."

"Yes I am," Kathleen responded, liking her immediately.

There were introductions and hugs and kisses all around.

"I have to go back to work," Dennis said reluctantly, as they were hustled through the barriers and out of the station, "I'm on early turn today, but I'll be home at four o'clock this afternoon. Nellie will take you home to Stanley Terrace, it's not very far. You must be tired out travelling all that way!

"Did you get any sleep on the boat?" Nellie spoke with a broad Lancashire accent and they all had difficulty understanding her.

"We did sleep a bit," Maureen replied, "but it was very hard on the seats."

"Well never mind love, you can have a good rest when you get to our house. This is what they call Station Brow and we live round the corner down Fishergate."

Arriving at number ten they were taken to the rooms at the top of the house.

"Little Thomas can sleep in with you," Nellie suggested, "and the three girls can sleep in this room. It'll just be for a few days, I think Dennis has got you a house in a street near here, he'll tell you about it when he comes home. Dinner's at half past twelve so you can have a wash and a rest. Will you come with me Kathleen then I can show you where to get the water? Bring that big jug, love, so that you can fill it up, she indicated a large hand-painted jug in an enormous matching bowl. Kathleen picked up the heavy water jug and followed Nellie to the bathroom.

"We have guests staying here love," she explained, "so if you see strangers walking about don't let it worry you."

When Kathleen returned to Seamus and Maureen's bedroom with the jug full of cold water, she found the others examining the curtains and beds, and the heavy polished mahogany furniture. They were opening drawers and peering into cupboards totally fascinated with their new surroundings.

"Isn't it lovely?" Maureen handled the bedspread and the multi-coloured patchwork quilt. "Look at this Seamus, you have to pour the water into this bowl to wash and here's the soap; the towel is hanging down here at the side." Kathleen instructed them, indicating the marble-top wash stand, "You have to put your underclothes in these drawers and hang your dresses and coats in the wardrobe."

"Can I wash in that water Mammy?" Oonagh pleaded whilst standing on the bottom of the big bed and leaning over the brass knob.

"What time did she say dinner was?" Seamus asked, "I could eat an 'orse."

"Oh dear I forgot," Kathleen said, "I have to go down to get some tea and porridge. Will you come with me Peggy?"

The two girls found their way down to the kitchen, a short time later they returned, carrying two trays laden with steaming hot porridge and a pot of tea. They relished the breakfast and the rest of the morning passed by very quickly.

After they had enjoyed a delicious meal of soup, roast beef, and rice pudding in the big dining room, Nellie bustled in. "I bet you feel better now. Did you enjoy it?"

"Oh yes thank you," they replied in unison.

"Now then love," she spoke to Kathleen, "I want to talk to you about work. I don't want you to do anything today because you're tired, but if you could start tomorrow working in the kitchen - you have worked in a kitchen before haven't you?"

"Yes I have, at Muxnaw Lodge," Kathleen replied.

"Well there's a lot to do here. Your Uncle Dennis thought it would be a good idea if you worked for me. Start in the morning at six o'clock. You'll get your meals, have a nice bed to sleep in and good wages."

"Thank you very much," Kathleen smiled gratefully. "That's all right love. I was very sorry to hear about all your trouble, losing your mam and dad and being put out of your farm. It's terrible what happens these days isn't it?"

They all nodded in agreement, the tragic memories of Kilgarvan seemed to be fading away already.

Although the days working at Stanley Terrace were very full, Kathleen's heart was heavy with a sorrow she found difficult to understand. Her working hours were much the same as they had been at Muxnaw Lodge. The house had rooms for ten guests; most of them were commercial travellers. She would get up at five thirty to prepare breakfast, but now however, her work was no longer confined to working in the kitchen. She also had to wait at the tables, clear the dining room after meals, change the beds, empty the chamber pots, help with the laundry, do the washing up and keep the kitchen fire going. An older woman came in three times a week to do the rough work, scrubbing floors and polishing and Aunt Nellie also worked very hard.

Kathleen was glad when the first weekend came and she was given a half day off on Saturday. Most of the guests had gone home for the weekend. Determined to make the most of her free time, she went round the corner to the next street where Seamus and Maureen were striving to make their rented cottage into a home. It was in the middle of a row of two up and two down houses, with a back yard, outside WC and coal shed. Kathleen spent the afternoon helping Maureen to make new curtains, her light-hearted chatter belying her real feelings.

She was desperately missing the familiar sights and sounds of Kilgarvan, but never having heard anyone talking about homesickness, she did not know why she felt so tense at times. The beautiful mountains, fir trees and green fields of

County Kerry had been replaced by big cotton mills, with tall chimneys belching out thick black smoke, noisy cobbled streets with rows upon endless rows of grimy houses. Wherever she looked she was faced with bricks and mortar. She had never realised how much she would miss the colourful sunsets and the people and animals of her village.

She suspected that Seamus and Maureen were feeling the same as herself, but no one mentioned anything, no one said, "I wish I was back home in Ireland."

Peggy and Oonagh talked about their new school and about their daddy starting work as a railway engine fireman on Monday.

Later that day, on leaving church after confession, Uncle Seamus suggested they should all walk up to the town centre. He had heard about the Saturday night pot fair and he was curious to find out what it was like. The sights, sounds and smells they experienced that night helped lift their spirits considerably.

They all gazed in wonder at the beautifully lighted colourful shops. They pressed their noses against the windows of the rich gown shops, ooghed and aaghed in mesmerized delight at the sparkling colourful jewels. They watched as the ladies and gentlemen came out of the flower shop with arms full of gorgeous blooms, the like of which they never suspected the earth could produce.

They found the fairground, and Seamus paid three half pennies for admittance into the tent of performing fleas. They all laughed as they watched the Russian man, with a long black beard, harnessing the tiny creatures to miniature gilded chariots and placing them on the table covered with a green baize cloth. They could scarcely believe their own eyes as the fleas raced in straight lines across the table. After the flea circus they ate delicious hot black peas from earthenware cups and watched as the hawkers auctioned the shining glass and pottery wares. They breathed deeply when their nostrils sniffed the delicious aroma drifting from the coffee grinding shop and the pie shop. Oh yes the pies, and the whiff of freshly cooked Lancashire hotpot made their mouths water.

Their sight seeing ended with a meal of unforgettable fish and chips laced with salt and vinegar, wrapped in newspaper. The chips burned their fingers as they blew on them, their breath going out into the cold night air.

That night, Kathleen went to sleep feeling more contented; she felt better still after they had all been to mass at St. Wilfred's the following day. Aunt Nellie did not go because she was a Methodist and Kathleen worried in case such a nice woman should be damned into hell.

The first letter from Francis arrived by first post on Tuesday. Kathleen waited until her afternoon break before opening it. Then at two thirty she sat on the side of the bed in her tiny room and read:

My dear Kathleen,

I do hope your journey after I left you, went well. It was wonderful being with you on the ship. I will never forget the day I came to England and I hope you feel the same.

I want to be near you my dearest and I think about you all the time. When can I see you again? I count the hours until the day arrives.

Please write soon and tell me you are longing to see me.

It is a very grand place here at Alderley Park. I am working in the stables and assisting the groundsman. I hope, as I told you, to eventually work as a librarian. I am living in the lodge gatehouse with my Uncle John and Aunt Louise. My aunt is very poorly with tuberculosis.

Please tell me about your life at Preston and what you are doing. I love you my dearest Kathleen. I am your slave, an ever-loving one.

Francis James Duffy.

Kathleen read the letter over and over, taking in every word. She then realized that she had neither pen nor paper with which to reply, so she pushed the letter into the top drawer of her dresser, removed her apron, picked up her shawl and rushed down stairs through the front door. All the time she wondered what she was going to write in reply?

From that time the letters went to and fro regularly each week. The more they dropped through the letter-box, the more Aunt Nellie and Uncle Dennis, looking upon themselves as her guardians, asked questions.

"What does he do?" her uncle asked.

"He's a groundsman" Kathleen replied, "but he hopes to be a librarian."

"He must be very clever if he wants to be a librarian. Is he?" Dennis questioned.

"Yes he is," Kathleen replied, not really knowing what he was.

"Who does he work for?" Nellie wanted to know.

"Lord Stanley," Kathleen told them, "Lord Stanley of Alderley."

"Lord Stanley indeed," Aunt Nellie and her husband stared at Kathleen and rolled the name around their tongues.

"Before you know it we'll be hob nobbing with royalty," Aunt Nellie preened.

For the next two months Kathleen continued to fall asleep every night, exhausted and often in tears. She would gaze in sorrow at the moving fingers on the face of her mother's black marble clock, which ticked away next to the oil lamp on top of the chest of drawers in her room. She felt so lonely and longed so much for her loved ones who lay sleeping beneath the soil in the tiny churchyard at Kilgarvan.

Falling asleep she would dream she was milking Dolly, running barefoot across the fields, riding over the mountains with her father, James and Billy the donkey, to Bantry Bay.

On the evening of 24th December, Francis arrived in Preston complete with overnight bag. "Kathleen," he breathed as she opened the door.

She blushed when he kissed her on the cheek.

"Come in please," she stood back shyly, "I was just making afternoon tea."

"Am I just in time?" he quipped with his customary confidence.

"This is my Aunt Nellie, Mrs. O Sullivan," Kathleen introduced him.

"Hello young man, I've heard a lot about you. Did you have a good journey from Alderley Edge?"

"Yes thank you, Mrs. O 'Sullivan."

"You're just in time for tea young man. May I call you Francis? Come this way, I'll show you to your room first and then you can come down into the kitchen for tea."

Later, as Kathleen and Francis ate cake and drank tea together, they felt like two strangers. That same evening they walked to the next street on a thin layer of snow to see Seamus and Maureen. Stepping under the light of the gas lamp at the bottom of the street they halted. Francis took her in his arms and kissed her.

"I'm going to ask your Uncle Dennis if we can be married," he told her. "You want to marry me don't you my love?"

Her whispered, "Yes" caused her heart to beat faster with joy, especially so as he kissed her again.

Before the festivities were over Francis had made his honourable intentions known to her aunts and uncles, and requested her hand in marriage.

"Do you have a home to take her to?" Dennis inquired.

"We can have three rooms in the lodge gate house" Francis informed them.

The couple became engaged on Boxing Day 1882 and

the wedding date was set for 2nd June.

Seamus and Maureen's fourth child made her debut in April. She was a 'carrot head' all right but not a boy as Seamus had hoped for. They named her Kathleen Helen.

Kathleen walked down the aisle on her Uncle Dennis's arm at St. Wilfred's Church. She was a beautiful virgin bride all dressed in billowing white. A quiet reception was held afterwards at the Bull and Royal Hotel. In spite of the fact that she hardly knew the man to whom she had vowed to spend the rest of her life, Kathleen believed herself to be deliriously happy. A passionate two-day honeymoon at Blackpool followed the wedding, then they returned to Preston to collect her luggage for the journey to Alderley Park.

Before they left for Cheshire, she received her first envelope, post marked Virginia USA, containing a letter each from Eileen and Sheelagh. They had left Ireland, sailing from Cork, in March and they sounded excited about their new home. Kathleen wrote to tell them about her wedding and gave them her new address at Alderley Park.

The stately home of Henry, the third Lord Stanley of Alderley, and its surroundings were to the young Irish girl, places of enchantment. She was thrilled with her new home, which consisted of three rooms in the lodge house, standing close by the massive iron gates. The lodge house was most unusual. Built in Italian style in 1816 it had thick stone walls, small casement windows and a small tower. All the windows overlooked the small garden and the beginning of the tree-lined driveway to the big house. There were no windows at the back of the gatehouse, overlooking the main road, because Lord Stanley fully intended his staff to be looking where they were supposed to be looking and giving all their attention to the big gates and the driveway.

The couple soon settled into their love nest. Francis's Aunt Louise was very sick, and slowly fading away. She lived in the other part of the lodge house, with his Uncle John. Kathleen found herself being called upon more and more to attend to the desperately sick woman, who was dying from tuberculosis.

Before the autumn, Kathleen was asked to carry out the duties of gatekeeper. She was required to put on ceremonial gauntlet gloves and to go out in all weathers, day and night, to open and close the big gates. The carriages, occupied by His Lordship and his family, visiting dignitaries and friends, were constantly entering and leaving through the gates. If she were late, keeping anyone waiting, she would be chastised in no uncertain manner.

The snow was deep on the ground when Aunt Louise was laid to rest, the funeral being attended by most of the servants and tenants on the estate.

Kathleen did not like Uncle John, she always felt he was undressing her with his eyes; not the way an old man should look upon a young girl at all. She was always glad when he was out of the way, but she did not like to tell Francis how she felt about his uncle.

On Boxing Day, they had called it St Stephen's Day at home in Ireland, all the staff were invited to a party in the servant's hall at the big house to partake of the remains from the master's festive table. Kathleen enjoyed herself immensely. It was so long since she had attended any social gathering and she was happy to entertain everyone by a display of Irish dancing. Towards the end of the evening she noticed that Francis was well intoxicated, she was disturbed because he was paying a lot of attention to a young blonde kitchen maid.

"What's the matter with him," she thought. "I'm just

as good looking as she is, doesn't he know he's a married man, showing me up like that. How dare he?"

As they walked back home she sulked all the way, a full quarter of a mile. The cold light of the moon shone and glistened on the leaves and the frosted blades of grass.

"What's the matter Kitty?" he asked, putting his arms around her shoulders when she shivered. She refused to answer, so he stopped and pulled her towards him and kissed her full on the mouth.

"Come on Kitty," he purred, "pull your claws in and smile like a Cheshire cat."

Relenting, she laughed at his taunt and he kissed her again. He always called her Kitty when he was ready to make love to her.

As the winter blossomed into spring and the hot summer came and faded to autumn, she thought the babies would never come. Then, by the end of October she knew that all their lovemaking had not been in vain.

The news of the impending birth helped to cheer Francis out of his depression. It was two years since he had arrived from Ireland, full of high hopes that all his book learning would lead him to the work of his choice. He found it impossible to swallow the bitter pill that he was an Irish catholic, and therefore expected to be capable of nothing more than working with his hands like a navvy. The estate manager would nod and smirk whenever he attempted to broach the subject of less menial employment. Kathleen realized he was gradually becoming more morose. She would save her pennies to buy him new books and she would try to encourage him to write poetry as she herself often did.

In early March she persuaded him to dig the garden and they planted vegetable and flower seeds together. Eileen and Sheelagh wrote from America to say how happy they were at the prospect of becoming aunts. Michael McCarthy was making fine money as a thatcher and could afford to keep his adopted girls at school.

Just before midnight on 18th May 1884, Kathleen felt a short sharp pain at the top of her abdomen. Francis was asleep by her side. By two o'clock she was certain the birth of their infant was imminent. Calmly she got out of bed, lit the lamp and began to rouse him.

"Francis wake up, the baby's coming."

Quickly, he sat bolt upright in bed looking at her in disbelief.

Smiling at him reassuringly she requested gently, "Will you go and tell Mrs. Hook?"

He jumped out of bed and pulled on his trousers, tucking in his shirt lap only partially.

"Tuck your shirt in properly."

He did as she asked, pulled on his socks and boots and rushed off down the stairs. The night was warm with a full moon, and the father to be did not bother to put on a jacket. He ran out of the house and away down the road, a distance of over a mile to the village. Over half an hour later he returned, sitting with the midwife in her pony and trap.

Kathleen had been busy laying out the baby's clothes in readiness and tidying up the three rooms. She had only had three pains since Francis left. When she heard the pony's hooves she sat down at the bottom of the bed with her left hand around the brass knob on the iron bedstead.

The tall stout midwife puffed her way up the narrow staircase. Stomping into the room, completely out of breath, she gestured and grunted to Kathleen to lie down on the bed. Clumsily she examined Kathleen, and then with obvious disgust she whipped back the blanket to cover her naked abdomen. "You're not ready yet," she spoke in a gruff and almost manly voice, "you shouldn't have sent for me in the middle of the night when you're not ready."

"I'm sorry," Kathleen protested weakly, "I had the pain."

"It'll be a lot worse than that before you've finished," the midwife growled - "A lot worse."

"Oh I see," Kathleen replied without showing the fear that gripped at her heart.

"I'll give you this bottle," the woman said. She opened her black leather bag and took out a flat cork topped bottle.

"It's castor oil, it should do the trick, drink it all down now," she removed the cork and handed her patient the greasy bottle to drink from.

Kathleen took it and after gulping a mouthful she pulled her face at the taste and oiliness of the revolting stuff.

"Go on, get it down. I'm not going to go till you've drunk it all," she smiled trying to be a little friendlier.

Kathleen closed her eyes and poured the oil down her throat, almost making herself sick. She wiped her greasy mouth with the back of her hand and held out the empty bottle.

"That's right lass," she said slapping a heavy hand on her patient's shoulder. "I'll be back in the morning, you won't be having it till tomorrow. It's your first one isn't it?"

Kathleen nodded.

"Well first one's always worst, it's a bit better when you've had a few, then you get used to it. I'm not trying to frighten you love, you'll be all right, don't worry, it'll soon be over."

Kathleen nodded again, said "thank you," and watched with wide open eyes as the woman picked up her bag, snapped it shut and walked out of the room plodding heavily down the stairs.

The time was now 3.30 a.m. Francis came up the stairs, undressed sleepily, got into bed beside her and went off to sleep, leaving the oil lamp lit for Kathleen, who found it impossible to sleep, her mind was too active and her body too restless.

By six o'clock when Francis got up to go to work she was outside using the latrine. She could hear old Uncle John moving around. He had taken on her work as gatekeeper whilst she was confined.

It was 9.30 a.m. when Mrs. Hook returned to examine her again, "It's not coming yet love," then, she pointed to the little black marble clock on the dresser, "you watch that clock and when I come back you tell me how often you're getting the pains."

Three hours later Kathleen still lay on the bed, her eyes watching every movement of the hands of the clock. The contractions came regularly every twenty-five minutes; as each one began she panicked and stiffened herself up, like a ramrod. In her ignorance and dire loneliness she expected her infant to appear at any time. How she longed for her mother, and how she prayed that the woman would come back to her soon.

The midwife returned; Kathleen went into labour with more frequent contractions at one o'clock. The long ordeal began as Mrs. Hook positioned herself at the bottom of the bed. She sat at Kathleen's right hand side close to her legs, with her back toward the bottom of the bed. Each time a contraction began she would place her hands, clasping hold of Kathleen's bare feet by her insteps. Raising her legs, she would push forward, pressing Kathleen's knees and thighs up hard against her lower abdomen, instructing her to bear down with every contraction. The whole performance being a total contradiction to everything nature intended.

Lying on her back and holding on tightly to the brass rails of the bedstead above her head, Kathleen screamed and yowled every time the infant in her womb attempted to move on its way, through the birth canal. Her feet pushed hard against the woman's hands and as the screaming hours wore on, her legs and feet became cold and pained with cramp. Her body was stiff and aching from lying on her back in almost one position for many hours.

No conscious victim ever went through more torturous hours on the rack. Her face was contorted with the agonizing pain, she screamed and wept, sometimes flailing demented as the heavy woman pushed and panted, and told her that she thought she was in hell at the time her one and only child was born.

With each contraction Kathleen imagined the child would appear, but it did not, and the dreadful pains continued. Holy Mary please help me," she screamed and cried.

Then she heard Francis on the stairs and she shouted for him to come up, and he did.

"You get down it's not decent!" the midwife yelled.

"No please Francis please," Kathleen howled, "PLEASE let him stay."

"If he stays I'm going," the woman yelled back.

Kathleen reached out frantically for her husband, as another contraction took hold. She held him, bruising his arms, completely crazy with the head of her unborn child, as it seemed to her, refusing to appear. Then the woman, still strongly protesting that in all her years as a midwife, she had never before had a husband present in a labour room, became more red-faced and angry. The two young people, the man unwashed, clung to each other, trying in vain to find solace and comfort.

"Come on, you've got to start pushing properly now," the midwife yelled.

"What do you think I've been doing all afternoon?" Kathleen protested.

For almost another hour she pushed and screamed, loud enough to put the fear of God into any black hearted heathen, and Francis wept. Then with unimaginable relief, at five minutes past six, she felt her infant slither into the world.

James Francis Duffy, weighing a hefty eight and a half pounds, was well and truly born. His mother smiled at him as she had never smiled before.

As baby James grew older he became the image of his grandfather Daniel O Sullivan. When he was eighteen months old his mother became pregnant again, something his father had sworn would never happen, but Kathleen did not mind she loved her baby and wanted more.

The snowdrops and crocus were in full bloom when Francis's Uncle John died. He left his few worldly possessions, including a Steinway piano to his nephew. Kathleen was delighted to move into the larger division of the lodge house, which he had occupied. She had helped to keep it clean when the old man was alive but now she was happy to arrange the furniture and other things to her liking.

It wasn't long before she bought herself a Smallwood's Tutor music book, and with the help of Francis's friend Albert, who played the euphonium in the local brass brand, Kathleen learned to play the piano. In the springtime she was thrilled when Albert moved, with his young bride Marie, into the empty rooms of the lodge house where she herself had come as a bride.

"At last," she thought, "I'll have a friend, someone of my own age and sex to talk to."

The task of gate keeping was a very trying one to say the least. She had hardly ever been able to move away from home in case his Lordship or some other important person should require the gates opening. Now, she could share the task with Marie, she would at last have some free time to herself, instead of having to wait until Francis came home before she could go shopping in the village, or walking with James in the woods.

One day Francis came home with a scrumptious bundle of creamy white fur, a Cairn terrier bitch whose name was Bonny. Not only was she bonny by name and looks, she was indeed bonny by nature as well, her mistress adored her.

Shortly after the young couple had moved into the

62

adjoining rooms, Francis persuaded Albert, content in the knowledge that the two wives were at home together, to spend more and more time with him in the local Inn. Kathleen did not mind at first because Francis was funny when he came home merry, and he was more loveable, but soon his drinking habit began to affect the family purse. Kathleen had to scrimp and scrape to provide the layette for the unborn child. She started to crochet and to use the inherent skills from her Irish ancestry more than ever in order to save money.

Marie doted on Kathleen. She was a very simple girl who had been reared in an orphanage, and she was very anxious to learn everything she could from her newly found friend. She found Kathleen to be a very patient and humble teacher. As a token of her gratitude Marie bought her friend a lovely book of poetry. The gift inspired Kathleen to write a poem herself, she wrote:

The Gift

'A gift'! A friend once gave to me
A book! And oh what ecstasy,
Pages and pages with poems filled
To the inmost depths
My soul was thrilled,
It lifted me to a higher plane
Where none but those who ken may gain
Insight, into the minds of men
To satisfy – with stroke of pen.

One afternoon in June 1886, Kathleen prepared herself and James for a walk in the grounds and woods of Alderley Park. Flaming June was for once living up to her

63

reputation, being very hot and dry. In the seventh month of her pregnancy Kathleen was bubbling over with energy and good health. Her skin glowed with the freshness of her twenty-one years and her hair shone with a sheen she had never known before.

She pushed James in his bassinet along the bridle path through the woods. Bonny ran behind at her heels. She was such a loveable and obedient dog, Kathleen never had to tell her twice, Bonny always obeyed. They had been walking for an hour and she felt so near to nature. Despite Francis's craving for drink they were happy. She had a lovely child and another one was soon to be born. She loved the beautiful countryside, although there were no mountains it reminded her so much of Kilgarvan. She stopped by a stream and removing her stockings, she twiddled her toes in the cool running water. It would take her another hour to walk back to the lodge house but she would be home in time to prepare Francis's evening meal.

James was asleep in his pram and suddenly she realized that Bonny was nowhere to be seen. "She's probably off after rabbits," she thought. Then, anxious for her beloved pet, in case she should be lost or worse still worried by foxes, she called her name, "Bonny, Bonny, Bonny where are you?"

Then she heard her response as she barked excitedly.

"Bonny," she called, "Bonny," and again she barked and Kathleen followed the sound. Running through the long green grass and stumbling through the thicket she found her pet prancing around her master who was lying face downwards, half naked, on top of a golden haired, half naked girl.

Kathleen stared astonished for a moment, then she squealed through tightly closed lips as she realized what she had stumbled upon. The guilty pair tried their best to conceal their faces and nakedness. They squirmed like snakes in the grass, all their passion drained and dried up. The forbidden

64

fruit had suddenly turned into gall.

Kathleen saw enough to realize her husband's lover was no kitchen maid. The flouncy yellow frills and knickerbockers, strewn around in the grass and thicket, smacked of a richer and more elegant variety.

She turned and stumbled away, leaving her dog panting and licking her master's mortified face. The hot tears stung and choked her as she groped her way back to James's pram. He had wakened and was trying to sit up. In her anger and bitterness she pushed him down, released the brake and hurried with the clumsy bassinet along the bumpy bridle path. The tears streamed down her lovely face, her heart was pounding and thumping in her breast. She was trying to persuade herself to go back to claim the man she loved. But no, she continued on, her pride maintaining the upper hand, until she eventually arrived home, walking in as though nothing had happened to spoil her dream.

Marie came round as she always did, Kathleen pretended that she had injured her shinbone on a log. Yes, she reasoned, that was the cause of her tears – perhaps her dear friend Marie would take care of James whilst she prepared her beloved husband's evening meal. Marie was only too pleased to oblige and suspecting nothing at all despite Kathleen's blotchy face and erratic behaviour.

Left to herself, Kathleen was sorely tempted to flop down on the sofa and sob her heart out, but her fighting spirit came to her rescue and despite her tears she held her head up high and resolved to battle on. If only she wasn't pregnant then she could fight her voluptuous rival at her own game, but why, she reasoned, should she have to fight? She was his legal wife and he had no right to touch another woman. He vowed before God, in church, to keep to me alone, and now there's nothing I can do to stop him from taking another woman if that is what he wants to do. I'm his wife and I have to live with him so I'll have to make the best of it.

She started to prepare the meal as she did every other day, and eventually he came home. He grinned sheepishly as he walked in with the dog in his arms, and that she could not stand. All the resolutions she had made to remain calm, now left, she wanted to scream. She made some excuse to go outside and in the garden she searched for some serenity. She felt like strangling him, but she prayed to her God to forgive her for such an evil thought.

Returning into the house, she remained silent, and they both kept up an ice-cold masquerade.

Mrs. Hook attended again at the birth of Kathleen's second child. This time the ordeal was just as painful but not as long. The child was a girl, born August 10th 1886, and they named her Elizabeth. She was dark with a rich Irish beauty like her mother, to whom she was destined to bring much comfort and joy.

After the birth of his daughter and the episode of his exposure with his golden haired lover in the woods, Francis took to the whisky more and more.

It was after one of his more vicious drinking bouts that the priest appeared on the doorstep one Monday morning. He wanted to know why Kathleen and her husband and children had not been to Mass on the previous day. She was up to her eyes in the washing - possing, boiling, scrubbing, mangling, creaming and dolly blueing.

"Oh yes please Father – please can you help?" Kathleen appealed as the squat fat dark eyed Father O Shea sat on the sofa drinking tea and eating buns, whilst Kathleen tried to pacify Elizabeth.

"It's my husband Father, he's drinking the whisky all the time and taking all the money – and err – other things too,"she ventured to say. She did not believe that Francis would have confessed but she did not know for certain.

"Well now Mrs. Duffy, if it's takin' a drink that your husband's doin' then surely it is that the man's entitled to his pleasure; and wouldn't you be knowin' that, an' you bein' a good Irish woman an' all?"

"But surely Father," Kathleen tried to protest.

The priest replied emphatically, "No my child, you are trying to usurp your husband's place."

Elizabeth cried out loud and Kathleen felt sick with frustration as the priest blatantly refused to condemn her husband's wrongdoing. Listening to the screams of her newborn infant she became infuriated.

"I'm sorry Father, I don't agree, and if you'll be leaving my house before I'll be possin' you in the tub, I'll be much obliged."

The man looked at her in amazement. He put his cup and saucer down on the floor, looked at her again, saw she was in earnest and made his way towards the door.

"You'll regret,"…..he began.

But Kathleen's determined and angry expression stopped him, and he walked out through the door for the last time, never to return.

Having no stomach to eat humble pie at the feet of Father O Shea, Kathleen began to attend the Services at the Church of England. St Mary's was very close to Alderley Park and her friend Marie was happy to go along with her. They loved to watch the aristocratic Stanley family in their beautiful clothes as they attended at Church. Kathleen would spend many hours day dreaming about life with the Lords and Ladies. She would often imagine herself sitting in an open landau, with a handsome gentleman riding up to the big old Georgian mansion. She would enjoy tea and play croquet on the lawn, have a Nanny to help her to care for her children and dance at the balls in a beautiful gown, to wonderful music.

Then she would sigh, and come down to earth with a bump, "Such things are not for the likes of me," she reminded herself.

Francis usually spent every morning of the Sabbath with a hangover and it was two weeks before she told him of her break with the Catholic Church. When she did tell him his face became red with anger, and she thought he was going to burst a blood vessel, but as Kathleen had discovered to her sorrow, he was a weak character and his anger was short lived. She continued to attend Matins and Evensong with Marie unhindered.

Her relationship with Francis settled down to one of resigned tolerance. He would still demand his marital dues, especially when he was inebriated, and she had no choice but to continue as a dutiful wife. She found solace in her children, her dog, her music, reading and gardening. Occasionally she would write letters to Eileen and Sheelagh and her Aunt Maureen. Sometimes she had to wait months before receiving any replies. She longed to visit Preston but there was never enough spare money to afford the train fare.

In July 1888 her third child, Rosie was born. The young midwife was new to the village. Kathleen was very surprised when she did not start to push on her feet when the labour pains came as Mrs. Hook had always done.

In the winter after Rosie's birth, James and Elizabeth had the mumps and Francis caught it from them becoming seriously ill. It was a desperate time and Kathleen had to go begging at the poor house. After many weeks of suffering Francis recovered but the disease had left him sterile.

Rosie was a toddler when the letter came from America telling them all about her Auntie Eileen's wedding, Kathleen wept. How much she would have loved to be there with her sisters. Eileen had married an Irish immigrant from Galway named Patrick Finnerty, and Sheelagh was bespoken to Alexander Zaltowski, the son of a Russian immigrant farmer.

They had been living at Alderley just over ten years when Francis came home one night with a big surprise for his family. "We're moving to Bury," he announced.

"Moving to Bury?" Kathleen laid her crochet work down on her knee and gazed at him astonished. "What do you mean?"

"I've been offered the job as caretaker at the Bury Athenaeum Theatre and I've accepted."

Kathleen didn't know whether to laugh or cry. "Where is Bury?" she asked.

"About ten miles north of Manchester, it's a cotton mill town like Preston."

"That probably means no garden," Kathleen thought, and the last thing she wanted to do was to leave her precious garden.

"Will we be nearer to Preston?" she asked.

"Yes we will," he answered.

"Is there a house?"

"No, we'll have to rent one, I'm going up to see about everything next Monday. The main thing is we'll have more money."

"Oh I see," said Kathleen, as she tried to take it all in.

The Bury Athenaeum Theatre had been opened in 1853 by another member of the Stanley family, the first Lord Stanley of Alderley having been the younger brother of the first Earl of West Derby.

It was the second Saturday in August when the wagon, drawn by four handsome shire horses, stopped outside the lodge house, the time was 6:30a.m. After the loading of the furniture and all their belongings, Francis and Kathleen with their three young children, and Bonny, said goodbye to Marie and Albert. They left Alderley by train for their terraced house in Haymarket Street, almost in the centre of the thriving cotton town.

The house had a hall, front parlour, living room, kitchen and three bedrooms. There was a small back yard but no garden. The cooking was done on the large open living room fire, which had an oven and a high mantle shelf above. There was a clothes rail above the fireplace which could be let down by a rope pulley. The house was lit by modern gaslight.

James was now a big boy of eight, he would have his own small bedroom over the hallway and his sisters would share the back bedroom. Fortunately for Kathleen, the previous tenants had left the house and the windows shining and spotlessly clean, so whilst they were waiting for the removal wagon to arrive they went to shop for groceries at the indoor market hall.

The same evening, after they had managed to get the children off to bed, they sat amongst the chaos of their belongings drinking a well-earned cup of coffee.

"Kathleen," Francis started.

"Yes."

"I want to make a new start."

"How do you mean?"

"Our marriage."

"Oh" she said, not making it easy for him.

"You know I haven't been doing right by you and we haven't been very happy."

"No we haven't, she emphasized each word.

"Well I'm going to try to do better from now on."

"Turn over a new leaf you mean?"

"Yes that's it. Will you help me?"

"I'll try," she said, "I promise I'll try."

That night Kathleen went to bed in the strange front bedroom of the house feeling more secure in her marriage than she had done for a very long time.

The next day was spent unpacking and moving the furniture into place. They pinned newspaper up at the windows until Kathleen could make some curtains.

"I'm going to buy you a sewing machine," Francis said as he fastened the paper up with drawing pins.

"If you do I'll be able to make more dresses and clothes for the children."

"Which school are they going to?" Francis asked.

"The nearest Church of England school. Do you know where it is?"

"Yes, I think it's nearby the Parish Church. Are you taking them to see the headmaster tomorrow?"

"Yes," she replied.

"I'm coming with you."

"Are you?" Kathleen queried.

"Yes, I want James to have a good education. He's a clever lad, I don't want him to end up like me in a hole in the corner job."

"I'm glad you're going with us," she stated pleasantly.

The following morning at five o'clock they awoke to the most horrendously infernal din. Kathleen lay motionless with terror.

"What the heavens is that?" he queried.

"Come on Maggie, time to get up," the high pitched eerie old woman's voice shouted from the street below.

Deafening rapid banging of metal against glass sounded. Francis jumped out of bed as the harsh clamour continued, and pulling the newspaper aside he peered out through the window into the summer dawn.

"It's the knocker up," he announced, as he spied a shawl-clad woman carrying a long pole with a metal bit tied to the end. As she rattled and shouted by the houses on both sides of the street her clog-clad feet clip clopped across the cobbled street, and the weavers responded from their beds.

"All right Nellie," each one shouted as they heard the call, loud enough to waken the dead.

Kathleen had been accustomed to rising at the first cockcrow but this was the rudest awakening anyone could possibly have. Did they have to get used to that terrible din every morning from now on, except for the Lord's Day? Any further attempt at sleep was impossible as the workers began to leave their houses, banging the doors behind them. At first there were just a few pairs of rattling clogs on the cobblestones, and it was fascinating to listen to some of them approaching from way off in the distance.

The first factory whistle blew at five thirty, and soon the hundreds of clog-clad feet resounded, like an army on the march. Men, women, and children from the age of eleven were hurrying to the cotton mills. Some were carrying cold bacon or marmalade sandwiches they called butties, wrapped in red spotted handkerchiefs, which they would eat, by their looms, at eight o'clock for breakfast. Other workers, who lived close to the mill, would return home to spend the half-hour break. Some of whom would be nursing mothers returning to breast feed their babies, who were cared for during working hours by their grandmothers, or some other woman fortunate enough not to have to earn her living in a cotton mill.

The Duffy family arrived at the school and the headmaster was pleased to see them after morning assembly.
"My name is Kirkman," he introduced himself shaking hands with Francis, then showing them into a tiny cramped room, where he asked them to be seated opposite his desk.

"I'm Duffy sir, Francis Duffy, this is my wife and these our children." Francis gestured towards Kathleen and the children as he pulled Rosie up to sit on his lap. "We moved last Saturday from Cheshire to Haymarket Street.

Mr. Kirkman was tall, middle aged, with greying hair and moustache. He looked stern but spoke kindly. "How old is the little one?"

"Rosie is four," Kathleen answered, "and Elizabeth is six."

"This is James our eldest, he is eight" Francis added, gently moving James closer to the master's desk.

"So you are James, are you my boy?"

"Yes sir."

"And you're going to come to our school with your sisters?"

"Yes sir," James nodded.

Then his father spoke, "I would like James to work hard at school Mr. Kirkman. I think it is very important for a boy to have a good education."

"And quite right you are too Mr. Duffy. Err, will you be employed locally?"

"Yes, I'm starting work as caretaker at the Athenaeum Theatre. I didn't get the work I wanted," Francis added quickly. "That's why I'm anxious for James to have every opportunity, for the boy's sake of course."

"Yes of course, very commendable too if I may say so Mr. Duffy. I can assure you we will do our very best with the boy." He stood up in order to end the interview. "I'll take the details from you tomorrow Mrs. Duffy if you'll bring the children about half past eight in the morning. I have a class to take now so I hope you will excuse me?"

"Oh, yes sir, thank you," Francis held out his hand.

The headmaster shook the hand again. "Thank you for coming to see me Mr. Duffy, goodbye now."

"Goodbye sir, goodbye."

The following day Kathleen collected them from school at four o'clock. The girls were happy but James did not speak. By the time he arrived home he was almost in tears.

"What's the matter James?" his mother asked.

He turned his head away to hide his tears. "What's the bog?" he mumbled defiantly.

"What do you mean?"

"They called me Duffy the duffer out of the bog."

"Come now, sit down here and tell me all about it. Who's been calling you names?"

"He's called Billy," sniffed James. "He called me an Irish pig from the bog. What's the bog Mammy?"

It's the field where we used to cut the peat to burn on the fire in Ireland. It's nothing to be ashamed of. Do you know what he is?"

"What?"

"He's a silly Billy and a horrid boy," James grinned through his tears.

"Was Mr. Kirkman making a fuss of you?"

He nodded.

There you are, he's jealous of you. Duffy is a good name and you are English not Irish, so if he wants to call you names he can call you a Cheshire cat. Ireland is a very beautiful country so don't you be taking any notice of him."

The boy's eyes shone and his self esteem and confidence were restored, he was glad to have a mother who made him feel so good. "Will you help me with my sums Mammy?" he asked.

For the next two years the family prospered. Francis kept his promise to be a better husband and curb his drinking habit. Although Kathleen deeply yearned for the countryside and the hills of Kilgarvan, she contented herself by trying to be a good wife and mother.

They were able to visit Preston where they enjoyed a

very poignant reunion with Kathleen's relatives. Aunt Maureen bought her a silver plated cameo brooch to commemorate the event after all the years of separation.

There was plenty of entertainment for the Duffy family in Bury, including regular visits to the swimming baths. The males and females had to attend on different days of the week, as mixed bathing was quite unacceptable.

In June 1895, Francis and Kathleen celebrated their thirteenth wedding anniversary, by a memorable day trip to Blackpool on the train.

In November of the same year, Francis had gone out one cold frosty night to the 'Jolly Hatters' public house. Kathleen sat bent over the sewing machine, she looked up at the clock it showed a quarter to eleven. She heaved a great sigh, stretched her aching back and stood up to put some wood and coal on the dying embers of the fire.

Francis would be home soon, cold, perhaps hungry and maybe the worse for drink. She sat down again determined to master the setting of the sleeve into the dress, it was her second attempt but tired as she was she refused to give up trying. I must have it ready for the theatre tomorrow night she kept telling herself. Francis had promised to take her to see the Shakespeare play 'Macbeth', as a special treat, and she was looking forward to it so much. It was such a long time since they had been out together. She was earnestly hoping that Francis would not change his mind and that nothing would happen to stop them from going. Bessy Hargreaves, a weaver who lived across the street, had offered to come in to sit with the children.

She had just finished the sleeve when Francis walked into the living room. She held up the dress to examine it. It was a deep cyclamen silk, the colour would set off her dark hair and green eyes.

"Do you like it?" she asked him.

"Yes it's fine," he replied with only vague interest,

"What's for supper? I'm hungry."

"There's some broth in the pan left over from dinnertime."

"Broth, who wants broth! Can a man not come home to a good supper? Pity you couldn't do some cooking instead of sewing that dress all night. I suppose you're tired out now?"

Kathleen felt deeply hurt at his unkind words. She so very rarely neglected his interests and did he not realize she was only making the dress to save him money, and she wanted so much to look nice for him.

"I could just eat some chips. Have we got some lard, peel a couple of potatoes will you, he ordered.

Instead of responding immediately as she normally did, she sat looking down despondently at the dress. She really was so tired, that peeling potatoes now was the very last thing she wanted to do.

"I'll light the kitchen mantle," he said as he took a taper down from the mantelpiece and lit it in the fire.

Returning from the kitchen he spoke aggressively. "You go to bed, you might as well, I'll cook the chips myself."

Kathleen tried to protest.

"Go on," he commanded, losing patience "Go to bed."

By the time she had put her sewing machine away and was ready to go upstairs, he had peeled the potatoes and was melting the fat in an iron pan on the fire.

Picking up the little black marble clock to take upstairs, she walked to the kitchen door. He was standing by the slop stone slicing the potatoes into an enamel bowl.

"I'm taking the clock up," she spoke with an apologetic tone hoping he would turn to smile or to kiss her goodnight, but instead he just grunted like a hungry bear. "Goodnight," she said unhappily, then as an afterthought she added, "Bonny's in the yard, don't forget to let her in."

Getting into bed she shivered between the cold cotton sheets, and tried hard to warm her feet on the earthenware hot water bottle. Hearing a loud hissing noise coming from downstairs she raised her head quickly from the pillow.

"KATHLEEN!" Francis's screams came to her through the open bedroom door.

She jumped out of bed and ran along the landing and down the stairs as fast as her bare feet and nightdress would allow. She opened the living room door at the bottom of the stairs to be confronted by a nightmare scene. The smoke came at her through the doorway and she could vaguely see Francis trying to beat at the flames.

Through the choking smoke he coughed and screamed at her, "Get the children down – get them down."

Fleeing back up the stairs she shouted, "James oh God James, get up, the house is on fire." She ran into the room where she had to shake him to arouse him from a deep sleep. Then scarcely knowing what she was doing she went into her bedroom to pick up, like some sort of talisman, her mother's black marble clock. With the clock in her hand she rushed into the back bedroom and somehow managed to get a protesting Elizabeth and Rosie out of bed. Pulling off a blanket she wrapped it around Rosie and half carried, half dragged her down the smoke filled staircase, with James and Elizabeth coughing and screaming behind her.

Reaching the open front door she saw a man in the street throwing his overcoat around her husband, who by now was a blazing human torch.

She screamed as she came up against a helmeted policeman whom she saw and heard blowing his whistle, then mercifully, she collapsed unconscious at his feet on the freezing cold pavement.

When she regained consciousness she was lying covered with a blanket on the sofa in Bessy Hargreaves's living room. Feeling icy cold she was shaking violently. The tears began to come to her eyes and she started to scream and tried to get up from the couch to go to Francis.

"There now," the policeman said as he held her with restraint.

She screamed again repeatedly and hysterically so that he was compelled to slap her face. She became quieter but continued to sob and to shake.

"Come on now lass," the constable said quietly, "we know it's bad. Look at the children, try to be brave for them." He was crouching beside the sofa still wearing his helmet and cape and he tried to direct Kathleen's attention to her children who were sitting on the fireside chairs.

Elizabeth and Rosie were wrapped together in a blanket holding each other. They both wept quietly whilst staring in disbelief at their mother and the policeman. James sat opposite them, he was shaking but not crying, and the black marble clock, which he had rescued from the chaos, rested on his knees.

Bessie Hargreaves came hurrying from the kitchen and announced, "I'll put the kettle on." She stopped in her stride as they all listened to the galloping horses and the clanging bells of the fire engine coming down the cobbled street. "Is somebody seeing to him?" Bessy asked the policeman, quietly but anxiously.

"Yes, the sergeant is, and that other chap, they've taken him to Doctor Mann's house."

"Oh I hope he'll be all right, what a terrible business," Bessy whispered.

They need some hot sweet tea," the constable said. "You see to them will you, I'll have to get the people out from next door if they're not out already."

As the constable opened the front door Kathleen could see her blazing home across the street. She screamed again and shouted, "Francis – please - where is he?"

"It's all right love," Bessy knelt by her side. "They've taken him to Doctor Mann's, they'll be lookin' after him, you mustn't worry." Bessy was trembling herself and she kept fighting back the tears. There was such an awful commotion going on in the street outside.

The front door opened again as the policeman returned with Doctor Mann's assistant. "What is her name?" the doctor asked Bessy as he walked around the sofa in the middle of the room to attend to Kathleen.

"Kathleen Doctor, Kathleen Duffy, she can't stop shaking."

"Hello Kathleen, I want to help you and the children," the doctor spoke quietly.

"Where is my husband, can I see him Doctor?"

"No, not tonight my dear, they are taking him to the infirmary. Perhaps tomorrow, maybe tomorrow you can see him." He took hold of her wrist to test her pulse. "I want you to swallow these two pills with some hot sweet tea and then I want you to try to sleep."

"They must be kept quiet, they're suffering from shock, keep them warm," he quietly instructed Bessie.

"Yes Doctor, thank you Doctor, I'll do my best."

The policeman took out his notebook and addressed the doctor, "We need to know about relatives sir."

"Well she's in no fit state to tell you anything now, but I'll try." Turning back to Kathleen he said, "Mrs. Duffy, have you any relatives living in Bury?"

Kathleen shook her head violently.

James spoke up, "Uncle Dennis." his voice squeaked.

"What's that lad?"

"Uncle Dennis and Auntie Nellie, they live in Preston and Uncle Seamus O Sullivan too."

"Good boy. Do you know the street where they live?"

James looked blank.

"Stanley Terrace," Elizabeth volunteered.

"Good girl. There you are constable, Mr. and Mrs. O Sullivan, Stanley Terrace, Preston."

"Right Doctor, we'll get word to them right away." The constable walked towards the door.

Before he reached it Elizabeth screamed, and began to cry, "Bonny! Where is Bonny?"

James and Rosie began to cry as well, anxious for their loveable pet.

It's our dog Bonny," James sobbed looking pleadingly at the policeman, "she's a little white one."

"I'll go to look for her," he assured them as he departed through the door.

It was early morning before he returned with the wet shivering bundle of fur. Kathleen and the children were asleep but Bessy sat poking the fire. The constable whispered to her that a fireman had found the dog huddled up in terror behind the outside lavatory of the burning house. The dog whined as she crept up to the fireplace and Bessie picked her up to cuddle her on her knee.

The next few days to Kathleen were almost a blank in her mind. She could not eat and was only able to sleep with the aid of sedatives. Seamus and Maureen left their children in the care of Auntie Nellie and arrived in Bury on Sunday afternoon. The neighbours living next door to Bessie offered to put them up, and they visited the hospital with Kathleen right away. Francis was very poorly in Bury infirmary. He had third degree burns to his face, chest and arms. He was on the 'danger list' and the doctor would not even allow Kathleen to see him. Whenever he regained consciousness he was in too much pain to communicate lucidly with anyone, and had to be given morphine continuously.

"We're doing our very best," the doctor informed them, "but he is very poorly."

Two days after the fire, the estate agent offered Kathleen another house for the same rent around the corner at number seven Garden Street. After calling at the office for the keys, Seamus, Maureen, Kathleen and the children went to see the house. It was a three-bedroomed terraced house, very similar to the one in Haymarket Street. It was cold, damp, and completely empty, Seamus had bought some coal and wood to light a fire and they had only three orange boxes to sit on.

Then it was that things began to fall, as it were, completely out of the blue. Maureen answered a knock at the front door only to find an elderly woman, who stood beside a small chest of drawers carried there by two young boys.

"It's not much love," the woman said, "but it's no worm, and you can 'ave it if you want it, ee I'm sorry fer all yer trouble. Carry it in lads, don't stand there gawpin'."

The boys obediently lifted the chest of drawers and carried it into the hallway and disappeared with the woman, whilst Maureen stared after them in disbelief.

Less than half an hour later, a man came with a large jug, inside which were two knives, two forks and a bottle opener. He did not bother to knock but lifted the latch and walked right into the back living room, where they were sitting in front of the fire.

"There's a jug here love, I expect you'll be able to use it. Don't worry now, you'll be all right, God's good. If there's any help you want just let me know, I only live down t' street."

Bessy managed to find a second hand double bed mattress and a single bed, and on Friday, almost a week after the dreadful fire, Kathleen and the children were able to move into their new home. The following day Seamus and Maureen had to go home to Preston, as Seamus could not afford to stay away from work any longer. Uncle Dennis would give Seamus some money to help to compensate for the wages he had already lost.

As the tears continued to roll down Kathleen's cheeks, and her heart was bursting with the pain of her sorrow, the gifts poured in to her newly found home. Everything imaginable was brought to the house by these generous compassionate Lancashire folk, both the rich and the poor. They all wanted to give whatever they could to the unfortunate family who had lost their home, their clothing and almost all of their possessions.

There were bundles of clothing, there was bedding, fruit, books, money, food, flowers, furniture, pots and pans, ornaments and cushions, and even an enormous aspidistra plant.

The gifts were either left outside on the pavement or the benefactor would simply tip the latch and call out "Hello, I've just brought you a little bit of something love, it's not much so you throw it away if you don't want it."

Kathleen would rise from a donated chair and go out to the front door to say, "Thank you,'" as she choked back the tears. Their generosity made her cry all the more, how could she ever thank these dear people for all their kindness? If only she could tell Francis how wonderful they were.

Every night after she had finished working at Armstrong's Mill, Bessy Hargreaves would come round to help. She would make a meal and afterwards she would help them to sort out the various gifts of clothing and other things.

"These trousers are too big for you James but they'll be all right next year, so we'll keep them on one side for you." Best of all she would sit and talk. Even though Kathleen was unable to answer her most of the time, she would still keep on talking, consoling, friendly, soothing, talk. She would tell stories to the children, always making sure they were stories of happiness and joyous things, helping them to forget if only for a short time, the dreadful situation in which they now found themselves.

Many gifts of money were left by theatre patrons at the Atheneaum. They had read in the *'Bury Times'* of the fire, and of Francis's terrible injuries, and the news of his death when it mercifully came, spread almost as fast as the fire that had caused it.

The inquest was an extremely painful experience. Bessy stayed away from work in order to accompany Kathleen.

How had Francis been burned? How did the fire happen? That dreadful night had to be re-lived all over again.

"We are sorry to distress you Mrs. Duffy but these questions need to be asked."

The pompous little man, they called the Coroner, spoke the kind words, as it seemed to Kathleen, without the slightest depth of feeling, as though he was reciting them like a Polly parrot.

"Do you know what your husband was doing and how the fire started?"

"He was cooking chips on the fire sir."

"Speak up Mrs. Duffy, the Court must be able to hear you."

"Cooking chips sir, cooking chips on the fire."

"Where were you at the time?"

"Upstairs in bed."

"Did your husband try to put out the fire?"

"Yes sir."

"Did he use water?"

"I think so sir."

"Why do you think so?"

"I beg your pardon?"

"Why do you think your husband used water to put out the fire?"

"I heard a loud hissing noise before my husband shouted for me."

"Dear me, that was the very worst thing he could have done, tut tut tut. Did you know that pouring water on to boiling fat is a very foolish thing to do?"

"No sir."

The man gestured with his hand, "There we are," he addressed the Court, "is it any wonder there are so many tragedies with so many ignorant people around?"

Kathleen winced at his scorn and pompous tone and Bessy bristled visibly.

The questioning continued, "Was there wet washing hanging above the fireplace?"

"Dry sir, dry flannelette sheets."

"And was your husband attempting to beat out the flames when you came down the stairs?"

"Yes he was."

"The Fire Officer's report tells us there were cinders from the open fire splayed all around the room, and therefore it is understood, throwing water on to boiling fat, caused the fire to effuse, as it would of course," the Coroner added.

The result of the inquest was announced solemnly at the end of the proceedings. Francis James Duffy had died from injuries sustained during a fire at his home and the verdict was **"Death by Misadventure."**

In spite of the bitter cold the mourners at the Manchester Road cemetery on December 15th were many. For the second time in her comparatively young life, Kathleen found herself being supported in her grief between Seamus and Maureen O Sullivan. She sobbed quietly as the mourners sang the well-known words of the hymn, *"Change and decay in all around I see, Oh thou who changest not, Abide With Me."*

CHAPTER 3
DAYS OF DESPERATION

January 1896 was no less cold than the previous month. Somehow Kathleen, with a heart that ached so desperately, struggled through each day. The kindness of her neighbours, and the strangers, who persisted in showering her with gifts, was overwhelming. Her loneliness was always worse at bedtime, and she would sit up late into the night until she was exhausted, rather than face the night alone without Francis by her side.

The house was only very sparsely furnished, but they had the absolute necessities, and thanks to the generous gifts, she was able to pay the rent and buy food and coal. Her nimble fingers proved to be a blessing, not only could she occupy her mind and her time knitting and crocheting, but also altering the garments which had been given them, to make them fit.

She would sit with Elizabeth and Rosie, at the table in the middle of the living room, teaching them the handicrafts she had learned in Ireland as a child. She passed onto them the fine intricate skills handed down from their female ancestors.

James would keep a good fire burning and the room cosy and warm. He would read aloud to the others – *'David Copperfield'* was his favourite.

What will you do when we go back to school Mammy?" Elizabeth questioned, deeply concerned for her mother's welfare.

"I'll be all right Beth."

"I'm going to start work," James asserted, " we need

the money, and Bessy says that I'm the man of the house now!"

"Your father wanted you to stay at school. I'll go to work in the mill with Bessy, so you can be educated."

"No Mammy, it's awful in the mill, terribly noisy and cold. I know Harry's mam works at Rostrons, and she says it's awful."

"Now don't you be worrying about me James, you carry on with your book learning, and leave the worrying to me. Besides we must think about father's wishes."

"Why don't we go back Ireland?" Rosie piped up with the unexpected, "or Cheshire? Lancashire is dirty, the teacher says it's all cotton mills and smoky chimneys."

"We don't have enough money to go back to anywhere," her mother replied. "Anyway there's work here in Bury."

"Did you like Ireland Mammy?" Elizabeth asked.

"Yes I did, it's really beautiful. I used to run across the fields with bare feet, and climb the hills with my brother James. We had a donkey called Billy and Dolly the cow. I used to milk her early in the morning."

"How do you milk a cow?" they all asked laughing.

Ignoring the question Kathleen said dreamily, "The milk was thick and creamy, and we made butter and cheese."

"Why did you keep the pig in the house?" James asked indignantly. "It must have smelt awful."

"No it didn't, but when she had piglets – we called them bonhams – she would sometimes roll over on her babies and squash one of them."

"Oh no," Elizabeth squealed, and the others shook their heads in wide-eyed amazement.

"We kept them in the house so that we could watch that the bonhams didn't get squashed."

"Will you sing us some Irish songs Mammy, like you used to do?" James asked wistfully.

"I like *Danny Boy*," Rosie said, and she started to sing in a high pitched voice, and the others joined in the chorus.

"Are there any songs about Dublin, where Daddy came from?" Elizabeth asked.

"Yes I know one," Kathleen recalled, and she started to teach them. *'In Dublin's fair city, where the girls are so pretty, I first set my eyes on sweet Molly Malone.*

For the next ten minutes they sang *'Cockles and Mussels'* to their hearts content, and Kathleen thought to herself how strange it was that she remembered only the good things of her homeland, and could scarcely recall the bad.

They were now engrossed in singing and learning this song:

> *Molly Kennedy, ennedy, ennedy,*
> *I love you,*
> *Every morning and night and noon*
> *With you Molly I long to spoon.*
> *Stop your taisin' me,*
> *Start a plaisin' me*
> *Say you love me do.*
> *Molly Kennedy, ennedy, ennedy,*
> *I will marry you.*

When Bessy walked through the door after her day at the mill to find them all singing, "I am glad to hear you sing tonight, you'll have to teach me that song."

"Yes, and we've been singing *'Cockles and Mussels'* too, Rosie told her.

Bessy was relieved to find, for the first time since the fire, some semblance of relaxation and a happy atmosphere in the home. She also was a widow; her husband had died four years ago when she was thirty-six. She had not been blessed with children of her own, although she herself came from a very large family. She was a plump motherly-type of woman, with dark brown hair and brown eyes. During the past few months, and more especially since the tragedy, she had grown very fond of Kathleen and her children, finding great satisfaction in being able to comfort them.

She picked up the kettle from the hob and carried it to the tap in the kitchen – Kathleen followed her.

"We've been talking about work this afternoon Bessy. So you think I could get a job at Armstrong's Mill?"

"Yes I think you could. You'll have to do something soon or else you'll all end up at the workhouse. The money you have now won't last very long, will it?"

"No, it won't, it would be good if James could stay on at school like Francis wanted him to."

"You must face facts Kathleen, you won't be able to keep him at school much longer, you won't be able to afford to."

Kathleen sighed as she realized the truthfulness of Bessy's words, "No, I suppose you are right, he'll have to leave school in May when he's twelve. Do you think you could ask for a job for me at Armstrongs then?" she ventured.

"Yes of course, I'll see Mr. Howarth the manager tomorrow. You wouldn't earn very much at first, but I'm sure you could soon learn how to weave. Perhaps you could start next week when the children go back to school?"

"Thank you Bessy, I would be glad if I could work at the same place as you."

Bessy did see Mr. Howarth, and on Monday morning, after the children had left for school, Kathleen made her way along Rochdale Road to the big factory. She pushed open one of the big wooden doors, where the notice said 'OFFICE', and knocked on the 'ENQUIRIES' window.

A young boy, aged about fourteen opened it, "Yes, can I help you please?" he asked.

"Mrs. Hargreaves asked if I could see Mr. Howarth about a job."

"What name please?"

"Mrs. Duffy, Kathleen Duffy."

"I'll see if I can find Mr. Howarth," he said and closed the window.

There were two further big swing doors leading into the massive weaving shed. The noise emanating from the six hundred looms, driven by pulley shafts and operated by steam engine, was deafening. After standing waiting for over half an hour Kathleeen was almost in tears. Her hands and feet were icy cold, and she was beginning to think that they had forgotten her. Occasionally workmen would pass through to go in and out of the weaving shed. As they opened the massive doors she would catch a glimpse of the weavers standing by their looms. The noise was so loud, she was glad each time the doors closed again. She started to blow on her hands in a vain attempt to warm them, and stamped her feet continuously.

If only Francis could come walking through the doors, take her in his arms and away from this dismal place, she thought. She was trying to muster up the courage to knock again on the window, when the boy came through from the weaving shed and beckoned to her. Following him round to the left, she was shown into a warm office, where a nice looking man aged about forty, sat behind a big mahogany desk.

"Good morning Mrs. Duffy, my name is Howarth, sit down will you please? Very cold morning isn't it?"

Kathleen nodded as she sat down on the spindle-backed wooden chair, saying 'Thank you."

He smiled at her, and she felt a little better after her

long miserable wait.

"What is your Christian name?"

"Kathleen sir."

"Your age?"

"Thirty-one sir."

"Thirty-one," he repeated, writing it down. "Is your husband working?"

"I'm a widow, my husband was...." Kathleen gulped as the words stuck in her throat, and the tears welled in her eyes.

"I do beg your pardon," he looked startled. "I am sorry, I remember now, Mrs. Hargreaves told me about you. I really am sorry. You're from Ireland aren't you?"

"Yes sir."

"Mrs. Hargreaves told me you're a good seamstress, is that right?"

"Yes," she nodded.

"Well now, that will certainly help you with the weaving. Can you start tomorrow?"

Kathleen's heart lifted, then sank in quick succession. "Oh yes sir."

"We'll give you two looms to start, and one of the weavers will teach you. You won't be paid this week as we work a week in hand. The wages are made up to Wednesday night, which means that you'll have two days pay next Friday, and a full week's pay the following Friday. You'll be on piecework, which means you will only be paid by the yard for the cloth you weave, after it has been examined by the Passer; you understand? You will eventually be able to earn as much as thirty shillings a week, depending on how hard you work of course."

"Yes sir, thank you," Kathleen sat uncomfortably on the edge of the chair.

You start work at six o'clock in the morning, you have half an hour for breakfast, from eight to eight-thirty, three-quarters of an hour for dinner from twelve thirty to one fifteen, and you finish work at five thirty. Saturday is half day of course, six a.m. start and finish at twelve noon, is that understood?"

"Yes I understand."

"Very well then Mrs. Duffy, that will be all for now. If you're unhappy about anything come to see me, I'll help you if I can."

He stood up to open the office door for her, and she walked out through a large outer office and into the weaving shed. She was just about to pass through the swing doors, when a hand grabbed her arm from behind. It was Bessy.

"Have you got the job," she mouthed the words into Kathleen's ear in order to be understood above the noise of the looms.

Starting tomorrow," Kathleen shouted back.

"That's good love." Bessy's face lit up with pleasure. "I'll be coming to see you tonight, all right?"

"Yes," she replied. "Yes all right," and she walked out through the big swing doors.

The same evening, when the children came home from school, James handed her a letter from the headmaster, which read:

> *Dear Mrs. Duffy,*
>
> *My wife and I were deeply distresssed to hear of the very sad and untimely death, of your dear husband. Please accept our sincere condolences.*
>
> *I would be very pleased if you will allow me to call at your home tomorrow evening, at approximately 7.00 p.m., to discuss your son's educational progress.*
>
> *I am,*
>
> > *Your humble servant,*
> > *James E. Kirkman.*

"Mr. Kirkman coming here – whatever does he want

91

– do you know James, you haven't been doing anything wrong, have you?"

"No Mam I haven't and I don't know what he wants, he never said."

Kathleen got out of bed at five o'clock the next morning feeling sick with apprehension. She had hardly slept through worrying about the weaving and how the children would fare without her being at home to care for their needs. She was paying Miss Duckett, an old maid, to look after the children and to give them their mid-day meal. She lived a few houses away down the street with her widowed sister who went out to work. Kathleen would leave her front door unlocked when she left for work at five thirty, and Miss Duckett would come in at a quarter to eight to get the children up and ready for school. They would go to her house for dinner, and again when they came home at four o'clock, then they would see their mother when she came home from the mill at ten minutes to six.

Kathleen arrived at the mill with hundreds of other workers, wearing a blue overall underneath her black woollen shawl. Unlike the other women, she wore shoes rather than the customary clogs. Although she never thought herself to be in a class above the others, she was nonetheless determined to preserve a pride in her appearance, promising herself never to become dirty or common in any way, either physically or morally. Her brush with the aristocracy at Kilgarvan and Alderley encouraged her to hope for a better life than the one she now endured, although any such relief seemed to be far removed from her present circumstances.

She was given her weaver's number, 413, and told to sign the attendance book. Not all the weavers could write their names but would sign with their own special mark. The engine started up at six o'clock, coinciding with the blowing of the factory hooter. Kathleen was to be taught to weave by a tall thin woman named Alice. At first the looms to Kathleen were nothing less than monstrous machines.

"How can I learn what to do when I can't hear what she's saying?" she wondered. She watched fascinated as Alice, after examining the warp and weft, threaded the shuttles and showed her how to tie a weaver's knot, using her thumb. Then placing Kathleen's hand around the icy cold steel handle of her two looms, she demonstrated how to slowly start each one. The deafening rattling noise became louder and louder as each loom was brought into action around the weaving shed.

Alice tapped her on her shoulder and then pointing to her own mouth she mouthed the words, "Watch my lips."

The cloth they were weaving was bed ticking, to be used as casing for flock and feather mattresses and pillows. The tiny black and white stripes in the cloth dazzled Kathleen's eyes until she became accustomed to them. Amazingly the next eleven and a half - hours passed quickly. She was cold, tired and hungry, having had only a cup of tea, a cheese sandwich and an apple for dinner. In spite of this, walking home with Bessy that night, she was overcome with a strange and elating sense of achievement, a feeling of belonging to a hardworking class of warmhearted people.

When Kathleen arrived home after her first day at Armstrong's mill, the children came running into the cold house.

"Mammy, what was it like?" James asked.

"Look at your hair," Elizabeth remarked,"it's all covered in fluff."

"Yes it's lint. Come on now James, help to set the fire, and girls, wash the breakfast pots and lay the table for tea. I bought a loaf and some potted meat and a simnel cake."

She placed her wicker-shopping basket on the table and took out the grocery items. "How did you get on at school today, did you have a good dinner at Miss Ducketts?"

"Yes, we had beef steak pudding and all the children at school wanted to know about the fire."

"Oh I see," Kathleen answered, not wanting to be reminded.

After tea they all sat warming themselves by the fire whilst James struggled with his homework.

"Will you set the fire every night in future James so I can light it as soon as I get home? JAMES!"

"Oh what's that Mam, yes the fire, yes I'll do it. What's the capital of Finland? I know it's Helsinki. What a funny name," he muttered to himself.

Before they had cleared the table there was a knock at the front door.

"Oh no," I'd forgotten, it must be Mr. Kirkman. Hurry up, clear the table, everything looks such a mess. James, answer the door, quickly it's cold outside. Don't keep the man standing waiting."

Elizabeth and Rosie rushed around clearing the table and tidying the house, whilst their mother dashed into the kitchen, whipped off her cotton overall and flicked the lint from her hair.

"Come in please sir," invited James, as he stood with the front door wide open.

"Hello James. Is your mother in?"

"Yes sir, my mother's been working at the mill to-day"

"Oh has she, I expect she'll be feeling very tired then?"

James showed Mr. Kirkman into the living room and asked him to be seated beside the table, as his mother emerged from the kitchen.

"Good evening Mr. Kirkman," she greeted as they

shook hands. Kathleen seated herself at the opposite side of the table.

"Mrs. Duffy," he began, "I'm so sorry about your husband and the fire, but I will try to come to the point without delay. I know how concerned your husband was about James's future and his education."

"Yes he was," Kathleen agreed.

"Well, my wife and I have talked over the matter. You see we have no children of our own and," he continued quickly, "you would be doing us a great favour if you would allow us to be responsible for James's education, financially and everything I mean."

James stared at the Master his eyes wide open.

His mother began, "You mean," she hesitated "You mean you want James to stay on at school?"

"Yes I do, I don't really like to say it in front of the lad but he's clever and hard working and," he paused, "I think he's going to go places, given the right opportunity of course."

"Do you really?" Kathleen was overwhelmed and astonished. Then overcome with emotion and tiredness, the tears welled, "I'm sorry," she apologized and sighed deeply.

"Please Mrs. Duffy, don't apologize, perhaps I shouldn't have come so soon after all your trouble," he started to get up from the chair, "it's too upsetting for you."

"No please," she gestured for him to sit down again, "please, I'll be all right," she took a deep breath and smiled. "It's been my first day at the mill today, err – please, will you have a cup of tea?"

"I would love a cup of tea, thank you so much," he said knowing she needed a break, some time to regain her composure.

Turning to the girls she said, "I'll make your cocoa, it's almost your bedtime." Putting the kettle on the hob and going into the kitchen for the teapot and cups and saucers she quickly glanced in the mirror over the slop stone, in an attempt to improve her appearance. She was trembling slightly with emotion and fatigue. She returned to the living room carrying a tray with the tea and cake, and made a firm attempt to regain her self-control.

She did not underestimate the man's generous proposal, and after pouring the tea she took the initiative. "I understand what you've said Mr. Kirkman," placing the refreshment in front of him. She sat down again before continuing, "I know I could be too proud to accept your generous offer."

"But Mrs. Duffy err…"

"No, I'm not going to refuse, I would be very foolish if I did, especially as I know how much my husband would wish me to accept."

"You are a very wise woman, if I may say so. I've grown very fond of James," who by this time had lost interest in the adult conversation, and was engrossed in his geography homework. "He's such a clever boy, it would be a dreadful waste of talent if he were to leave school now."

"I was trying to keep him at school until his twelfth birthday in May, but then I'm afraid he would have had to start work."

"Yes, he told me, 'as the man of the house' he was going into the mill to keep the wolf from the door." James looked up and listened at the sound of the familiar words. "Err – before we go any further Mrs. Duffy, you realize this could mean he would not be earning money for the family for possibly another ten years?"

"Ten years, as long as that!"

"Yes, if he is, as I believe, good university material, then yes, he would be twenty two before he graduates. Of course he could earn some money for himself out of term but…"

"And would you be willing to finance his education

for all that time?" Kathleen interrupted.

"Yes, more than willing, it would be a privilege and there are scholarships you know," he added. "So if he continues to work hard he could get a grant."

"Well I can't believe it, it's like a miracle, a once in a lifetime chance."

"It is and I'm glad you see it that way."

"There's just one thing," Kathleen said.

"What is that?"

"I hope you won't mind but – well – sir, I'll agree to the proposition, if you will allow me to contribute as much as I am able myself, even if it is only a very little, would you?"

"Yes of course," he beamed. I know you take your parental responsibilities very seriously; pity all the other parents are not like you, but I'm sure we can come to an amicable arrangement. Now, perhaps we could talk to the boy?"

"Yes of course, James," she said.

"Yes Mam," the boy looked up.

"Mr. Kirkman wishes to talk to you."

"Yes sir," he stood up straight with his hands behind his back.

"How like my own father he is," Kathleen thought. "I wish he could see him now."

"Your mother and I," the schoolmaster reiterated slowly, "your mother and I have decided you will continue your schooling. You will have the opportunity to pass for Bury Grammar School, and then if you work hard, you could possibly go on to university. Now what have you to say to that young man?"

"Oh yes sir, I would like that very much, that would be very good, but sir?"

"Yes James?"

"Well sir – since my father died sir," he looked down at the floor and swallowed hard, "I am the man of the house now and I want to work for my mother – sir."

Kathleen stood up and moving towards her son placed her right hand on his shoulder saying, "James – Mr. Kirkman has made a wonderful offer."

"Yes Mam."

"He is going to help us with the money. I mean so you can stay on at school, and then, when you are older, you will be able to earn a lot of money and be a real man of the house with a very good position. Will you do that for me James?"

The boy bowed his head and thought for a few moments then looking up at his mother he said "Yes Mam I'd like to stay on at school and I will work hard at my lessons, I promise.

"That's a good son," Kathleen said, she felt like hugging him but refrained.

"So there we are," Mr. Kirkman said as he stood up, addressing Kathleen. "I'll get the necessary papers for James's entrance to the Grammar School. You will need to sign them, so perhaps I could bring them round on Saturday morning?"

"Saturday morning, no I'm sorry, I'll be at work."

"Ah yes, I forgot, shall we say afternoon then, about two o'clock?"

"Yes sir, thank you very much, and please will you thank Mrs. Kirkman for us?"

"Oh dear me, I almost forgot, my wife would like you all to come for tea. Would a week on Sunday be all right?"

"Thank you very much, that would be lovely" Kathleen accepted, very surprised at the honoured invitation.

"My wife was very upset when she knew about your tragedy, she naturally wishes to help as much as she can."

"Everyone has been so wonderfully kind," Kathleen sighed deeply. "It isn't the first time I've experienced a great loss in my life. I lost my parents and my brother and sister after our home was taken from us, then my two sisters were taken to America."

"So you've had more than your share of tragedy then – I am sorry Mrs. Duffy, but you must keep bearing up with the help of the Lord and you'll get through."

"Yes I'll try Mr. Kirkman, I will try."

"I'll see you on Saturday then," he said as she opened the front door. "Goodnight Mrs. Duffy, Goodnight my boy."

"Goodnight sir," James called out from the living room as his mother closed the door on the schoolmaster and the cold night air.

Not every day at Armstrong's mill passed as smoothly for Kathleen as the first one. The heavy steel-pointed shuttles, which sometimes whizzed out from the side of the looms, were a dangerous hazard, and then there were the floats when the threads were all tangled, and she had to spend interminable and unprofitable hours re-joining them together with weavers knots. Her fingers became cracked and sore with the cutting threads, and the backs of her hands were often chapped and bleeding due to the constant damp and cold.

There were many times when she gazed at the moving cloth, watching carefully for a flaw, she would daydream of the green hills of Ireland and the countryside where she had lived around Kilgarvan. She was a fast learner, but dreaded having to send for a tackler when one of her looms broke down, especially a horrid man named Joe Buckley. He would scowl and curse her and she cringed at even the thought of him.

She was thrilled one day when one of the loom tacklers came to her at dinnertime, "What part of the old country do you come from?" he asked.

"Kilgarvan, County Kerry," she smiled as she listened to his rich Irish brogue.

I'm John Fitzpatrick from Dunmanway, West Cork," he said offering her his hand, which she grasped with joy, meeting with one of her own countrymen was like meeting an oasis in the desert.

"How long have you been over here?" he asked.

"Nearly fifteen years, I lived at Preston and Alderley Edge before we came to Bury. Have you ever been to Bantry Bay?" she inquired.

"Yes I went there when I was a lad, lovely place isn't it, wish I was there now."

"So do I." Kathleen enthused. She knew she had found a friend, and whenever she needed someone to mend her looms she would go looking around the weaving shed for John Fitzpatrick, who always helped her as much as he possibly could.

As those early days at the cotton mill turned into weeks and the weeks into months, Kathleen became a very proficient weaver until, by the end of the first year she was running four looms and earning good wages. Most of her leisure time, what little she had, was spent with her children, only occasionally, she would visit a theatre with Bessy who continued as a firm friend. The fact that she was a beautiful young widow sometimes brought unwanted attentions from men, but she would always resist any lewd advances with good humour and dignity. She found it difficult trying to be father and mother to the children but she devoted her whole-hearted attention, to bringing them up with loving discipline. She insisted on good manners at all times always telling them that 'manners maketh man'.

She taught Elizabeth and Rosie to cook, to sew, and to clean the house, and James did his best as a handyman around the home. She trained him to take good care of his clothes, to be neat and tidy and to attend to the fires, which was no mean task, especially when it came to black-leading the living room fireplace, which had to be done every Thursday after school.

It was a thrilling time when they were able to purchase a second hand piano, not a fine one like the Steinway, but nevertheless it had a good tone and Elizabeth learned to play well. They would spend many happy hours during the long winter evenings playing and singing around the piano in the front parlour.

They would go for walks together after church on Sundays. It was a very rare occurrence when they could afford to spend a day at the seaside, visit their relatives at Preston, or go for a long ramble over the Pennine hills. Such days when they came were a delightful treat, and they would talk about such times for years afterwards.

They were often invited to tea with Mr. and Mrs. Kirkman at their big house on Walmersley Road. Mrs. Kirkman was very entertaining and they thoroughly enjoyed her company. James passed the entrance exam to the Grammar School, and true to his word, Mr. Kirkman allowed Kathleen to contribute towards the school expenses for books and uniform. James was the light of his mother's life.

Elizabeth was also a clever scholar who possessed a remarkable literary talent. When she left school in the summer of 1898 she started working at a flower shop in Princess Street. Her working day began at 8.00 a.m. and ended at 9.00 p.m. On Friday and Saturday nights she had to work until 10.00 or 11.00 p.m. Mr. Kirkman consoled himself that at least she was not condemned to life in a cotton mill, as so many of his bright eleven and twelve-year old pupils were. Rosie spent most of her time sewing, she hoped to be an apprentice dressmaker when she left school.

James would often ask his mother to help with his homework. One night the subject was history when he turned to ask, "Mam, did you know that Pope Adrian gave Ireland to England's King Henry the Second for a birthday present?"

"No I didn't, is that what the book says?"

"Yes it does, Mother."

"Yes?"

"If the English are so cruel to the Irish in Ireland, why do you want to go back to live there?"

Thoughtfully Kathleen replied, "I would love to go back because it's home where I was born. It's clean and green and so beautiful with mountains, lakes and rivers. I've told you about it so many times James. We must try to get some pictures from somewhere. You should have seen the salmon leaping out of the River Roughty!"

"But you hardly know anyone there after all these years," James reasoned.

"No I don't but I would still love to go back."

"What about religion, would you still be a Roman Catholic if you had stayed in Ireland?"

"Yes of course."

"Why?"

"Well Ireland's a Catholic country like Spain, France and Italy."

"Do the priests rule over the people and tell them what to do?"

"In a way, yes."

"So how could you go back to live there now that you are Protestant?"

"Oh, I hadn't thought about that. I know, I could go to the Church of Ireland."

"What's the difference?"

"What do you mean?"

"I mean, what's the difference between Church of

Ireland and Irish Catholic?" James asked, somewhat exasperated.

"Church of Ireland is like the Church of England, you don't confess your sins to the priest, and you don't say prayers to Mary."

"And there's no statues," James added.

There was a thoughtful pause before Kathleen said, "Anyway we can't go back, we haven't enough money."

"When I leave school, I'll get a job in Dublin." The idea intrigued him, "Then I'll take you back," he added confidently.

"That would be fine, but you'd better get on with your homework now or you won't be taking us anywhere."

"All right Mam, but can I just read your Irish poem first?"

'Cottage in Kerry', you mean she replied, whilst taking out the hand written poem from the top drawer of the sideboard, she handed it to him and he began to read aloud:

"I fain would retire to my 'cot by the sea
Where the roar of the billows comes clearly to me,
And when dusk has fallen, the scent of the flowers
Comes in through the window to brighten the hours,
The shades of night lengthen, the cottage fire glows
Peace, in my heart gently steals, morning dawns misty,
Then clear the light grows and the glory of Kerry reveals.
I'd wander along 'twix the hedgerows bright
Where the musk roses bloomed afresh o'er night
And the cool morning breeze fans my cheek as I go
Down to the sea where the tide is low,
Friends of my childhood, there to meet
Seagulls – just back – with the fishing fleet."

"Thanks Mam," James said as he handed back the piece of paper, "I wish I could write poetry too."

Kathleen had worked for more than three years at Armstrong's mill when she became friendly with a young married woman named Elsie Bennett. Elsie had straight strawberry blonde hair, a round pink face, saucer blue eyes and a wide mouth, constantly opening and closing in an endless stream of nonsensical chatter. Kathleen found her very amusing. As well as working as a weaver at the mill, Elsie also worked part time as a barmaid at the Derby Hotel, which was situated on a prominent corner in the centre of Bury, opposite the imposing Parish Church, and next door to the Derby Hall. There was a tram shelter in the centre of the square the locals called 'top't town', and the monument to the man Robert Peel, former Prime Minister and founder of the Police Force, looked down on the scene.

One dinnertime, in the summer of 1899, a group of weavers seated on low wooden boxes by Bessy's looms, listened whilst Elsie talked about her work at the hotel. One of the apprentices had just returned from the pie shop with individual pies baked in enamel dishes, for the weavers. Kathleen was ravenously hungry and began to tuck into her hot meat and potato pie. It smelled delicious. As she cut into the steaming hot pie she let out a scream, and quickly put it down on the floor.

"Whatever's the matter," Bessy and the others started to laugh? "What did you do that for?"

"It's a cockroach, a big one, I 'ate 'em," Kathleen shouted.

"You mean you nearly ate him," Elsie joked. "Is 'e dead?" "Eooh! What a big one 'e's dead all right. Take it back to the shop, they'll have to give you another pie. Tell 'em we don't pay for cockroaches. There's plenty of free ones in Bury."

"Yes, take it back," Bessy urged, "they'll probably give you two instead of one." She picked up the white enamel dish, with the cockroach planted firmly within the pie, and handed it to her friend.

Taking it from her, but holding it at arm's length, Kathleen marched off angrily along the alleyways between the looms, through the weaving shed towards the big swing doors. Pushing open one side of the door she was knocked completely off balance by a tall, blond, handsome young man. Coming from the opposite direction he sent the pie flying right out of her outstretched hand. Exasperated, she felt like screaming at him.

"Oh I am sorry," the young man apologized as he dived to rescue the pie. "Is it your lunch?"

"No leave it," she shouted, feeling embarrassed.

Objecting to her tone he looked surprised. Kathleen knew him to be Garth Armstrong, the mill owner's son. He was not accustomed to a weaver raising her voice at him.

Realizing her rudeness she tried to apologize, "I'm sorry, I didn't mean…"

"No it was my fault absolutely," he bent again to retrieve the pie, and on observing the cockroach embedded therein, his expression changed to one of disbelief and astonishment.

The look on his face made Kathleen see the funny side of the whole affair and she started to giggle, nervously to begin with, then he smiled at her and they both began to laugh. "I'm taking it back to the shop," she managed to explain between the convulsions of laughter.

"And so you should indeed," he emphasized.

Her spine tingled as their eyes met and she blushed.

"Look here," he said, taking a gold fob watch from his pocket, "it's now ten minutes to one and you haven't had your lunch yet. What is your name?"

"Kathleen sir, Kathleen Duffy."

"Mrs," he questioned?

"Yes, well, I mean," she stammered "I'm a widow."

"I see," he said, whilst making no attempt to hide his admiration for her. "Well now Kathleen, I suggest you take another half hour off, with my express permission."

"Oh thank you very much sir," she replied.

"And you make sure they give you a decent pie next time or I'll be after them," he grinned broadly, handed her the somewhat battered pie, and pulled a wry face at the cockroach. "You enjoy your meal when you finally get it Kathleen." He smiled at her as he walked away, raising his hand in friendly salute.

Walking to the shop across the street, Kathleen forgot her pangs of hunger and laughed to herself all the way. "What a lovely person he is, and so handsome. I wonder how old he is - about thirty-one, I suppose. The others will be surprised when I tell them who I bumped into. You turned out to be a friendly cockroach after all she chuckled, looking down at the dirty, dead black vermin in the pie."

It was at this time, that everyone was talking about an impending war in South Africa; when she told the weavers she had been talking to Garth Armstrong, she learned he was rumoured to be volunteering for the army.

In the autumn Elsie's children became poorly with the measles, and she was compelled to stay at home to look after them. It was one foggy night in November when she arrived breathless at Kathleen's house. She knocked on the door then walked in.

"Hello Elsie," said Kathleen, surprised to see her. "What's the matter, how are the children?"

"They're bad Kathleen, very bad. You can't put a pin between our Nellie's spots, we have to keep the curtains drawn all day, they can't stand any light on their eyes and we've got two beds downstairs. Doctor Mann's been ever so good. Have yours had the measles?"

"Yes, they've all had them. Is there anything I can do for you Elsie?"

"Yes love, there is. You know my weekend job at the Derby?"

"Yes."

"Well I can't go this weekend, and I don't want to lose the job, so I wondered if you would stand in for me?"

"But Elsie," Kathleen protested, "I don't know anything about bar work."

"I know you don't, but it's easy when you get used to it, and it's good money too."

"Oh I don't know, I really don't fancy the idea."

"I'd be ever so grateful if you did go for me Kathleen. Bill Wolstenholme's the manager, he's ever so nice and he'd show you what to do. Can I go round to see him now to tell him you'll go tomorrow night?" Elsie pleaded. "You wouldn't need to be there till seven, its interesting meeting different people."

"All right then Elsie, just this once. He'll probably end up kicking me out."

"Don't be silly, you'll be every bit as good as me, probably better. I am grateful love, thanks ever so much. I'll have to go now or else my Fred will think I've got lost. I'll see you at the mill as soon as the children are better. Goodnight Kathleen, what a terrible night it is."

"Goodnight Elsie, I hope the children are better soon."

The following evening Kathleen walked through the revolving doors into the Derby Hotel and across the luxurious red carpet to the man behind the bar. "I'm Kathleen Duffy," she said quietly, "I've come in place of Elsie."

"Oh have you now," Bill Wolstenholme smiled, eyed her up and down and seemed to be very pleased with what he saw. "I'll show you where to hang your coat."

When Elsie's children were recovering from the measles, Elsie became ill with influenza so Kathleen's first weekend as a barmaid extended to every weekend in December. She enjoyed the job, and as usual was a good worker.

"We're going to be very busy over Christmas, and especially the New Year,"Bill remarked one night. "Will you stay on for Friday and Sunday nights?"

"Yes I will," Kathleen agreed.

Kathleen busied herself behind the hotel bar the night would be a long one. She was thinking about Rosie who was suffering from a bad cold. "I must remember to buy a miniature bottle of whisky to take home, if I put some in her tea it will help her to sleep." Because Bessy also had a cold, she had asked Miss Duckett to come in to sit with Rosie. Elizabeth would not be home until eleven o'clock tonight and she would go straight to bed. James had gone to stay for the weekend with Mr. and Mrs. Kirkman; they were taking him to a pantomime at the Manchester Palace Theatre. "Most likely it will be after midnight before I get home tonight," Kathleen mused whilst polishing the wineglasses. She examined each one in the glow of the gaslight candelabra, twirling the stems between her fingers.

"This place is so grand," she thought wistfully, as she admired the crimson velvet curtains adding to the ambience of warmth and wellbeing. The small round wooden tables were highly polished and the comfortable pink plush chairs invited relaxation. She particularly appreciated the central heating. The weaving shed had been so bitterly cold all day and dreadfully damp, it was Friday, the next to the last day of the old year, *and the old century*, it had seemed unending. It was sheer heaven to be in this lovely warm place.

She was feeling good tonight wearing her new white satin, long sleeved blouse, with a high neckline, frilled centre front and pearl button decoration. Her straight black ankle length skirt emphasized her trim figure. She wore her thick dark hair coiled high at the back of her head, held in place with glittering slides and combs. A black velvet choker ribbon, worn with the lovely silver cameo brooch Aunt Maureen had given her in the centre, enhanced her slender throat. She was modest without being coy, charming but not pretentious.

Every few minutes she would be conscious of the swish of the revolving doors as the customers began to arrive, taking their overcoats off, and shaking them to remove the snowflakes clinging to them.

"Only a few of them here yet," Elsie said as she hustled in from the cloakroom and around behind the bar. "Is that the time, quarter past seven? I'll be late for me own funeral I will. Snowin' like mad it is," Elsie continued, "I never thought I'd get on that tram, packed out it was, everybody goin' out enjoyin' themselves. New Years Eve tomorrow, they'll all be drunk as Lords hangin' round that Bobby Peel monument singin' *Auld Lang Syne*."

"Two scotch please love," an elderly fat man with a jolly face grinned at Kathleen from the other side of the bar. Good finish to an old century eh, trams won't be runnin' tomorrow and arf of workers won't be in t' mills. Nothin' like that in my day mind yer, we had to be at work even if we had to walk miles, hail, rain, snow or blow."

Kathleen nodded in smiling agreement as she took his

money. "Oh look, a nineteen hundred new penny," she noticed as she held up the bright shining new coin. She wanted two for the girls, one each to put in their shoes tomorrow night, when they left them behind the door for 'Mother New Year' to fill them with an orange and an apple each, and the customary new penny. "I hope there will be one more before closing time," she said to Elsie as she placed the treasured coin safely on top of the till, intending to replace the three new pennies later with old ones.

"I do wish I could go to the ball tonight," whined Elsie as she filled a tray with drinks for Tommy, one of the waiters.

"No use you dreamin' about that now Elsie, you won't be any fairy godmother tonight love, you'll be too busy pullin' them pints and pourin' them whiskies."

"You be quiet Tommy Tucker," Elsie quipped back at him. "Don't you be so cheeky."

"What is it like at the Derby Hall?" Kathleen queried.

"Oh it's lovely, just like a palace, beautiful red carpets, oak panels, lots of mirrors and a big wide staircase, - real grand it is," she sighed.

"Some of our customers must be going there tonight. Just look at all them lovely dresses. Just fancy it'll be fifty years in February since Lord Derby opened this hotel and the Derby Hall; that was before our time that was. You weren't even a twinkle in yer father's eye then Kathleen. You can bet there'll be some lords and ladies and fancy gentry going to the ball tonight."

Kathleen smiled and listened between serving drinks as Elsie gabbled on.

"It's a charity do tonight you know I reckon it won't start till nine and finish at two in the mornin'. Mayor and Mayoress 'll be there, 'im with 'is gold chain and that chap with that big gold mallet thing."

Kathleen laughed, "You mean the mace bearer!"

"Yes that's him, Mr. Mace Bearer."

Kathleen sighed, "It's no use us fretting about the ball, we won't be doing any dancing tonight."

There was a slight lull in the bar activities and Kathleen looked up through the large high windows, watching the snowflakes now falling thick and fast. If she stared hard at the flakes she had the illusion of speeding upward in the opposite direction. The trams were trundling down Market Street, full of potential revellers coming into town. Her thoughts went out with sympathy to the poor horses, "They'll be skidding all over the road if it keeps on snowing."

Whilst she was thinking she became conscious of a tall, khaki-clad figure in army officers uniform, leaning against the bar. Her senses reeled as she caught the look in two big deep blue eyes.

She stepped forward automatically, picked up a pint glass and said, "Can I help you sir?"

Garth Armstrong smiled, and sensing her embarrassment quickly sought to put her at ease. "Hello Kathleen, I didn't know you worked here."

"Good evening Mr. Armstrong, what will you have sir?"

"A pint of mild please Kathleen," he stated as he repeated his disarming smile.

"Come on Kath, I'll never get these drinks," Tommy called out impatiently.

"It's all right, I'll serve 'im, no patience 'e 'asn't," Elsie offered.

As Kathleen poured the pint of golden liquid, making sure of a good amount of froth on the top, she thought to herself, "I haven't seen Garth Armstrong since that pie incident months ago, and now, just because he's remembered my name I'm acting like a love sick maid."

"Will you have one with me Kathleen?" he offered as she handed over the glass of beer."

She hesitated.

"A sherry or something?" he suggested.

"Thank you, yes I'll have a sweet sherry please." Turning to reach for a glass she caught his admiring glance through the mirror at the rear of the bar, and felt herself coming all over hot and bothered again. She was glad when she had to move away to serve someone else so she was able to regain her composure.

She turned back to speak to him again, this time with smiling confidence, "Are you home for long?" she enquired.

"I'm afraid not, I leave on Monday night from Manchester, 11.45 train from London Road Station."

"Just a short leave then?"

"Yes embarkation. I'll be going out to South Africa soon."

"Its good to see the big wide world I suppose, but I'm sure I'll be glad to be back in good old Bury again."

Kathleen's heart sank as he spoke about going away. "I am a silly woman," she scolded herself. "Why should I be concerned where he goes?"

As she went to and fro whilst serving other customers, they continued to talk whenever she came near to him.

"You haven't left the mill, have you?"

"No I only work here on Friday and Sunday nights."

"You must be tired out working at the mill all day long, then coming here?"

"Yes it is tiring sometimes, but I enjoy the change."

"Have you any children?"

"Yes, two girls and a boy. James is fifteen, he's at the Grammar School."

"Is he indeed?" Garth raised his eyebrows.

As the night wore on the hotel became noisier and Kathleen became busier. Garth persuaded her to have two more glasses of sherry, she was surprised each time she looked and he was still sitting on the same bar stool. She expected him to drift off somewhere to find other company. He was handsome enough to attract any woman in the room.

At 10.30 p.m. Bill came to help behind the bar. Kathleen glanced at the clock, "Another hour to go before closing time." she thought.

Twenty minutes later she noticed Garth talking to Bill, they both looked in her direction and then the manager came over to her, "Go and get your coat, there's a gentleman waiting for you," he nodded towards Garth.

"Me, are you sure?"

"Yes I'm sure, hurry up before I change my mind," he joked. Taking hold of her shoulders from behind he pushed her firmly beneath the flap of the bar counter. "See you Sunday!"

Kathleen could scarcely believe what was happening, her mind was in a whirl.

The handsome soldier was waiting for her when she came out of the cloakroom. "Kathleen, I'm sorry I didn't ask you myself, but you were so busy. May I see you home?" His voice was soft and caressing.

She nodded and smiled and he guided her through the crowded room and out of the revolving doors. They both cringed and gasped as they moved out into the icy air. The snow was quite deep and he placed a protective arm around her and she took shelter close to his broad shoulders. They crunched and slithered down Market Street, laughing and gasping as the large snowflakes stung their faces. Before she realized what was happening he had manoeuvred her into the doorway of the Derby Hall and through the revolving doors.

"Tickets please sir," the doorman requested.

"I'm sorry, we have no tickets. I'm home on embarkation, can we go in?" Garth pleaded, whilst simultaneously taking a half sovereign from his pocket and slipping it to the man.

"Oh thank you sir, and you miss," he said as he

113

beamed his obvious delight at the very benevolent bribe.

As the haunting strains of a Lehar waltz drifted down to them Kathleen tugged at Garth's sleeve in dismay, "Please, please, I can't go in here, I'm not suitably dressed," she pointed down to her laced up shoes and black serge skirt.

"You look beautiful, you'll be the belle of the ball," he spoke softly, then guided her up the wide red carpeted staircase. "Call me Garth, will you?" he whispered.

He was waiting for her as she emerged from the ladies' cloakroom, and she glanced at her reflection in a long mirror. "You look lovely," he reassured her. "Don't be scared. Come on let's find some food. Are you hungry?"

"Yes I am," she said.

They walked into an anteroom where there were three long tables laden with bowls of punch and delicious refreshments. The room was almost half full of people, and the women dressed in ball gowns, made Kathleen feel like Cinderella, *before* she met the fairy godmother.

"I don't care," she told herself, "I'm too happy to worry about them."

As a couple they were well matched, and everyone was too polite to stare at Kathleen's unconventional attire. They ate and drank their fill. Garth nodded and said good evening, to a few people whom he knew.

"Where do you live?" he asked Kathleen as they made their way into the ballroom.

"In Garden Street, just around the corner."

"So we haven't very far to go home then?"

"No," she said, "not far." Then in sudden consternation she said, "Oh dear, I forgot."

"What is it?" he asked.

"I was going to buy some whisky for Rosie, and I forgot my two new pennies."

"Who is Rosie?"

"She's my youngest, she has a cold."

"And the whisky is for her?"

"Yes."

"And the new pennies did you say?"

"Yes, one for each of the children."

"I'll see if I can get some," he replied.

The master of ceremonies announced the next dance, and the tall handsome officer and his very attractive lady, began to waltz amongst the social elite of the northern counties of England. All of them arrayed in their finest attire would grace any gathering in the land. The music was enchanting, the night romantic, the wine flowed freely, what more could anyone wish for?

Garth had eyes for no one but the lovely Kathleen. He did not care that she was only a barmaid and a weaver in his father's mill. She was beautiful and he wanted to possess her. Whatever he wanted in life he had never been denied and most of all he wanted this colleen. This mature Irish woman, this merry widow whom he was sure had so much to give. Come with me and be my love was uppermost in his mind.

Kathleen was utterly swept off her feet. Everything about him was wonderful, he danced superbly and he was a gentleman in the truest sense of the word. He pampered to her every whim. His voice and his touch were strong, and yet caressing. The desire to spend every waking moment with this dream of a man, was her dearest wish.

They longed to hold each other close but protocol insisted that he hold her delicately, almost at arm's length, as though she were some Dresden china doll. They both loved dancing and were enraptured by the tuneful melodies coming from the superb orchestra, but by one o'clock the strong desire for close physical contact became unbearable, and so in their eagerness to be alone together, they left the Derby Hall.

The snow was deep and falling fast. Standing outside Kathleen's house they embraced passionately.

"Can I come in my sweet, it's too far to walk home in this weather and I'll never get a cab now?"

Kathleen brushed the snow from the front of her hair she felt giddy with the wine, and thrilled to be loved after all her lonely years. "You'll have to be quiet," she whispered "Miss Duckett's in the house."

"Miss who?"

"Miss Duckett, she's sitting in with Rosie, you'll have to wait in the front parlour. Ssh, we must be very quiet."

Slowly she pressed the front door latch and after softly closing the door, they crept along the hallway and she led him into the dark front room. "Wait here," she instructed, "I won't be a minute."

Finding Miss Duckett asleep by the living room fireside, she awoke her gently and after apologizing for her lateness she took the woman's shawl, wrapped it around her shoulders and bade her goodnight from the front door. She waited to make sure the elderly woman reached her own home safely, then shivering, she closed the door with a sigh of relief.

She walked back down the hallway to fall eagerly into Garth's arms and they clung together in a long embrace. "Darling, you're lovely," he murmured.

Leading him into the warm living room she helped him to remove his khaki greatcoat. He took a flask of whisky and a bottle of sherry from the deep pockets.

"Is Rosie asleep?" he asked.

"Yes, I'm sure she will be."

"Give her some whisky tomorrow then, and we must try to get some new pennies tomorrow too. Will you have a drink darling?"

"I've really had enough already," Kathleen said whilst producing the only two wineglasses she possessed from the corner cupboard.

He filled both glasses and they drank together standing before the fireplace.

"Drink to me only with thine eyes and I'll not ask for wine." They laughingly repeated the words of the popular song together.

"You love music don't you?" he stated.

She nodded, taking a sip from her glass. "How do you know?"

"It's very obvious," he replied.

They emptied their glasses and he placed them on the red plush tablecloth.

Turning to Kathleen he held her face between his hands looking down at her, "You have green eyes," he remarked.

"So I should have, I'm Irish," she replied jokingly "And yours are blue, typically English, blond hair and blue eyes."

"Yes," he laughingly boasted, "one of the famous Armstrong's of Westmorland, all the better to hold you with my dear," he smiled pulling her close in his arms again, he kissed her repeatedly as she responded to his warmth and passion. "Darling please, I love you – you are so beautiful – Kathleen please – please be mine – my sweet – no darling please – don't – no – you mustn't deny me."

"No Garth, NO!"

"But you're so lovely – please my dearest." He kissed her neck and whispered to her to give him what his body craved.

"NO, DON'T!" she spoke aloud as his fingers began to fumble with the tiny buttons on her blouse, and then, without warning, she placed the palms of her hands full square on his chest and pushed him away from her with all her strength.

Overbalancing, he fell back against the table.

Picking up the large poker from the hearth she raised it menacingly.

"What are you doing?" he mocked her with total disbelief.

"I am not a whore," she hissed defiantly. "I'm not a whore," she repeated as her eyes began to fill with tears. "I don't have men here every night," she sobbed.

Garth held up his hand in protest and was about to speak, but before he could do so she spat out the words, "I've never been intimate with any man only my husband, he died more than four years ago, and now you come here thinking you can use me." Sitting down heavily she dropped the poker down on the hearth. Her cheeks were flushed and she looked more attractive than ever.

"You hardly gave me such a virtuous impression did you?" he replied with scorn.

"She looked up at him, the tears of remorse and shame welling in her eyes. "I thought you were an officer and a gentleman and," she hesitated, "please, I'm sorry, I've drunk too much wine, I'm not used to intoxicating liquor."

Regaining his composure he stood quietly looking down at her; she looked so pathetic and vulnerable, all his sympathy went out to her. Instinctively he knew she spoke the truth and impulsively he knelt beside her, taking her hands in his he kissed her fingertips. "Darling I'm so sorry," he said 'I've been such a cad, please forgive me, please," he pleaded.

Kathleen kept him in silent suspense, "I will," she finally conceded "only if you give me your solemn promise to behave and stop drinking."

"I swear, hand on my heart," he gestured.

"It's half past two," she announced, looking across the room at the black marble clock. "I'm very tired," she stifled a yawn. "I've been up since five o'clock yesterday morning."

"Darling, so you have, I am selfish. You go to bed,

I'll sleep down here."

"Elizabeth would scream if she found a man in the house when she gets up to go to work."

"I'll sleep on the sofa in the parlour then."

"No you can't, it's too cold in there. James is away, you can sleep in his bed."

Garth was surprised at her offer, "She really does think I'm an officer and a gentleman after all," he thought, then he said, "You're so sweet, I wish I had known you years ago."

"It isn't customary for the mill owner's son to associate with one of the weavers."

"Don't say that darling, anyway you're different."

"What do you mean?"

"You're refined and...no, I'm not going to say it, you'll only accuse me of flattery."

"Oh thank you sir, I'm honoured indeed," she laughed with him and then she said as if suddenly remembering the real world, "I should be going to work at the mill this morning."

"Oh no indeed, you can't go to work, I'm leaving on Monday night, I want you to be with me till then. Will you come to London Road Station with me?"

"Yes if you really want me to, but what about your family?"

"I'll telephone mother tomorrow. She'll probably be very annoyed but I'll get round her somehow."

Bonny roused herself and jumped down from the opposite fireside chair. "I'll have to let her out in the backyard," Kathleen said.

"She looks a good dog, how old is she?" he asked.

"She's fifteen, she was a lovely dog once, we've had her since she was a puppy and I dread losing her."

"Yes, I'm sure you do."

After seeing to the dog Kathleen said, "I'll show you

upstairs before I turn the gas mantles down. Please be quiet, we must not waken the girls, they sleep in the back bedroom."

"Please may I kiss you goodnight?" he whispered.

"Yes all right, just a little peck," she consented mischievously as she held out her cheek.

"Thank you for a wonderful evening, good night my love, sleep well."

"Goodnight Garth."

Elizabeth went off to work later that morning believing her mother had already left for the mill. Kathleen had been up at six o'clock, she had given Rosie some lemon tea, laced with whisky, and then she went back to bed, finding it hard to convince herself Garth Armstrong was sound asleep in James's room. Getting up at nine thirty she re-kindled the living room fire and also the back bedroom fire for Rosie. Garth came downstairs at a quarter past ten and whilst he was enjoying a good cooked breakfast, Kathleen ventured out into the deep snow to buy him shaving soap and a razor.

Unable to keep her news to herself, she called to see Bessy who was not well enough to go to the mill. "Guess who came into the Derby last night?" she asked with rapt excitement.

"I'm too old for guessing games Kathleen, tell me!"

"Lieutenant Garth Armstrong, in officers uniform, of course," Kathleen enthused. "And guess what happened?"

"I don't know, tell me."

"We went to the County Ball at the Derby Hall, and then he took me home."

"Kathleen Duffy, I do not believe you!"

"It's true, he's round at my house now."

"You don't mean he stayed all night?"

"Yes it was snowing, I mean…" Kathleen stammered, "he slept in James's bed."

"And so he should, well I never, what next, I am surprised. How long is he home for?"

"Till Monday night. He wants me to go with him to Manchester to see him off. If you're feeling better, do you think you could sleep at our house on Monday night to look after Rosie? Garth's train doesn't leave till nearly midnight, so I'm bound to be late home."

"Yes, you know I will love. How is Rosie?"

"She's staying in bed again today, I gave her some whisky this morning. I should have brought some for you shouldn't I? It's bitter cold outside, can I bring you anything from the shop?"

"Yes, if you would please Kath, just a few things, it won't take you a minute. Mr Garth will be wondering where you've got to, I expect you want to get back to him. Just fancy him being at your house, I can hardly believe it."

"Don't tell anyone will you Bessy, I don't want to be the talk of the mill."

"You can trust me love, I won't tell anybody."

Completing the shopping for Bessy, Kathleen returned home, and after Garth had finished shaving in the mirror above the kitchen slop stone, they sat talking in the living room.

"Will you wait for me?" he pleaded. "It could be twelve months before I'm back home, depending on how long it takes to beat the Boer's. It's a long way to South Africa, can you wait so long?"

"Yes I can wait," she replied with no doubt in her mind.

"How long is it since you left Ireland?" he asked.

Surprised at the question she replied, "Eighteen years. "Have you ever been there?"

"No, I would like to go. What is it like?"

"Tis like heaven on earth," she sighed, reverting back to her Irish brogue. "Especially where I come from."

"It sounds as though you would like to go back. Don't you like Bury?"

"I like the Lancashire people, they've been very good to us, but I miss the old country, it's so beautiful. You can't compare the green fields of Ireland to the dark satanic mills, although," Kathleen hesitated, "there is some lovely countryside in Lancashire too, it isn't all doom and gloom."

"Marry me and I'll take you home again Kathleen," reciting the words of the popular song he continued, '*Across the ocean wild and wide, To where your heart has ever been, Since first you were ---*'

Interrupting the song Garth asked, "What was your name before you were married Kathleen?"

"Err," she answered, "O Sullivan, Kathleen O Sullivan."

Garth paused, and acting solemnly, going down on one knee before her, he clasped both her hands in his. Proposing to her he said, "Miss O Sullivan, will you, being a woman free to marry, will you do me the great honour to be my beautiful bride. I mean it Kathleen, I love you, will you be my wife?"

Looking with deep sincerity, into his big blue eyes Kathleen gave her answer, "I'm honoured by your proposal sir, I'll give you my answer when you return from South Africa."

During the afternoon they went out shopping together. Rosie stayed comfortably in bed with plenty of books to read and some dolls' clothes to make. At Garth's request, they trudged through the deep snow to the flower shop to meet Elizabeth who was astounded to see her mother accompanied by such a fine handsome lieutenant.

Introducing her gentleman friend to her daughter, Kathleen felt like some errant schoolgirl, but Garth soon put them both at ease, and Elizabeth thought her mother looked more radiant than she had ever seen her before. Kathleen was amazed, but needless to say delighted, when Garth bought her a very expensive, necklace of pearls. They stopped by the music stall in the indoor market hall as Kathleen usually did, and he bought her the sheet music copy *'I'll take you home again Kathleen'*.

"Play it for me when we get home," he requested.

That same night, the last one of the old century, they went out to the Royal Hotel in Silver Street.

Garth telephoned his mother who was extremely annoyed, "Surely you could come home Garth, you know we're having a farewell party for you tonight."

"I'm terribly sorry mother, I couldn't possibly get home in this weather, give my apologies to everyone there. I'm staying with a friend. I can't tell you on the telephone, I'll explain when I see you on Monday."

They returned home early to be with Elizabeth and Rosie, it was New Years Eve and the beginning of a new century, they would all enjoy a festive drink together. They spent Sunday, the first day of January, nineteen hundred quietly. The snow was still thick on the ground and so they stayed by the fire in the front parlour, enjoying plenty of food and drink and music around the piano.

In the evening Kathleen had to go to work at the Derby Hotel at seven o'clock. Garth went with her and seated himself at the bar. Being Sunday, it was early closing night and so Kathleen would finish work shortly after ten p.m. She was glad it was Elsie's night off. As she had said earlier to Bessy, she did not want everyone at the mill to know about herself and Garth Armstrong and Elsie would be the last person to keep such knowledge to herself.

Leaving the hotel at ten-thirty they returned home to Garden Street, and by midnight, they had all retired to bed. Garth had kept his promise, behaving all weekend as a gentleman should, but later that night, when he was sure Kathleen was fast asleep, he crept into her room. Closing the door stealthily, he slipped into bed beside her. Stifling her startled cry with his lips and seducing her surreptitiously, she gasped as he induced her surrender to his ardent desire.

Garth left the house at ten o'clock on Monday morning, promising to be back no later than four o'clock in the afternoon. He walked to Bolton Street Station to inquire about the times of the trains.

"You'll get to Manchester all right sir," the man in the ticket office told him, "they've cleared the line to Manchester, but we can't promise you'll be able to leave for London tonight. It depends if there's any more snow or if the points freeze. We're clear as far as Crewe sir but we can't say what it will be like in the Midlands. Train leaves here at 7.40 p.m., that'll get you to Victoria in good time, then you'll have to cross Manchester to London Road to catch the London train."

Garth thanked him and calling a hansom he headed for home, with mixed feelings of elation at the recent conquest of his loved one, and trepidation at the prospect of facing his mother. He would have to call at the mill later to say goodbye to his father. "It would take an earthquake to keep that man away from the factory," he mused.

The inquest with his mother was not at all as bad as he had expected. He did not venture to say where he had been staying and she did not ask. She was in fact quite tearful, as

124

would be expected of a mother saying goodbye to her only offspring who was going thousands of miles away to do battle.

"Don't worry mother, I'll be back I promise – there's no corner of a foreign field going to claim this Englishman!"

To Kathleen the day seemed endless waiting for Garth's return. The sky was black and heavy as it seemed with more snow, and it was freezing cold.

Garth arrived back after a strenuous day at three thirty, giving Kathleen a long kiss in the hall. "Darling, why do I have to leave you?" he whispered.

Rosie peeped around the living room door, astonished to see her mother in the arms of a man.

They were half way through a hot meal when Bessy came in, behaving rather shyly when she saw the distinguished lieutenant 'Mr. Garth' seated at Kathleen's table. "I've been home to get my nightdress, you did say you wanted me to stay the night didn't you love? Ee, isn't it an awful night?" she said as she nodded and smiled at Garth.

"Hello Bessy," he greeted, "yes it is dreadful weather, come near to the fire and warm yourself. Is it foggy outside?"

"Yes that fog's coming down all right, going to be a bad night it is. Will the trains be running do you think?"

Instead of answering her query Kathleen said, "Come on now Bessy, sit down, I've cooked some roast beef and Yorkshire pudding and roast potatoes. Are you hungry?"

"Hungry? I could eat an 'orse, that does look good and it smells good too. How are you Rosie, are you feeling better love? There's a lot of influenza going around, no wonder with all this bad weather."

At seven o'clock the couple were ready to leave for

the station. Garth had a large kit bag and a suitcase to carry. Kathleen had bought him a fountain pen and propelling pencil in a case, hoping of course that Garth would use the pen to write to her often.

"Ooh it's not fit to turn a dog out," Bessy ejaculated as she opened the front door, ready to see them off. "Goodbye sir, come back safely won't you?"

"Thank you Bessy I will. Take good care of Kathleen for me."

"Yes sir I'll do my best. Will you be all right Kathleen, what time will you be home?"

"I don't know Bessy, don't wait up for me, I'll see you tomorrow."

"Goodnight love," she kissed Rosie, "be a good girl."

"Yes Mammy I will, goodnight."

Arriving at Bolton Street Station they were pleased to take refuge in the general waiting room, where there was a big coal fire burning in the grate. The fog wasn't too bad, more like a mist, but even so the seven forty train did not shunt into the station until eight o'clock. As the train approached Manchester, the fog became like a thick dirty yellow pea soup. The passengers peered through the windows, trying in vain to penetrate the dense blanket of fog. The atmosphere was tense as they listened to the slow pounding of the iron wheels on the rails. Finally, the train snaked into Manchester Victoria Station at ten minutes past nine and the passengers alighted with relief at having arrived safely at their destination. Garth lifted his kit bag on to his shoulder.

"Let me carry the case," Kathleen offered, "it isn't too heavy."

"Carry your bag sir?" a cheery porter offered. "Want a cab, going to London Road sir? Dreadful night isn't it?"

The porter found them a cab, the horses were stomping and snorting in the bitter cold night air. How the cabby manoeuvred the hansom along the crowded streets to

126

the other side of the city whilst avoiding an accident, was incredible.

"The horse probably knows his own way," Kathleen said as she snuggled close to Garth to keep warm.

The cab came to a halt outside London Road Station at ten minutes to ten. Kathleen's heart sank when she realized that Garth would have left her in another two hours time, his train was due to leave at eleven forty five. Walking towards the booking office, they stopped to read the train departures notice. The trains were running only as far as Crewe, all other trains were cancelled due to the fog and freezing points. Except for a few other soldiers, the station was unusually quiet.

"Does it mean you can't go tonight?" Kathleen asked hopefully.

It was as Garth had hoped and expected. His eyes shone as he smiled down at her, "No, I can't go tonight darling, it means we have more time together."

They noticed as they passed waiting rooms. Soldiers were lying on the seats and some on the floor, using their kit bags as pillows.

"Do we have to go back to Bury?"

"I hope not darling, come on, we'll try the Grand Hotel, at least I have a good excuse for not getting back to camp on time."

They walked quickly up London Road, which by now was very quiet, for the fog had become thicker than ever. The few remaining cabs were full, most of them having turned in for the night. Garth gave Kathleen his big white handkerchief to hold over her nose and mouth. He was unable to cover his own mouth as his hands were so full. The dirty black moisture was settling everywhere as the smoke from thousands of house, and dozens of factory chimneys, could not get away into the outer atmosphere. It hung in the air, to be breathed into nostrils and lungs, dripping from hair and eyebrows and clinging to clothing in filthy wet globules.

Crossing the road, they came to the Grand Hotel. "Sorry sir we're full," the hotel doorman informed them, "Try the Midland, you might get in there. Sorry sir, madam, horrid night isn't it?"

"How far is it?" Kathleen asked, after they had thanked the man.

"I'm sorry darling, can you make it, hold on to me, we must try not to talk in this filthy stuff."

Finally, after groping their way across Piccadilly and along Moseley Street they arrived, dirty and exhausted in the grand and opulent foyer of the Midland Hotel. Without hesitation Garth booked a double suite in the names of Lieutenant and Mrs. Armstrong. Kathleen was mortified at the dreadful lie, then quickly consoled herself, the clandestine affair was not so bad after all, Garth had proposed marriage to her she reasoned, was she not to be his future wife?

The experience to Kathleen was so unreal, as they moved along the sumptuous corridors and into the luxurious suite, with wonder of wonders, a splendid bathroom with lots of hot water and lovely warm towels, it was just like a miracle!

After they had bathed, Garth had food and wine sent up and it was after midnight when, between the soft pink sheets, she gave herself to him in sweet abandon. The two bodies joined together, thrilling to the exquisite delight of the age old joy of man with woman, the two becoming deliriously one flesh.

Unbelievably next morning the sun was shining and the snow melting. It was mid-day on January 3rd when Kathleen said goodbye to her beloved one as he leaned from the window of the train door.

"*Goodbye Kathleen I must leave you,*" he whispered the words of the popular song in her ear, "*Though it breaks my heart to go*" They clung to each other until the moving train tore their grasping hands apart and they waved farewell through blinding tears. Kathleen watched and waved as the train wound out of the station and she could see him no more.

Feeling as though she had left part of herself behind, she made her way with a heavy heart back home again to Bury. Before leaving, Garth had insisted on giving her a cheque for £30, instructing her to take it to Martins Bank in Silver Street, and to open a Bank Account. She decided she would do it today as the Bank was always closed when she was home from work.

Bessy came round to Kathleen's house after work, she was eager to hear all the news. "Where did you stay last night?" she asked.

"The Midland Hotel in Manchester."

"The Midland!" Bessy gasped. "I bet you felt like Queen Victoria herself."

Kathleen told Bessy everything except for the dark secret that she and Garth had slept together. No one – she was determined – would ever know that.

Once back at work, Kathleen found it hard to believe the wonderful weekend had not been a dream. She would return home to gaze at the glittering pearls, and to examine the bankbook to convince herself it had all really happened.

Four days after Garth left, she received a big bouquet of yellow, white and bronze chrysanthemums with a card which read, "Wait for me, I Love You, Garth."

She decided to leave the money in the bank to make interest until she needed it. She had never dreamt she would ever possess such a small fortune, she would have to work for months to earn £30.

The days soon changed into weeks, and as they did she became more anxious and worried. Apart from her three pregnancies, her monthly menstruation cycle had always been every twenty-eight days, as regular as clockwork. January 18th had passed by without a sign, and then as each day dawned in February, and nothing happened, she became more tense and worried. Pretending she was happy, she would sing with the other weavers during the day, then at night after doing the housework, she would bury herself in a book or *'The Sunday Companion'*, anything to take her mind off what she dreaded most.

She would snap at the children and if Elizabeth played, *'I'll take you home again Kathleen'* on the piano, she would shout at her, "Leave it, leave it, can you not find something else to play?"

There was no sign of a letter from Garth. Insidiously the thought began to creep into her mind, she had been completely fooled. His talk of marriage had been a deception. The expensive pearls and the money had been the wages for her services as his harlot. He would have no conscience, she had been well paid. There would be other women in Capetown with whom he could play the 'love game'.

As the days before February 15th came, she would comfort herself with the idea that it sometimes happened that a woman might completely miss her period for one month, and revert to normal again the next. February 15th came and went with the stark realization; she had been fooling herself!

She arrived home from work one day in the middle of March to be greeted by James in gleeful mood. "Mother, guess what's happened?"

In a dull tone she responded, "What is it James?"

"I've been told I can take the exam for a Kay Scholarship to Queens College, Cambridge – Cambridge Mother Cambridge!" He danced around and hugged her so she was forced to smile.

"Mother what's the matter, I thought you'd be thrilled to bits, are you ill?"

"I've got a headache," she lied. "Yes of course I'm pleased, it's wonderful news. Did the postman come today Elizabeth?"

"Yes Mother, a letter came."

"A letter!" Kathleen's heart leapt and she held her breath.

"Here it is!" Elizabeth picked up the letter from the back of the sideboard "It's postmarked Preston," she pointed out.

Kathleen sat down, overwhelmed with the disappointment of dashed hopes, the tears came to her eyes.

"Are you going to open it Mother?" Rosie asked.

"All right," she sighed, "give it to me, I'll see what it says." She opened the envelope, which held not a letter, but an invitation card. "It's cousin Oonagh, she's getting married on April 24th, and we're invited."

"A wedding!" The girls pranced around excitedly. "What shall we wear? I'll have to have a new dress Mammy," Rosie insisted.

Kathleen's tears welled again as she imagined herself disgracing her family at her cousin's wedding, looking like an unmarried pregnant floosy.

James sensed his mother's unhappiness. "What is it Mother, I know there's something wrong. Is it Garth Armstrong?" He must be too busy fighting those Boers, they've been telling us all about the war at school, it must be jolly hard. He should still find time to write to you though, shouldn't he, especially if he's an officer and a gentleman." He held his Mother's hand, doing his very best to console the woman he loved.

His Mother managed to smile at him through her tears "Yes James, you're right, especially if he's an officer AND a gentleman."

It was later the same night when Kathleen told Elizabeth, "I'm going round to Bessy's, I won't be long."

"Can't you stay in with me when I've come home early?"

"Not tonight love, I have to talk to Bessy, I promise I won't be long."

Her friend greeted her in her usual affectionate manner, "Hello love, I didn't expect to see you tonight. Sit down, I'm just going to put the kettle on for a nice cup of tea." Coming through from the kitchen with the kettle in her hand she asked, "What's the matter Kath, you look down in the dumps. Have you still not heard from Garth?"

"No I haven't, but that isn't the only problem Bessy, I don't know what you'll think of me," she paused, taking a deep breath before she added, "I'm going to have his baby."

"OH NO!" Bessy stood with her mouth open wide, kettle in hand. "Ee love I am sorry, are you sure, are you not mistaken, when will it be?"

Kathleen shook her head sorrowfully, "No I'm not mistaken, end of September I suppose."

"You haven't been to see Doctor Mann yet have you?"

Kathleen shook her head again.

"You know them boats take weeks to get to South Africa, you might get a letter even yet. I'm sure you will," Bessy tried to console her friend.

"I hope you're right, but it's more than ten weeks now since he left, and even if he does write, he won't be home before September will he? It will be at least December before he comes home." Then tightening her lips she voiced the thought never far from her mind. "That's assuming he doesn't get shot or something else as dreadful."

Bessy was silent as her friend continued to confess.

"I feel so wicked, I ought to have had more sense. It was just one night at my house, and then that night at the Midland, and now he's gone and forgotten all about me."

"How did he sign the register?"

"What?"

"The hotel register, at the Midland, what did he sign?"

Kathleen choked on the words as she answered

"Lieutenant and Mrs. Armstrong."

"Are you sure?"

"Yes I saw the signature. I felt so guilty about it. Why what about it?"

"Well they usually sign a false name when they're trying to get away with it, don't they?"

"I wouldn't know about that."

"You see you can prove he's the father from that register."

"Oh I see," Kathleen answered vaguely, although she could hardly see how that register was going to help her situation. Then she voiced the question, "How can I possibly tell the children and all the rest of the family? Oh Bessy, I wish I were dead! Cousin Oonagh's getting married in April and James wants to go to Cambridge University, whatever will he say when he knows?"

"I don't know love, but he's bound to know soon when the baby starts to show. You go home now Kathleen, it's getting late, leave it to me, I promise I'll think of something."

The next day Bessy caught hold of the office boy's arm as he passed by her looms. She handed him a sealed envelope marked 'private' and addressed to Mr. William Armstrong. Pointing to the name she mouthed the words, "Give it to him," as she gestured towards the office. Later the same day she sat with the mill owner in the very imposing factory boardroom.

"I received your note Mrs. Hargreaves, would you mind telling me what is so urgent, I'm a very busy man. He was a tall, stout, handsome man of late middle age and Bessy trembled inwardly at his very superior manner. He was

133

immaculately dressed and smoking a cigar.

"It's Mr. Garth sir, have you heard from him?"

"Really Mrs. Hargreaves, that is no concern of yours, none whatsoever."

Bessy took a deep breath whilst saying a quick prayer "It's my friend sir, Mrs. Kathleen Duffy, she's going to have a baby."

"Please will you come to the point, I don't understand what you're talking about."

"My friend's having a baby and Mr. Garth's the father."

The man stared at her in astonishment without speaking, so she continued, "It was that weekend before he went away, New Year when it was snowing. He took her to the Midland Hotel in Manchester, there's proof in the register, he signed it Lieutenant and Mrs. Armstrong."

"Really, if your friend is that kind of woman, what does she expect," he said scornfully, "she has only herself to blame."

"No she isn't, she's a good woman." Bessy raised her voice in anger. "She works hard in the mill, she's never had a man since her husband died from that fire, and that's five years ago, and Mr. Garth said he wanted to marry her."

"All right Mrs. Hargreaves, calm down now, we don't want all the staff hearing do we now?" He spoke in a more kindly manner. "What you have said has come as a great shock, that's if it's true, of course."

"It's true as God's my judge."

"Have you told anyone?"

"Nobody."

"I suppose your friend sent you to me?"

"No sir, she doesn't know I'm here, I didn't tell anyone."

He stubbed his cigar in an enormous glass ashtray and standing up he pushed back his heavy chair. "Now then as you know, my son is a grown man and I cannot be responsible for his actions."

"No sir, I understand that."

"But," he paused looking at her thoughtfully, "If you promise me not to say a word to anyone, especially to Mrs err?"

"Duffy sir, Mrs. Kathleen Duffy."

"To Mrs. Duffy, I will try to see what I can do but mind you now, I'm not promising anything at all, only that I will do my very best to help. Where does she live by the way?"

"Garden Street, number seven, opposite the Hippodrome."

"Number seven Garden Street," he repeated, taking a notebook from his pocket, he scribbled down the address.

"Thank you very much sir," Bessy sighed with great relief, feeling as though she had overcome some insurmountable obstacle. "She's a good girl, and bonny too."

He smiled at her, "Yes I expect she is, all right Mrs. Hargreaves, I'm pleased you had the courage to tell me," he said as he showed her from the office.

On the Saturday afternoon following Bessy's disclosure to William Armstrong, Kathleen was alone in her house. Responding to a knock at the front door she was confronted by a tall, well-dressed, middle aged woman whom she had never seen before.

"Mrs. Kathleen Duffy?" the woman inquired haughtily.

"Yes."

"May I come in, I wish to talk privately?"

"Yes please, do come in." Kathleen led her into the

front parlour, wondering all the time just who she could be? "Will you have a seat?" Kathleen offered.

"No thank you, I prefer to stand," the woman replied in the same haughty manner.

Kathleen seated herself on a fireside chair and the woman stood beside the piano. "Can I help you?" Kathleen queried politely.

"I believe you've been spreading nasty rumours about my son," she said.

"Your son, I'm sorry, I don't understand. Who is he?" she asked, thinking her to be the mother of one of the Grammar School boys.

"My name is Gertrude Armstrong."

Kathleen gasped, her face turning bright red. She recognized the facial resemblance to Garth.

"You've been saying my son has fathered you a child?"

Shocked into silence Kathleen found it difficult to speak. Then she replied, "It is true, I am carrying Garth's child. Have you heard from him?" she ventured.

Ignoring her question the woman asked scornfully, "When is your bastard expected?"

Kathleen cringed at the dreadful slur, "The end of September," she answered hardly knowing where to put herself in the face of such contempt.

"Did Lieutenant Armstrong pay you handsomely?"

Kathleen winced, "He gave me £30," she said, regretting the words as soon as they were out of her mouth.

"£30! My goodness, how benevolent. What have you done, squandered it I suppose?"

"It's still in the bank," Kathleen felt her anger beginning to rise.

"Then I see I've wasted my time. I was going to offer you five pounds for the operation, far more than adequate I'm sure."

"Operation?" Kathleen was puzzled.

"Come now, don't tell me you're so naïve, there are women who only require a small fee for the effective use of soap and water. I've heard it aborts an unwanted foetus."

Kathleen stood up, and facing the woman, she placed her hands on her protruding abdomen. The woman's words had shocked a furious response from every fibre of her being. Her voice shook as she spoke with suppressed rage. "I'm going to have this baby Mrs. Armstrong," she glared at her and swallowed hard. "And when it's born it's going to be loved. It's not going to be choked with carbolic soap and water, that's to be kept for nasty women like you, to wash out their filthy mouths!"

Gertrude Armstrong humped her shoulders indignantly she glared as though she were ready to strike at the younger woman, who had dared to address her in such a manner. "Very well," she said as she turned on her heels, "I came to help and…"

"Get out of my house or I'll call the constable," Kathleen shouted at the woman. "Get out!" Her arm went out passed the woman's shoulders, her finger pointing to the door. Kathleen was quick to detect a flash of fear in her eyes before she marched off down the hallway with her long skirts swinging, she went out through the front door which she did not bother to close.

Gertrude Armstrong disappeared down the street and Kathleen closed the front door. She heaved a great sigh, leaning against it to rest her emotion racked body. Realizing how she had reacted to the woman's despicable suggestion, she suddenly felt elated, totally relieved from the misery which had engulfed her for several weeks past. The new life forming inside her body had been a burden and a dread. Now she knew the precious life she bore within her was there to be cherished and treasured. She spoke out loud to convince herself even more. "I'm going to love my baby, it's mine and I love it and I don't care who knows about it."

She went into the living room exulting in her newly discovered joy. She began to tidy the house. Then, almost without thinking, she took up a piece of paper and a pencil and started to scribble the words:

My Precious One.

"Long the travail
Till waiting time is o'er
Maybe the soul
Must touch some distant shore,
Yet all the glory
Of Motherhood I'll own
If through pain and darkness
My Little One I've won"

Pushing the paper into the sideboard drawer with her other poems she reached for her shawl. Hurrying off to the baby linen and the wool shops, she bought two first size baby nightdresses, three vests, and some white cashmere wool to make a baby shawl. Then overtaken with curiosity as to how Gertrude Armstrong had known about the baby, she hurried to Bessy's house in Haymarket Street. The house opposite, which had been burned out in the fire, was now a thriving sweet shop.

Knocking on Bessy's door, she tipped the latch and walked in, "Bessy," she called out and walked through the house to find her friend pegging out clothes on the washing line.

"Hello love," she said, with a clothes peg in her

mouth. "Put the kettle on, I'll be in shortly when I've pegged these out."

Kathleen did as she was bidden and when Bessy came in she said "I've had a visitor this afternoon."

"A visitor? Anyone I know?"

"Garth Armstrong's Mother. How did she know?"

Bessy's face reddened, "Mrs. Armstrong – came to see you! How did she know what?"

How did she know about the baby?"

"It wasn't me," then reluctantly she added, "it must have been her husband."

"Mr.William. How did he know?"

"I went to see him on Wednesday, never mind him, what did his wife say?"

"She was going to give me money – blood money," Kathleen scoffed.

"Blood money?"

"Yes, she wanted me to get rid of the baby."

"Oh God love us, she didn't. What did you say?"

"I ordered her out through the door and threatened to fetch the police."

"Good for you."

"I told her she was the one who needed soap and water to wash her mouth out."

Bessy shrieked out loud, "Serves her right, the horrid old hag. What did she say to that?"

"Nothing, she just went out with her tail between her legs. I'll probably get the sack on Monday."

"Oh no you won't, I'll see to that."

"Bessy," Kathleen's voice was more subdued. "Please don't tell anyone, I would hate anyone to know how horrid my baby's grandmother is."

"You can trust me, I won't say anything. It's too disgusting for words."

"Look what I've got," Kathleen said as she proudly

held up the baby gowns and vests. "I'm going to make a shawl. By the way, what did Mr. William say, did he kick you out of his office? I don't know how you had the nerve to tell him."

"Well it's easier to stick up for a friend than it is for yourself. As a matter of fact he was kind, shocked and nasty at first – but he is going to do his best to help. He told me not to tell you, he doesn't want to build up your hopes but he definitely said he would try to help. I'm sure it wasn't his idea to send his wife, he didn't seem to be that kind of a man."

"I suppose that is something we will never know."

"No, I don't suppose we will, but it's surprising, things sometimes have a way of coming to light. Anyway, I'm glad I've got my happy Kathleen back. It's good to see you looking forward to this baby."

"Yes, I am now but I'm not looking forward to telling the children. I think I'll leave it till Elizabeth's home tomorrow. It is Sunday tomorrow isn't it?"

"Yes, all day," Bessy joked, "from morn till night." Then she added, "You know I said I would see Miss Johnson, about an apprenticeship for Rosie at the dressmaker's shop on Princess Street?"

"Yes."

"Well I saw Miss Scissie this morning, she would like Rosie to call to see her. There are three sisters who own the shop, but Rosie must ask to see Miss Scissie. I told her Rosie is a very good seamstress."

"Thank you very much Bessie, Rosie will be thrilled. Are you coming round tonight?"

"Yes, I'll be at your house about seven. There's a good show on at the Hippodrome next week, shall we go?"

"Yes all right. I'm giving up my job at the Derby, but I'll talk to you about that later, bye now."

On Sunday afternoon, after they had cleared the dinner table and washed the dishes, James put on his coat, "I'm going for a walk with George Mother," he explained.

"Wait a minute James, I have something to tell you, all of you, don't go James, it's important."

"Hurry up then Mam, what is it? I promised to call for George at two o'clock and it's five to now."

"You're going to have a baby brother or sister," Kathleen blurted out.

"What!" James shouted at her.

She tried to explain. "A baby, it's coming in September. It was Garth Armstrong, he said he wanted me to be his wife."

"Mother how could you – you're not married."

"I know James but – oh you don't understand – I was wrong, I know – but the baby – it's going to be born at the end of September."

"What will all the neighbours, and Mr. and Mrs. Kirkman think?" James was anxious to know.

"Please don't tell them yet James, you must please leave that to me, it's a very delicate matter."

"Oh Mammy," Elizabeth cried, and ran away upstairs.

"Can I make some clothes for it?" Rosie asked.

"Yes of course you can. JAMES PLEASE you must understand, I didn't mean…"

"I'm going out Mother, I'll talk about it later," James called out from the hall.

It was all confusion, so different to what she had intended. "I wanted to explain everything properly," she told Rosie.

"Yes Mammy I know, and they won't listen to you, they've both gone away."

"I'm going to talk to Elizabeth, read your book Rosie," Kathleen pleaded as she hurried upstairs to find out what was going on in Elizabeth's mind.

She found her lying on her bed with her head buried in her pillow. Kathleen sat on the side of the bed, silently for a while, and then she questioned her. "Liz, what's the matter, why did you run away?"

"Oh Mammy Mammy I don't want you to die, I love you, please don't die Mammy please."

"Who says I'm going to die?"

"The baby," she said between sobs. "Jane's Mammy died when she was having a baby. Mammy I love you. Tell me you won't die."

"Elizabeth no, I promise I won't die. Did I die when you were born, and James, and Rosie?"

"No you didn't," she reasoned. "Can I choose the names for the baby?"

Surprised at the unexpected request she replied, "Yes of course you can. What names do you like?"

Elizabeth thought whilst resting her head against her Mother's shoulder, "I like David for a boy, and if it's a girl I like," she paused quite a time before she said, "it's the name of a Greek goddess, I read it in a book, it's Diana."

"Mm. Diana, that's a lovely name. So that's settled then, David for a boy and Diana for a girl."

"Do you think it might be twins, one of each?"

"Dear me no, I hope not."

"What do you think it will be then?"

"I don't know, we'll just have to wait and see."

"Are you going to tell Mr. Garth?" Elizabeth asked.

"I don't think so, he doesn't want to know about me or the baby."

"That is awful, I thought he was a nice man."

Kathleen decided to go to her cousin Oonagh's

wedding, she could wear something loose fitting to hide the baby which wasn't showing very much yet. She would have to tell her Aunt Maureen, whom she loved almost as much as she had loved her own mother. She knew she would receive a sympathetic hearing, without fear of recriminations.

It was very enjoyable to meet with their relatives again. The wedding took place at St.Wilfreds, Preston, where Kathleen had married Francis. The whole affair brought back nostalgic memories, causing Kathleen to weep.

Cousin Peggy was chief bridesmaid to her sister, she seemed to be very happy although still unmarried, at twenty eight years old. Cousin Thomas, now a handsome twenty-one year old, reminded Kathleen of her brother James. Thomas was also the 'spitting image' of her Uncle Seamus. Oonagh's younger sister Kathleen, who had the typical Irish red hair, made a beautiful bridesmaid. Uncle Dennis and Auntie Nellie were both in their mid-sixties, and Uncle Dennis still suffered from chronic bronchitis.

In the evening, after the wedding reception, Kathleen managed to find a few minutes alone with her Aunt Maureen.

"You can count your blessings," Maureen chided her "be thankful you have some money in the bank and don't have to go knocking on the Workhouse door when the baby's born. You never know, you might hear from Garth yet, it's a very long voyage to South Africa, letters take a long time, especially when there's a war on."

Kathleen was very grateful for the kindness of her Aunt but refused quite stubbornly to believe in any such miracle.

CHAPTER 4
COME BACK TO EIREANN

The thick brown paper parcel, tied and sealed with red waxed string, finally ended its six thousand mile journey when the postman knocked at number seven, and Elizabeth answered the door. It was a beautiful morning in the middle of May and Kathleen had left for work two hours before.

When she arrived home at six in the evening, she was laying the table when Rosie came downstairs. "Close your eyes and open yours hands please," she stood with her hands behind her back, her face beaming. She could hardly contain her excitement at the prospect of surprising her Mother.

"What is it, have you got a present for me?"

Rosie laughed with glee, "Hurry up, close your eyes." Her mood was infectious and Kathleen laughingly closed her eyes, holding out her hands to receive the gift.

Rosie placed a parcel in her Mother's hands, "Look at the postmark Mammy, James says it's from South Africa."

Hearing the commotion James left his homework, entering the living room he was just in time to see the look of sheer amazement on his Mother's face. She gazed at the parcel and her head whirled.

James's voice when he urged, "Open it Mother, here's the scissors," sounded way off in the distance.

She laid the parcel on the table, its contents revealed no less than thirty-three long letters, written on thin rice paper in neat copper plate hand writing. She sat down at the table and began to read the letter at the top of the pile. It was dated January 6th 1900.

My Dearest Kathleen,

This, my darling, I pray will be the first of many letters, as I intend writing to you as often as possible.

The rest of the words became blurred as she tried in vain to hold back her tears. Her heart filled with joy and she wept copiously. James gave her his handkerchief and went into the kitchen to make her a cup of tea, brushing away tears from his own eyes as he did so.

Kathleen took hours to read all the letters, then taking a pink ribbon, she tied them all together. That night she carried them to bed, falling asleep with the love letters close to her breast. The next day she was too tired and excited to go to work. It was ten o'clock in the morning when she sat up in bed, staring contentedly at the bundle. They were such wonderful letters, so full of love they made her feel no other woman had been loved so much before. She must write to him to-day, telling him about their baby, but asking him not to worry about her, only to come home as soon as ever he could. She felt ashamed she had doubted him, not having any faith in his love.

The next day she went to the mill. She was a picture of radiant health and her heart was singing with the knowledge, her man really loved her. At nine fifteen she received a note, the message requested her to be in the office at ten thirty. It was signed William Armstrong.

She was nervous when she was shown into the office of the big man himself, "Whatever did Mr. William Armstrong want with her?"

"Good morning Mrs. Duffy."

"Good morning sir."

"Sit down please," he smiled, eyeing her up and down.

"Thank you sir."

His enormous desk was neat and tidy and he sat down opposite her. "I have some good news for you Kathleen, err may I call you Kathleen?"

She nodded.

"Garth has written to his Mother and me, saying he wants you to be his wife."

"Oh I see," she smiled with relief.

"I'll be very frank with you Kathleen," his eyes narrowed as he paused and took a whiff from his cigar. "You are not our ideal choice for our daughter in law. I believe you have three children already, but Garth leaves us in no doubt as to his intentions. "We could threaten to cut him off without the proverbial penny, but that would be a useless exercise, his grandmother left him a small fortune in his own right."

Kathleen listened intently, taking in every word.

"It would have saved a great deal of trouble for every one if he had told us about you before he left, however, we will have to cope with the situation in his absence, as best we can. "It's just as well, in your condition," he waved his cigar towards her, "that he does want to marry you. Wouldn't you say so?"

Kathleen took the jibe without flinching, "Yes sir," she answered calmly.

He had expected her to be some kind of flighty, go getting woman but she was nothing of the sort. She was calm, self assured and dignified. Even whilst wearing overalls and with lint in her hair, she was extremely attractive. "It isn't suitable for our son's future wife to be working in the mill, and err – we must consider our grandchild and your own health of course."

"That's very kind of you sir."

"I must insist you finish working here tonight." Kathleen's heart missed a beat. "We are not going to leave you without means of support, of course. You will be paid thirty shillings each week until your marriage."

"Thank you very much sir."

"Look Kathleen," his voice softening, "If we're going to be father and daughter-in-law can we please forego the formalities?"

"You must understand Mr. Armstrong, it isn't easy for me to stop calling you sir. I even found it difficult to stop calling your son, Mr. Garth."

He smiled at her humour, "Did you indeed?"

"Yes I did," she grinned back at him.

"I took the liberty of sending Garth a telegram telling him about the child. Did Mrs. Hargreaves tell you she had been to see me?"

"Yes, she told me after she had seen you."

"I did ask her not to tell you, I thought it might raise your hopes too much, but it isn't important now."

The thought flashed through Kathleen's mind that he had no idea of his wife's visit suggesting an abortion. "I'm not going to be the one to tell him," she thought. She listened as he continued.

"I also contacted a friend at the Foreign Office so," he paused, laying his fist on the desk, "even if Garth is not home in time, it may still be possible for you to marry before the child is born."

"By proxy you mean."

He stared at her know how. "Yes my dear, by proxy of course. But you never know, Garth may even be here in person."

"That does seem a great deal to hope for."

"Yes it does, I admit, but still, the age of miracles you know. You have other children I believe, by your first marriage?"

"Yes I have three, two girls and a boy. James is at the Grammar School, he hopes to take a Kay Scholarship for Cambridge."

"Cambridge University?" he asked with astonishment.

"Yes," she replied. Then anticipating his next question she volunteered the information. "The headmaster at the Parish Church School, he and his wife, they offered to finance James's education when my husband died."

"That was very fortunate, James did you say?"

"Yes James Francis, his father was Francis James," she added.

"Good, I look forward to meeting him," he paused to stub the remains of his cigar. "There is one other very important matter Kathleen, who is your Doctor?"

"Doctor Mann."

"We need to make arrangements for your confinement at Bealeys Maternity Home. You will have the best, and the most up to date private childbirth care, you understand?"

"Yes I understand."

"Then I would be pleased if you will go along to see Doctor Mann, and I will inform him accordingly. Will you do that Kathleen?"

"Yes Mr. Armstrong, I will."

Then pushing back his leather swivel chair, he asked abruptly, "How much do the other weavers know about the child?"

Kathleen was taken aback but quickly answered. "Perhaps one or two suspect I'm pregnant, but I haven't told anyone, only Bessy Hargreaves knows."

"The weavers know of your association with Garth I suppose?"

"No they don't, not that I know of, I haven't told anyone, neither has..."

Interrupting her he remarked, "That's very discreet of you, I must say," then he changed the subject saying, "You understand, we want nothing but the best for you from now on?"

"I am very grateful indeed for your kindness, I don't know how to thank you?"

"Tut tut don't mention it, nothing but the best from now on," he repeated as he smilingly held open his office door for her departure.

Kathleen walked out of the office and back to her looms literally shaking with ecstatic jubilation "I can't believe I'm leaving this horrid place tonight, I just can't believe it," she said to herself. "There'll be no need to tell the others about the baby now and suffer their sneers. I'm not going to tell them I'm leaving tonight, Bessy will tell them later. So it was, after almost five years of slavery, she walked out of the deafening, dark satanic mill.

On the way home she bought cooked roast pork, with sage and onion stuffing, and some cream cakes as a treat for the children, then she invited Bessy round for tea.

It was just after seven o'clock when James responded to a knock at the front door. "There's a lady to see you Mother," he said.

Walking into the hallway, Kathleen was very surprised to see none other than Gertrude Armstrong standing at the door. "May I come in," she asked quietly, her previous haughty manner conspicuous by its absence.

Kathleen nodded her assent, and showing her into the front parlour she closed the door.

Her visitor spoke again, "May I sit down?"

Kathleen gestured towards the sofa whilst remaining standing herself, she waited for the woman to speak.

"My husband tells me he has been talking to you today."

"Yes he has," Kathleen replied defensively.

"It was very discreet of you not to mention our previous encounter, but you realize of course, I was only acting in our son's best interests?"

"That's a matter of questionable opinion," Kathleen quickly retorted, whilst hoping another scene could be avoided.

"You must also understand, I would quite emphatically refute, as a blatant lie, any statement you may make concerning myself and the child," crossing her legs, she flung her arm across the back of the sofa as she spoke. "No one would ever believe your word against mine, of course."

"I can assure you Mrs. Armstrong," Kathleen answered tersely, "I have no intention of revealing such a deplorable episode, I am sure your son would not take kindly to the suggestion."

"That's settled then," the older woman chose to cut the incriminatory conversation short. I actually came with an invitation. "We, that is, Mr. Armstrong and I, would be pleased if you would come to dinner at 'The Gables', with your children, on Saturday night. We will send the carriage for you at seven o'clock. We do have to become related so we wish to get to know you better. Can I inform my husband to expect you on Saturday?" She had risen from the sofa, she was quite tall and robust and her fine plumes gave her the appearance of a mother hen.

Kathleen swallowed her pride, "Thank you very much for the invitation, we will be ready when the carriage calls at seven, goodnight Mrs. Armstrong, thank you for coming."

"Goodnight," the woman responded and quickly moved out to her waiting carriage.

Gertrude Armstrong rode back to 'The Gables' deep in thought. The fact that Garth was so determined to marry this offspring of an Irish peasant greatly exasperated and distressed her. In spite of her good looks, she was a mere weaver at the mill and far beneath their own social standing. She detested the idea of having to entertain the woman and her brats. Cambridge indeed – that's a tall-story if ever there was one. I'm sure Garth will regret his folly when he discovers their lack of breeding, perhaps he may even change his mind before it's too late. I really cannot imagine how he could subject his own mother to such humiliation? Of course, any pretty face can turn my husband's head, he will never learn.

Although Kathleen detested Gertrude Armstrong, she was in no position to refuse the patronage she and her husband were offering. There was no telling how long it would be before Garth returned, and so in the meantime, she must thankfully receive any favours they chose to endow. Before receiving Garth's letters, she had dreaded having to return to work in the mill after the baby was born, being compelled to farm it out to some back street child minder for twelve hours each day. She would have had to leave the mill in order to breast feed the baby at breakfast time and mid-day each day. She shuddered to contemplate such an ordeal. Now all such trouble was behind her she would be able to care for the child herself. "Who knows, perhaps I may even have a Nanny to help me," she mused.

Elizabeth had to ask for time off from the flower shop for Saturday night, and it was with no small amount of anxiety, and trepidation, that Kathleen rode to 'The Gables' with her children. They had never attended a formal dinner party before and even though Kathleen had learned a great deal from her work at Muxnaw Lodge, and with her Aunt Nellie at Preston, she was still afraid that one of them might commit some awful gaffe.

Over and over during the half-hour drive, she repeatedly stressed they must be on their very best behaviour. Continuously she questioned them as to good manners, table etiquette, and different foods and wine. Although they were well mannered and very polite, Kathleen knew without doubt that Garth's Mother fully intended to belittle them if she could.

In spite of her nervous anxiety and without even being fully conscious of the fact, she relished the challenge presented by the occasion. To bring Gertrude Armstrong down from her high horse without even appearing to try, was what she unwittingly hoped to achieve.

The journey ended all too quickly as the carriage turned into the driveway between the wrought iron gates, and the imposing spectre of the grey stone residence stood before them. They were shown into the opulent drawing room. The maid informed them their hosts would be down shortly, and asked them to, "Please be seated."

Kathleen wore a plain black silk dress, a white crocheted stole and her three-strand necklace of pearls. Elizabeth looked a picture in her green dress and darker green knitted shawl, she had worn this outfit for her cousin Oonagh's wedding. Rosie wore white silk with a crimson stole. James looked very smart in his school blazer, grey flannel trousers, white shirt with a stiff white collar and Bury Grammar School tie.

"Don't be nervous, sit properly," Kathleen encouraged as she noticed all three of them perched on the edge of their chairs.

Elizabeth's gaze repeatedly reverted to the baby grand piano in the corner of the large room. James's interest centred on the large bookcase. Rosie was delighted with the beautiful soft furnishings. They all sat quietly waiting, smiling occasionally at each other until the delicate tones of the Westminster chime clock, sitting high on the mantelshelf, startled them as it chimed a quarter to eight. How much longer are they going to keep us waiting, Kathleen thought irritably, at the same time reminding herself to keep calm.

Her thoughts were interrupted as the tall, handsome Mr. William approached her with outstretched hand. "Good evening my dear, I do apologize for keeping you waiting. We had to go to Manchester this afternoon, it's been such a hectic day. So these are your children Kathleen, I'm delighted to meet them. And you are?"

"Elizabeth," Kathleen introduced her oldest daughter.

"Ah, Elizabeth, I can see you have inherited your mother's Irish beauty."

He shook hands as Elizabeth blushed saying "Thank you sir."

"And this young lady's name is?"

"My name is Rosie sir, and this is my brother James."

"How do you do Rosie, and James, your mother tells me you are the studious one, hoping to get to Cambridge eh?"

"Yes sir, thank you sir."

James and Rosie shook hands and turned to see their hostess enter the room. She was elaborately clothed in a bronze satin, bustle and pannier dress. Her sandy hair did not have a hint of grey.

"There you are my dear. I was just apologizing for our lateness." He introduced the children to his wife.

She shook hands with each of them, but could hardly conceal her surprise at seeing them all so well arrayed. She smiled and nodded condescendingly to Kathleen.

William Armstrong turned to his wife, "Is dinner ready dear?"

"Yes, we can go in now," she replied.

They followed her into the hall and then to the oak-panelled dining room. This room contained a large oblong table surrounded by six high-backed dining chairs. An intricately carved dark oak sideboard stood opposite the large grey stone open fireplace. A profusion of decorative houseplants filled the bay window, facing a tall, glass display cabinet.

Kathleen was relieved because the children did not gaze around them but behaved naturally, as though they were accustomed to such elaborate surroundings. They took their places at the table as their hosts bade them. Kathleen sat between Mr. William and James, opposite the two girls, whilst Mrs. Armstrong sat at the opposite end of the table to her husband. Mr. Armstrong pulled the sash cord at the side of the fireplace to ring for service and then said grace.

The maid entered carrying a tray "Hors d'oeuvre ma'am?"

"Hors d'oeuvre?" Gertrude questioned, addressing Kathleen.

"No thank you, if you don't mind, soup perhaps?"

She smiled at the waitress who smiled back, sensing the surprise of her mistress at Kathleen's aplomb.

Kathleen heard a sigh from Mr. William on her left and caught a twinkle in his eyes, seeming to say, "Well done my girl, first round to you."

The rest of the delicious meal passed without incident. As each course was served, their hostess realized she was not, as she had imagined, dining with uncouth ignorant bumpkins. The more she became aware of the situation as it really was, the more she blundered into thoughtless errors.

She was listening to her husband questioning Kathleen as to what had happened after her arrival in England. "So after you left Preston you went to work for Lord Stanley of Alderley?"

"Yes. My husband had hoped for work as a librarian with Lord Stanley, but unfortunately, he didn't get the work he had hoped for."

She turned to Gertrude, who with dessert spoon suspended halfway to her mouth remarked, "Isn't that Lord Derby, his father was Prime Minister, he built the Derby Hall and Hotel and the Bury Athenaeum Theatre?"

"No," Kathleen said. "You see the Stanleys of Alderley descend from Sir John Stanley of Weever, the younger brother of Thomas, the first Earl of Derby."

"Oh yes I see, we've been to Derby, we saw the caves. Didn't we William?"

"Yes we did Gertrude, but I'm afraid that isn't quite the same dear."

"Oh isn't it, why not?"

"Because," he paused, "Thomas Stanley, who was the first Earl of Derby, came from West Derby near Liverpool, not Derby in Derbyshire. Lord Derby's seat is at Knowsley Hall near Liverpool?"

"Yes, that's right sir," James confirmed with a smile.

"Oh yes of course," Gertrude affirmed, "I had quite forgotten for the moment."

And you were saying about your sisters Kathleen?" Mr. William asked quickly, anxious to ignore his wife's faux pas."

"They live near Richmond, Virginia. Eileen married an Irish immigrant from Galway, and Sheelagh the youngest, a Russian wheat farmer."

"His name is Alexander Zaltowski," James said, and they all smiled at the unusual name.

"How very interesting your family is," William enthused.

After the meal they retired to the drawing room and soon Rosie told Gertrude, to whom she felt drawn, "My sister plays the piano."

"Does she now? Would you like to play for us Elizabeth?" Gertrude suggested.

"Oh yes please, may I? What a lovely piano." Her

155

eyes shone as she raised the keyboard lid and searched for sheet music beneath the lid of the piano stool. Then sitting down she played and sang:

> *Underneath the gas lights glitter*
> *Stands a little fragile girl,*
> *Heedless of the night winds bitter*
> *As they round about her whirl,*
> *While the hundreds, pass unheeding*
> *In the pleasant twilight hours,*
> *Still she cries with tearful pleading*
> *Won't you buy my pretty flowers.*

Everyone applauded, and then she played, whilst James and Rosie sang, the *'Londonderry Air'*.

The musical evening continued. Rosie had a lovely voice, she enjoyed singing a good smattering of Irish songs, and James recited *'The Wreck of the Hesperus'*. Elizabeth and Kathleen played a duet, and later Kathleen surprised her hosts by her accomplished rendering of *Handel's Largo* and *Chopin's Nocturne in E*.

They ate fruitcake and drank wine. Kathleen played whilst they all stood around the piano singing *'The Holy City'*. Gertrude was quite taken with young Rosie, and Mr. William chatted away to James.

Kathleen and the children rode away in the carriage just before midnight. Riding down Brandlesholme Road they talked animatedly about the wonderful time they had enjoyed, and how much they looked forward to their next visit to 'The Gables'.

"Mr. William said he hadn't enjoyed himself so much for years," James remarked.

"Mrs. Armstrong is a lovely lady isn't she mother?"

"I'm glad you think so Rosie," Kathleen replied with a deep sigh of satisfaction.

The night had been successful after all.

The news of the impending birth of his child eventually reached Garth at Pretoria, shortly after the relief of Mafeking. A combination of his father's attempt to pull strings at the Foreign Office, a mild attack of malaria, and his own plea for a compassionate return to England, ensured his hurried departure on the first thousand mile leg of his journey, destination Cape Town, and the first ship for home. It was a race against time so he could be home in time to marry Kathleen before the baby was born.

He cabled his father, **'Home in September. Stop. Take Care of Kathleen Stop. Many Thanks Stop. Love Garth.**

As soon as he arrived home, he would go to see his old school chum John Emerson, the vicar of Radcliffe Parish Church, to arrange for a special marriage licence. If all went well he would be home by the middle of September. It was now the middle of June, but he counted on making Cape Town in four weeks, which would give him another eight weeks to sail home. Britannia ruled the waves, so what had he to worry about?

What a blessing it would be to leave this blood, sweat and mosquito-ridden country. "Oh to be in England – Good old Bury, here I come." When he had been so determined to make love to Kathleen, the consequence of giving her a child had never entered his head. "What a damn fool I've been," he cursed himself, "leaving her in such desperate straits. I'll make it up to her when I get home, I surely will. I must send her a telegram from Cape Town."

Kathleen received the telegram reading it avidly, over and over again. It read, **"Home in September for wedding Stop Love You Stop Garth."**

The English summer was extremely hot. "I'm sure it can't be any hotter where Garth is," Kathleen thought. "I'm so glad, in my pregnant state, I don't have to work under that glass roof in the weaving shed, it must be suffocating."

She was nearly eight months pregnant, and whenever she ambled with her ungainly weight along the street, she could sense in no uncertain manner, the neighbours gossiping behind the curtains. Miss Duckett and her sister were quite disparaging at first, then later offered to take care of the house and children, when Kathleen went into Bealeys Home for her confinement. She had explained everything to them as best she could but she was sure they only half believed her.

She could imagine Miss Duckett telling her sister, "I think the shock of having a baby without a husband has made her go funny in the head. She fancies she's going to marry some rich man, but someone must be paying for her confinement. Life is funny isn't it, you never know what's going to happen next."

It was only when the wealthy mill owner's carriage began to appear at Kathleen's house, that the neighbours eyes really started to open wide with curiosity. The tall, immaculately dressed, middle aged gentleman with the cigar, and his lady, would spend maybe twenty minutes in the house and then leave. How mysterious!

It was six thirty in the evening of Sunday, September 18th when the tall blond army officer, alighted from the London train. It was the same platform, at Manchester

London Road Station, where he had said goodbye to his beloved, way back in January. He swung his kit-bag to his shoulder, picked up his suitcase, and walked with long determined strides towards the ticket barrier like a man with a purpose. It seemed impossible to believe his three month journey had finally come to an end, that soon he would hold his beloved again as he had dreamt a thousand times.

He inquired about a train from Victoria Station to Bury. He listened with rapture to the broad Lancashire accent, telling him beyond any doubt, that he was home at last.

"Leaves Victoria at arf past seven sur, yuv got plenty o' time, an it's a gud neet fur a nice walk o'ert city, bet yur glad tur bi back sur, aren't yur?"

"Yes indeed I am, very glad to be back, thank you very much my man."

He took up the ticket collector's suggestion to walk across the city, his pack was heavy but he felt as strong as an ox. It was a lovely balmy evening and as he strode down Market Street, his eyes feasted on all the familiar sights, and his exuberance was hard to conceal. He felt literally on top of the world. There was time for a good old pint of Bury Brewery beer in the bar at Victoria Station, he was sure he had never tasted anything so good.

He ignored the fetching eyes of the barmaid, subconsciously telling himself, "There's only one lass I want to be looking at tonight or any other night."

At last he stood outside the open door of number seven Garden Street. He could hear someone practicing scales on the piano in the front parlour.

He knocked and walked into the hall, calling out,

"Hello, anyone home?" He looked into the front room and the thought flashed through his mind "This is where I sat in the dark that night when it was snowing."

Elizabeth stopped her piano playing and gazed at the soldier as though he were some sort of apparition. "I think Mammy's lying down upstairs on the bed," she stammered. "Shall I tell her you're here?"

"Yes please Elizabeth," Garth replied as he resisted the temptation to dash up to his beloved.

Kathleen was resting on her bed. "Mammy he's here," Elizabeth almost squealed with excitement. "Did you not hear him come in? Come on quick, he's waiting."

"Yes all right, I'm coming," Kathleen whispered. "You go down," she gestured, and then rolled over sideways in order to raise her body, heavy with child from the bed. Trembling, she grabbed a hairbrush from the dresser and brushed it through her long thick hair. "What a sight I look to meet him, what will he think of me?" She walked unsteadily along the landing to the top of the stairs and began to descend.

Just like a man - Garth was totally unprepared for the sight that met his eyes. "Why? When he knew she was going to have his baby – when he had made a seven thousand mile dash from Pretoria to marry her before it was born – why, in the name of heaven, had he not realized what she would look like when he saw her?"

Kathleen sensed his dismay as she continued her ungainly plodding down the stairs.

Then he ran up to meet her, and baby between them, they laughed and cried with tears of joy. He put his arms around her and kissed her and kissed her protruding tummy as well.

"Kathleen, my darling, I love you, it's been so long, my brave sweetheart, I'm so sorry my darling."

"It's all right Garth, I love you too, no need to be sorry, I want to have our baby, let's go down shall we?"

160

He held her as they descended the stairs together and went into the living room and he kissed her, over and over again. "Darling, I have a close friend," he told her hastily, "he's the vicar of Radcliffe Parish Church. I'm going to see him tomorrow. When will the baby be born?"

"The Doctor said it would be the 29th or near. Did you get my letter?"

"No I didn't. I called in at the Cape Town barracks but my letters had been sent on to Pretoria. The Adjutant promised to forward them back home."

"So you haven't seen my little poem then?"

"No I haven't. Don't tell me I'm marrying a poetess, what is it about?"

"It was just a few lines about the baby."

"You must show it to me, but first of all, do you have some wine glasses?"

"Elizabeth, would you reach for the wine glasses please," Kathleen requested.

Garth went out into the hall, and took out a bottle of champagne from his kit bag. "I bought this in London, I need a cork screw. Where are James and Rosie, we should all be together for this?"

"James went to Evensong with his friends, it's after half past eight so he should be home soon. Rosie is at Maggie's down the street, will you go to tell her Garth is here Elizabeth?"

"Yes all right Mammy," Elizabeth said as she placed glasses and a corkscrew on the table.

The lovers were alone when Garth opened the bottle of vintage 1865, the cork shooting straight up to the ceiling, they both laughed excitedly as he filled two of the glasses.

"Here's to us darling and," he added, "to our son and heir."

"To us," she replied, raising her glass and taking her very first sip of champagne. "Don't you think it might be a girl?"

"It's a boy darling," he grinned mischievously, "didn't you know I have psychic powers?" he teased.

"Garth darling," she said, it seemed like a dream to be actually talking to him, "I hope you don't mind, I promised Elizabeth .she could choose the names for the baby."

"And has she chosen?"

"Yes, she chose David for a boy, and Diana for a girl." They had become so accustomed to the names, she hoped he would approve.

"Yes David, that's a good name – David William Armstrong." He rolled the names around his tongue.

"Do you think we might add Daniel too?" Kathleen asked. "Daniel was my father's name."

"Yes of course, we'll call him David Daniel William Armstrong, shall we?"

"Yes," she agreed. Garth was just about to kiss her again when in walked James. He looked every inch his sixteen years and so much like his grandfather, Daniel O Sullivan.

"You haven't met James, have you Garth?" Kathleen asked.

"Very pleased to meet you sir," James held out his hand.

"And you my boy, will you join your mother and me in a glass of champagne?"

"Oh yes please," James grinned. "Champagne, I say, I've never tasted it before."

"Well then, just a wee drop won't do you any harm lad," Garth said as he poured a full glass.

"Here's to your safe return sir," James raised his glass to drink.

"Thank you James, I'm very glad to be back in Bury I assure you."

"Did you kill any Boers sir?"

Kathleen cringed at the typical manly query.

"Indirectly, I've no doubt I did, there were many dead, and British too I'm afraid. War is a nasty business, you keep out of it if you can James."

"I'll remember that sir," he said emptying his glass to the dregs. "Mm., that was scrumptious. I've a bit of swatting to do yet Mam. Do you mind?"

"No, that's all right James. Put some more coal on the front room fire, it's turning chilly now."

"I hope he gets his sums right after that drink," Garth joked after James had gone into the parlour. Garth held Kathleen to kiss her again, when in walked Elizabeth and Rosie.

"Rosie my girl, so good to see you again." He took her in his arms and whirled her round. "How you've grown since January. How old are you now?"

"I was twelve in July and I'm working now."

"Are you indeed, so that means you're old enough to drink champagne does it not, and Elizabeth too of course?"

The two girls giggled and smiled at their Mother whilst Garth filled two more glasses, turning to Kathleen he asked, "Another one for you my love?"

"Just half a glass please, I mustn't have too much, we must consider the baby. We don't want him to be getting a taste of the hard stuff before he's born do we now?"

"Where are you working Rosie?" Garth enquired.

"I'm learning dressmaking at the Miss Johnsons' shop in Princes Street. When I'm grown up I'm going to have my own gown shop," she announced confidently.

"Are you now, it sounds very much like budding ambition. So then, how about we drink to Miss Rosie's Gown Shop?" Garth raised his glass whilst they all laughed and toasted the future 'Miss Rosie's Gown Shop'.

"Rosie is very determined," Kathleen thought, "so much like her father." Then she urged the girls, "It's time for bed girls, nearly half past nine." I'm never going to have any time alone with Garth tonight, she thought.

"All right Mammy," the loving and obedient Elizabeth responded, "we're going. Goodnight Mr. Garth, we're very glad you came back to us."

"Yes we are, very glad," Rosie added, "Goodnight sir."

"Thank you girls, goodnight, I'll probably see you tomorrow."

After James had also bidden them goodnight the lovers turned to each other. Garth held his arms outstretched with his hands waiting to receive hers, she placed her palms in his and their hands locked together. They stood for an age, devouring each other with their eyes, then opening his arms he took her to his heart and held her in a long embrace, kissing her repeatedly and passionately.

"I'm never going to leave you again," he cried. "We'll always be together from now on, I promise. I'm going to start looking for a house this next week darling with a big garden. You will be able to grow fruit and vegetables again, and we'll employ a gardener to do all the hard work for you."

Nestling in his arms Kathleen said, with no small amount of contentment in her tone, "I'm going to find it strange having servants, I've always been used to doing all the hard work myself."

He took hold of her hands and kissed the tips of her fingers. "No more hard work for these lovely hands from now on my love, you'll have to get used to being a lady of leisure."

"I hope I shall still find plenty to do darling," she said "I don't want to be idle."

"I'll keep you occupied, I promise," he said looking down at her with the boyish grin she loved so much. "I told my father I wouldn't be home until tomorrow sweetheart."

"And where are you going to sleep tonight, husband

to be?" she teased.

"Can I sleep with you my love?" the handsome Garth pleaded.

"No you can not," she chided humorously. "The children know we are not man and wife yet, so you behave yourself until we are."

"Can I sleep on the front room sofa tonight then, it's warm in there?"

"Will you be comfortable?" Kathleen relented.

"I've slept on so many bunks, camp beds and railway carriage seats, in the past nine months, one night on your sofa will be like heaven. Only six more nights and then, Mrs. Armstrong to be, you'll have to sleep with me every night of your life, and how will you like that?" he asked, kissing her on the end of her nose.

"I'll love it my sweet, I truly will."

"It's the 24th next Saturday, our wedding day, don't you go and have that baby before then will you?"

"I don't have much choice darling, but just to please my lord and master, I'll try very hard not to."

The following week was a bustle of activity for the prospective bride and groom. Garth left early on Monday morning, and after kissing him goodbye, Kathleen went to the dressmakers. It was to be a very tall order at such short notice, but she was paying them well and the Johnson sisters were all agog, knowing their apprentice Rosie was to be the step daughter of the wealthy Garth Armstrong.

On Monday afternoon, Garth visited his friend the vicar at Radcliffe and the wedding ceremony was arranged for nine o'clock, Saturday morning, September 24th .1900.

On Tuesday, he was delighted when discovering a vacant house for sale. It was situated in a very exclusive residential area, close to Stand Church, Whitefield, only three miles from the mill, and was exactly what he had hoped for.

It was later the same day when he drove with Kathleen in the brougham. They passed Stand Church and rode along Ringley Road to the house on the left surrounded by trees and a very high wall. The name of the house was 'Arbour Lea'. It had seven main bedrooms and servants quarters, ample stabling, spacious lawns and ornamental gardens. The whole place was completely secluded and utterly delightful. It was a blessed haven where they could live and love, as it were, in peace and tranquillity, concealed from the outside world.

Kathleen was determined to alter the servants' quarters. The bedrooms were more like horseboxes. The stable type doors, of these so called rooms, were no more than four feet high, over which anyone could peer at the occupants within. The rest of the house she loved, and so did Garth. The ground floor rooms had large bay windows with low window seats overlooking lawns. Kathleen could imagine herself sitting undisturbed with needlework, or writing poetry, a dream come true indeed, the house was a palace compared to number seven Garden Street. Garth was happy with the asking price of £950. 'Arbour Lea' was a mere forty years old.

As they drove back to Bury Kathleen was in further ecstasies when Garth inquired, "Do you think Bessy would make a good Nanny, darling?"

"Bessy?"

"Yes, we will need someone to help with the baby. Do you think she might be suitable? I was thinking she could possibly be good company for you during the daytime, when I'm at the Mill."

Kathleen was overjoyed at the suggestion. "I would love to have Bessy to help, she's so kind and loving."

"Do you think she would be willing to give up her

home to move with us to 'Arbour Lea'?"

"I would love her to move with us Garth. I'll go round after tea to ask her."

"Yes, all right darling, or better still," Garth added "perhaps we could ask James to invite Bessy to come round to see us, then we can discuss all the arrangements."

The morning of Saturday, September 24th was a glorious autumn day. Kathleen was awake at six o'clock. Bessy had promised to come at seven to help everyone to get ready for the wedding. The flowers were to be delivered at seven thirty and the first carriage would arrive at a quarter past eight. Kathleen got out of bed slowly, determined not to get too excited. She could see, in the early dawn light, the outline of the beautiful crinoline style ice blue gown, hanging outside the wardrobe door. The dress had a heart-shaped neckline and long fitted sleeves. The wide full skirt was tiered and scalloped and fell loosely from below the bust. She had chosen a bouquet of white lilies, and her headdress was a small tiara of white orange blossom. She would wear her hair, as her beloved preferred it, piled high on the top of her head. Garth's cousin Richard was to be the best man and James was to give the bride away.

"It's a very old church darling but not a big one, you won't have far to walk down the aisle," Garth assured her.

She woke the children at six thirty and they had washed and eaten their porridge before Bessie knocked at the door. She was wearing a fitted brown suit with orange accessories.

"Oh Bessy," Rosie cried as she opened the door, "you look just wonderful, what a lovely suit!"

"You'll soon put me in the shade young lady, when

you and Liz get your beautiful yellow dresses on, that's for sure".

"Hello love, how are you?" she greeted Kathleen. "Feeling nervous?"

"No I'm not too jittery Bessy, although I must say, I'm glad to see you. Have you had any breakfast?"

"Yes, I had a cup of tea and some gruel, I was up at five, I couldn't sleep with all the excitement." She helped the girls into their dresses, brushed James's suit, inspected his shoes and tied his bow tie.

The flowers arrived from the flower shop where Elizabeth worked. "I couldn't have done those better myself," she said, "they're gorgeous."

"Boasting again," James chided her.

"Now James, no unkind remarks please," their mother scolded as she descended the stairs.

"Come and look at your mother," Bessy called "Isn't she lovely?"

"Oh Mother you are, and the baby hardly shows at all." "That's our good dressmaking and design," Rosie the expert informed them, which was undoubtedly true. Kathleen was indeed a picture of radiant loveliness.

The first carriage came for Bessy and the girls at eight fifteen and the bridal carriage for Kathleen and James some five minutes later. Arriving at the gate of Radcliffe Parish Church at five minutes to nine, Kathleen was surprised and thrilled to hear the joyous peel of wedding bells. The bells were totally unexpected as it was meant to be an early morning quiet wedding.

Elizabeth and Rosie were waiting in the church porch, they listened anxiously after their Mother and James arrived, for the commencement of the wedding march. "Do I look all right?" they asked each other whilst each one nodded in assent.

The strident notes of Mendlesohn's Wedding March

resounded throughout the ancient edifice, Garth looked round to see his beautiful bride on James's arm.

Kathleen caught her breath at the sight of him, "How gorgeously handsome he is," she told herself.

His parents and his father's sister stood in the pew immediately behind Garth and the best man. The white robed vicar waited at the altar with benign expression.

Then it was the unexpected happened. Kathleen stopped her progress down the aisle momentarily as she felt the short sharp pain. James looked down at her with consternation as she tightened her grip on his arm. Flashing a reassuring smile in his direction she carried on walking down the aisle with her daughters behind her.

"All right Mam?" James whispered.

"Yes," she whispered back and smiled again.

They arrived at the altar and Garth took her right hand in his.

"We are gathered here to-day," the vicar's voice boomed out, as though he was addressing a large congregation, "to join together, this man and this woman in holy matrimony."

The couple made their responses – the congregation sang, *"The voice that breathed o'er Eden,"* and before the vicar announced, "Those whom God hath joined together let no man put assunder," Kathleen knew the birth of her fourth child was imminent! She felt a deep surge of elation that at last her waiting time was o'er together with consternation at finding herself in such a predicament.

The wedding breakfast for ten persons was to be held at the Radcliffe Boar's Head Hotel. Everyone kissed the bride and groom and wished them much happiness. Kathleen kept smiling pretending everything was quite normal. At the same time she clung to Garth as if to draw strength from his manly frame. "My other babies never came quickly," she comforted herself, "so why should this one be any different. I must wait till after the reception before I tell Garth."

The main participants moved into the vestry for the signing of the register. Afterwards the happy couple bade farewell to the vicar and thanked him for all his kindness.

Arriving at the hotel, Kathleen retired to the ladies room, she was in no doubt that she was entering the first stage of her labour. She felt like panicking and calling for Bessy but instead, she said a little prayer, vowing to keep calm so she would not spoil the enjoyment.

She patted her tummy and whispered, "Be a good baby now, don't you come too soon." .

The gaiety and merriment of the occasion was not marred by the impending birth. The meal was delicious and the champagne flowed freely. The best man and the groom made their speeches and William Armstrong announced that he wished to give 'Arbour Lea' and a grand piano as wedding presents. Everyone responded with oohs and aahs to the superbly generous gifts.

The bridesmaids were thrilled with the valuable jewelled pendants received from the bridegroom, and James's new grandfather-in-law gave him a gold fountain pen and pencil set and a leather writing case.

"You use that pen to pass all your exams for Cambridge my boy," the older man encouraged.

"Thank you very much indeed sir, I will do my very best."

Before leaving the reception Kathleen drew her friend to one side. "The baby's coming," she whispered.

"Oh the Lord love us, it isn't, are you sure?"

"Yes I'm sure, I'll have to go home to collect my things for the nursing home."

"Will you be all right?"

"Yes I think so, if you'll look after the children for me?"

"Of course I will. Have you forgotten, I'm working

for you now Mrs. Armstrong, I started my new job today, remember?"

"Oh Bessy, how can I ever thank you, you are such a dear." She kissed her friend and the tears came to her eyes, as she repeated "How can I ever thank you?"

"Get away with you now, that's what I'm here for isn't it? I'll go straight back to Garden Street and start on the packing. We might be able to move whilst you're in Bealeys Home. Hurry up and have that baby, I can't wait to see it."

Finally everyone waved goodbye to the bride and groom, and as soon as they were alone in the carriage Garth gave Kathleen a long lingering kiss, "Darling, you look wonderful, I'm so proud of you and I love you so much, I think my heart will burst with happiness."

"I love you too Garth, I love you so very much." "Even more than…" he waited.

"Even more than Francis? Yes my sweet, much more. But Garth, I have something to tell you."

"What is it my love?"

"You asked me not to have the baby before the wedding."

"Yes, well what about it?"

"Well I didn't have it before the wedding but it's coming now."

"NOW! You don't mean now – TODAY?" He sat bolt upright looking as though a tribe of dervishers were after him.

Kathleen began to laugh, "Garth darling please, it's all right, you mustn't worry."

"But what can we do, you're not going to have it now are you?"

"Garth please, sit back and listen to me carefully."

"Yes I'm listening." He started to kiss her.

"No you're not," she protested gently, holding his hands in hers. "Will we be passing the maternity home shortly?"

Garth had to think hard, then he said, "Bealey's Home that's on Dumers Lane isn't it?"

"Yes, that's right," Kathleen confirmed. "So would you please ask the driver to stop there? When we get there could you please go in to tell matron to expect me shortly? oops," she drew a sharp breath and closed her eyes, "this afternoon" she finished quickly. The mild contractions were increasing.

Garth's face was red and he panicked. The excitement of the wedding, the champagne, and now this baby coming, was more than any man could stand!

"Are you going into Bealeys now?" he asked.

"No darling, I have to go home to take off this dress and to collect my things for the baby. Don't panic please Garth, I'll be all right."

"But darling, it's the first time for me, I've never had a baby before. Look, we're nearly there, we're passing the church, and there's Close Park." He took out his gold pocket watch and tapped sharply on the window to ask the coachman to stop. The horses halted and the hired driver climbed down and opened the carriage door.

"Can I help sir, anything wrong?"

"Yes, I mean no driver, will you stop round the corner at the maternity home?"

"Bealeys Home sir," the driver looked astonished.

"Yes my man – Bealeys Home."

"Right sir – Bealeys Home it is sir."

The tears began to roll down Kathleen's cheeks with suppressed laughter, and Garth in his frustration and concern, mistook them for tears of pain.

"My darling, you must go in now," he said when the carriage halted in the driveway of the maternity home. "I can't bear to see you suffering."

Please Garth, PLEASE, just go in and tell them to

172

expect Mrs. Armstrong in a little over an hours time."

"One hour?" he questioned with amazement.

"Yes darling, one hour, hurry!" .

He jumped out of the carriage, up the few steps and through the double doors, re-appearing again three minutes later. "They're expecting you in an hour," he said.

"Good, then will you please ask the coachman to hurry."

"Oh yes, hurry please driver, number 'err, what number is it?" Garth questioned his wife.

"Number seven, Garden Street."

"Yes, number seven."

"That's right sir, number seven, where we were going at first sir." The coachman grumbled under his breath, "Thinks I don't know my job he does. Wedding and maternity homes – I ask yer – don't know what this world's coming to, I don't. Gid up me beauties," he said, whipping the two mares to a canter.

Kathleen continued to laugh, "He will be more surprised when we ask him to take us back to Bealeys."

Later that day, as Kathleen lay relaxed on the labour bed, anticipating the painful birth of their child, she began to breathe deeply when a particularly strong contraction began. As the labour progressed she discovered that deep breathing helped her to relax. If she tightened her body and attempted to resist the pain she was in agony. On the contrary, if she began to breathe deeply, immediately the painful contraction began, it happened, as if by some miracle, she was able to 'ride' the painful sensation. Continuing this very deep breathing during the contraction of the womb, she was able to relax when the contraction subsided. During these 'intervals' she began to move her legs and her body occasionally so she did not experience the terrible cramps due to lying in one position for hours on end.

It was unbelievable! But there she was when the nurse came into the room, puffing and blowing and breathing away to her hearts content. They had promised to give her 'Twilight Sleep', an anaesthetic recommended by Queen Victoria herself, but Kathleen did not need it. As she continued to breathe deeply immediately the painful sensation began, she found she could 'ride' the pain thereby helping, instead of hindering, the progress of her little one into the world.

The nurses, who had never witnessed such goings on before, thought she was quite eccentric. They were however, very happy to have a puffing patient instead of a screaming one, and so they left well alone. For the first time, Kathleen could truthfully say, giving birth was a wonderful experience.

David Daniel William Armstrong made his noisy debut, at four fifteen in the afternoon, weighing in at a hefty nine and three quarter pounds. His father was not disappointed - the baby was a boy!

Bonny died five days after David's birth and the children were heart-broken. Garth helped James to put the poor dead animal into a strong cardboard box and they took her to 'Arbour Lea' where they buried her beneath an old elm tree.

James carved her epitaph on a piece of wood which he nailed to the trunk of the tree, *"Here lies the body of our dear dog Bonny, dead in the flesh but always alive in the memory of those who loved her dearly."*

They had been so busy packing and getting their new

house in order that they had not noticed how ill their dear companion had become.

Garth was sitting beside Kathleen's bed in the maternity home when she asked, "How is Bonny?"

He had hoped to keep the death from her until she was stronger but he could not lie, and when he told her she broke into a torrent of weeping. She was inconsolable, constantly telling herself the dog would not have died, if she had been there to attend to her. Garth had no idea how much her four legged friend had meant to her. He decided there and then to have another one waiting for her when he took her home to 'Arbour Lea'.

He and Bessy worked like trojans arranging the new home. William Armstrong arranged a quick turnover with the solicitor so that Kathleen was able to move to 'Arbour Lea' at the end of her three-week confinement. She insisted that everything in the new home should be light and airy. The old-fashioned heavy Victorian furniture and dark colours were so depressing, she would have none of them. Garth had kept his promise, a little white poodle named Candy was introduced into the new household, and everyone became devoted to her.

They engaged a cook, a maid, a gardener and a coachman. A woman came in every morning except Sunday to do the rough cleaning and the laundry. As well as caring for the baby, Bessy was housekeeper and companion to Kathleen. It was no small task for the two women, ex weavers, to become used to giving orders to servants, but showing kindness and consideration achieved excellent results.

Elizabeth was happy to leave the flower shop to go off to a fashionable finishing school for young ladies, at St. Annes-on-Sea, but Rosie would do no such thing, her sewing was her life, and her gown shop she intended to have. Elizabeth would travel home on the train every other weekend, she would impart to her sister all the interesting things she was learning.

Garth was compelled to spend two weeks during November at Woolwich Arsenal to receive his official discharge from the Army. What a blessing the telephone proved to be, he made full use of it, sometimes phoning Kathleen twice a day, even though it was often quite difficult to be connected and the reception was very bad.

David was a remarkably good baby, happy and smiling most of the time. He was the image of his father with fair hair and blue eyes.

Kathleen wrote to her Uncle Seamus and Aunt Maureen apologizing for being unable to invite them to the wedding. She explained to them that everything had happened at such short notice. She invited them to come to 'Arbour Lea' for a long weekend as soon as they were able.

She also wrote a long letter each to Eileen and Sheelagh. She was very sorely tempted not to disclose that she had been a very pregnant bride, but decided honesty was the best policy, and so she told them everything. They would be greatly shocked but it was all over now, fortunately she was happily married with a very loving husband and a beautiful home. Both her sisters appeared to be prospering, in Virginia, U.S.A. and Kathleen earnestly hoped they would someday meet again. She ended their letters with the thrilling news, "Garth and I have decided that David is to be weaned when he is nine months old as we are planning two weeks belated honeymoon in Ireland. Bessy and Elizabeth will care for David and the house whilst we are away. As you can imagine I will be overjoyed to see the old country again. We are going to stay in Dublin, Killarney and Bantry. Garth is making all the arrangements."

It was Friday, August 1st when Garth and Kathleen left Whitefield by train for Liverpool, where they stayed at the Adelphi Hotel. The following day as they waited at the quayside, Kathleen's thoughts kept going back to that October day, twenty years ago, when she had landed amongst the bustle of this great city.

"Look darling, that building with the clock, I remember it," she said.

Garth was attending to the transfer of their luggage. "What's that darling? Oh you mean the Royal Liver Building."

"Royal Liver, is that what it is?"

"Yes come on sweetheart, we must get to the boat."

The River Mersey was a hive of activity with boats and ships of every shape and size passing to and fro. Ship's sirens and tugboat hooters were sounding off constantly, increasing the sense of excitement for the travellers. The day was very hot and Kathleen sweltered in her tight fitting, high neck, bustle and pannier gown.

"You have booked a cabin haven't you Garth?"

"Yes I have. Are you feeling unwell my sweet?"

"It's the heat," she murmured whilst thinking of her Aunt Maureen who fainted on the quayside at Dublin. Since her last pregnancy, Kathleen's waistline had expanded to twenty-four inches, whereas fashion demanded no more than eighteen. "Whoever designed these dresses ought to be made to wear them on a hot day like this," she muttered crossly.

"Never mind darling, we'll soon be aboard now." He held her arm as the hundreds of passengers queued and jostled to board. Once on the ship they received first class passenger treatment from the crew. As soon as their cabin door closed behind them, Kathleen started to fight for breath.

"Darling please, the buttons," she gasped. Her hands reached up behind her and her fingers stretched, as she struggled to unhook the twenty tiny buttons down the back of her dress.

"Here let me do it," he started to fumble. "It's no wonder women faint all trussed up like this."

"I will faint, if I don't get it off soon." She took another gasp of air whilst Garth undid each button as fast as he could. Gulping again for more air her fingers tore at the neckline of the dress as she pulled it away from her throat.

She felt dizzy, "Hurry, I can't breathe," she pleaded. She pulled her arms frantically out of the brocaded sleeves and the heavy dress fell to the floor. "Now the stays," she inplored, and pulled desperately at the tapes all crossed and pulled tight around her body.

Garth helped her and at last she was able to relax, and fell with relief into his arms. He held her, kissing her soft warm flesh whilst she relaxed even more. Then more passionately, he kissed her again, causing her to take more deep breaths.

"It's too – it's so – very hot," she said between the kisses, but the handsome Garth remained silent. His body was on fire with ardent passion for his beautiful wife, and she responded with elation to his touch. The ship's engines reverberated throughout the vessel as it sailed out of the dock, and blasts from the siren came loud on their ears through the open porthole. After Garth lifted her limp body on to the bunk they both became oblivious to everything except their love.

As the ship left the river Mersey, sailing for the open sea, the cabin became slightly cooler, but the prospect of having to dress again when they docked at Dublin alarmed Kathleen. They had only a bag of toiletries with them in the cabin. All the rest of their clothing was packed away in their two trunks in the hold of the ship.

After making sure his wife was discreetly covered with a cotton sheet, and pulling on his trousers, Garth rang for service.

A steward appeared two minutes later, tapping discreetly before entering, "Yes sir?"

Garth ordered wine and cognac and inquired, "What can you recommend for lunch?"

"The lemon sole sir, would that be suitable? All right at one o'clock sir?"

Kathleen nodded her approval and Garth responded, "Yes, thank you, that will be fine, lemon sole for two please."

"Thank you sir, madam," the steward replied, returning five minutes later with the liquid refreshment.

"What time is it?" Kathleen asked after Garth had locked the cabin door."

"Eleven thirty five."

"What time do we arrive at Dublin?"

"Six thirty this evening," Garth poured the drinks, popping a piece of ice into his mouth.

"Want some ice darling?"

"Yes please I most certainly do."

"I'll put some in your drink too."

"Thank you my love. I never expected to be going back to Ireland like this."

"Like what?"

"All naked and drinking wine."

"Neither did I." He sat down beside her, drink in hand. "You must blame the dress designers, not me sweetheart."

She smiled and answered demurely, "I'm not complaining darling."

"Seriously though my sweet, we must buy you some more suitable dresses in Ireland for this hot weather. I noticed some very cool fashions for the women in Cape Town."

"As long as you didn't look at the women inside them, I don't mind."

"I only have eyes for you sweetheart," he said,

putting down his empty glass and kissing her again.

At one o'clock they ate a superbly cooked lunch with strawberries and cream for dessert.

"Living a life of leisure isn't good for me," Kathleen said as she sipped another wine after the meal.

"Not good for you, why not?"

"I'm losing my youthful figure."

"Darling, how can you say such a thing, you have a lovely figure."

"I can't get into my dress."

"Don't worry darling, I prefer you as you are," he smoothed a hand over her shapely body to emphasize his point. "Really I do," he said laughing.

"Now you're making fun of me," she pouted her lips, pretending to sulk.

"You have such inviting lips my love," he said as he kissed her again and they laughed together.

It was more than four hours later, when Garth sat up on the bunk and reached for his watch. "Good gracious darling, it's a quarter past six, we'll be docking soon. We must get washed and dressed ready to go ashore."

Kathleen turned over beside him and groaned, "You'll need to help me with that dress," she said.

"Yes I will, never mind, it's a lovely dress and you look ravishing in it. Use plenty of talc and cologne and you'll be fine."

Kathleen finally dragged herself up from the bunk and washed and started to dress. It was still very hot and she dreaded putting on the stays and gown. "Will you help me with these corsets, just pull the tapes at the back and tie them in a bow."

"All right darling, breathe in."

"Pull tighter," she gasped. "Try putting your knee on my back and pull, not too hard darling," she cried. They both overbalanced as the ship rolled slightly and they fell laughing on to the bunk.

He kissed her again.

"Really Garth, this won't do, I'm so hot, I'll never get them on at this rate. Let's try again." When they eventually came to fastening the dress, she passed him a small buttonhook from her handbag. "I must change when we get to the hotel into something more comfortable. Where are we staying?"

"The Gresham."

"Well, the sooner we get there, the better."

They stood against the deck rail whilst the ship sailed into Dublin harbour and along the quayside.

"Home at last." Kathleen breathed a deep sigh of satisfaction. "I really cannot believe it."

"This time tomorrow we'll be in Killarney, then you'll really be home at last."

Their stay at the Gresham was immensely enjoyable, an experience they were to repeat many times, in the years ahead. They entered the building through folding doors, leading to a magnificent vestibule and hall, divided by graceful arches decorated in imitation of green porphyry. The grand palatial staircase rose by one broad flight to the first lobby, then ascended to the first floor in double flights. The banisters were of rich gilt bronze, supporting finely carved and highly polished oak balustrades. These were flanked by four exquisitely patterned 'twelve light' bronze gothic standards. An abundance of light and ventilation came from a large lantern light, which rose from an elaborately decorated ceiling.

Garth was accustomed to hotels of high standard, but this was something quite extraordinary. Their apartment was delightful, being more like home with individual taste, rather than a hotel room. "If this is Ireland," Garth said, "this is surely where I want to be."

Later the same evening, as they sat at a table for two,

waiting for dinner to be served, Garth reached across the table placing his hand over hers, his blue eyes twinkled. "This day has been really superb darling," his passionate look causing her to lower her gaze.

"You tease," she said. She looked ravishing in a pale lemon, off the shoulder evening gown, and his eyes devoured her.

Exultingly they clasped hands tightly, letting go as the waiter approached.

Spreading her napkin on her lap and taking up her soup spoon she said, "It's fortunate for me I am no longer a Roman Catholic."

"Why do you say that?"

"I would have to confess my enjoyment of the carnal sins of the flesh," she whispered.

"I don't believe it!"

"Yes I would," she insisted.

"But – this soup is delicious," he interposed "Surely God told Adam and Eve to be fruitful and multiply."

"Did he? I think it's asparagus," she replied.

"So it can't be bad to enjoy it, do you think?"

"No, I don't suppose it can," she smiled.

"If we didn't enjoy it, none of us would be here would we? I think it must be God's insurance policy to make sure we don't go extinct."

Kathleen laughed at the idea, "I suppose you must be right, I've never thought of it in that way."

"So why do you think we need to be married before we can do it?" Garth asked.

Kathleen was thoughtful before she answered "Probably because God wanted families, babies living with fathers as well as mothers, wouldn't you say?"

"Yes, that seems logical enough, we make a good pair of philosophers don't we," he joked. "Anyway, I'm glad I came back to you and David."

"Yes so am I, very glad. I wonder how he is?"

"He'll be all right. We'll try to telephone home before we leave in the morning, to put our minds at rest."

"Thank you darling, you are good," she replied.

The telephone call the next morning assured them David was still thriving. They left the Gresham looking forward to a further one night stay in the same hotel, at the end of their holiday. Had they not been two people very much in love, the train journey to Killarney could have proved quite tedious. They were thrilled when the mountains of County Kerry, finally came into view.

"Look darling, isn't it lovely," Kathleen enthused.

"Yes it is," Garth agreed. "I can see now why you wanted to come back."

Entering the Killarney Great Southern Hotel, situated close to the railway station, Kathleen did her utmost to recall the day she had passed this way before. It was however, a vain attempt to recapture her thoughts and feelings. It had been raining hard, she remembered that, and she had been wearing Charlotte Townsend's grey woollen dress. After arriving in England she had worn that dress until it became threadbare. It was almost twenty years since she had left Ireland, and now, as she entered the foyer of this splendid hotel, with its big grey marble pillars, the wife of a wealthy man, the past seemed another world away.

"Was it really me?" she wondered.

They were very pleased with the hotel and they spent the next day out shopping, and sight seeing, in the small Killarney town. They enjoyed coffee and cream cakes in a quaint little café in College Street, and spent a very pleasant hour in the bar of the Glebe Hotel. In the afternoon they found Moriarty's shop in the High Street. Such exquisite hand woven Irish gowns, shawls and skirts were indeed a sight to behold. Kathleen admired the lovely crepe de chine blouses for she longed for something cool and light to wear. Garth bought her two gowns, two skirts, two blouses and a shawl. He then succumbed to Kathleen's persuasion to treat himself to a smart fawn summer suit with matching cravat.

The following morning Kathleen looked very elegant, she was wearing a new beige gown, a deep yellow picture hat, and carrying a matching bag and parasol. All eyes turned as the tall handsome couple boarded the train for Kilgarvan. The single-track line ran from Killarney to Kenmare. The train halted at Headford and Loo Bridge and then, as they neared her home village, Kathleen's heart leapt in her breast. They alighted at the tiny Kilgarvan Station, three hundred yards from the village.

"There was no station when I lived here, no railway at all."

"Where shall we go first?" he asked.

"Would you mind, could we go to the churchyard please?"

"Yes. I think this man here is waiting for passengers," Garth indicated a pony and trap with an elderly man sitting, holding the reins, waiting for a fare. He looked as though he was prepared to wait for a month or more and if no one came, it would not matter, life would go on.

It was eleven o'clock in the morning and the day was hot. Kilgarvan village consisted of one main street lined with stone-built cottages, three small shops, a post office and three bars. It was situated on the main road between Loo Bridge and Kenmare.

As they rode down the gradual slope towards the village, Kathleen pointed with her parasol towards the valley on their right, "That's where the farm was," she said.

Apart from the songs of many birds, the village was very quiet. There were only a few villagers out on the street and they greeted the visitors as they rode by, "Good morning to ye, fine morning isn't it?" they said.

"Look," Kathleen was excited, "this is where I went to school," she pointed to the inscription '1858' written up above.

They alighted a few yards further on, opposite the school by a statue of the Lord Jesus Christ bearing the inscription above it, *'Thy Kingdom Come'*. Next they passed through a gate in the wall surrounding the tiny Roman Catholic Church and graveyard. Kathleen led Garth to a grave on the left, which was marked by an unusual headstone hewn out from a small boulder.

"This is it," she sobbed. "This is where they are buried."

They both stood silently together gazing down at the unattended grave. Kathleen rested her head against his shoulder. After a while he placed a forefinger under her chin, lifting her face to his.

"It's all right my love," she assured him, "I'm not going to weep, I'm much too happy for that but I do wish," she said wistfully.

"What darling?"

"I wish Mammy and Daddy could see you now, they would have loved you so much."

"I'm sure they were wonderful people darling," he said, whilst brushing his lips against her forehead.

Turning away from him, she held her parasol, balancing her body like a tightrope walker choosing her steps precariously between the closely set grave stones, she approached a low stone wall. Garth followed her with more manly strides.

As she was about to sit down on the rough stone, he whipped out a large white handkerchief from his pocket, flipped the bits of moss and masonry and spread out the handkerchief for her to sit on. "Careful darling, the moss will stain your dress."

They sat quietly together, both of them deep in thought as a pair of goldfinch sang out their summer song in the branches above.

"I ought to be very angry," Kathleen broke the silence. "They treated us dreadfully." She shuddered in a contemptuous gesture of disdain at the memory of her former persecutors.

"You have every right to be angry," he complied.

"But what upsets me Garth is the English, they are so self righteous. So full of land of hope and glory, as though they couldn't possibly do anything bad. They ought to be told what they did to my family and thousands of other Irish Catholics.

Garth nodded, "It's all part of man's inhumanity to man darling."

Kathleen's anger grew, as the nearness of her dead loved ones revived in her the injustice of the past. "They never tell them either," she said.

"Never tell who?"

"The people. We never read in the English newspapers the truth about what goes on in Belfast and Derry."

"What do you mean?"

"I'm talking about discrimination against the Catholics. They can't get jobs and Protestant Ministers raise the rabble against them, and Catholic shops and houses get burned down for no reason. Eileen and Sheelagh have something to tell me every time they write. They know all about it in America but the English are kept in the dark. She twirled her parasol indignantly in front of her.

Garth sat bemused at her unexpected tirade. "I suppose you must be right. Come to think of it, we never learned anything in history class about the English persecution of the Irish."

"Neither did James," Kathleen added scornfully. "I had to tell him myself. I'm sure he thought I was making it up half of the time."

"People are so cruel," Garth continued, "I went to South Africa waving the Union Jack, ready to kill and maim for the land of hope and glory, till I saw the stark reality." He swallowed hard and Kathleen listened sympathetically as he continued. "All the sickening, disgusting things men do to each other, just because they happen to be born a different colour, nationality, religion. My God Kathleen, you should have seen what they did to those poor black devils." He clasped his hands tightly and his body stiffened as he recalled the ghastly memories never far from his mind. "They called those persecutors Christian Soldiers," he sneered.

Placing her parasol on the wall, she took his big hands between her slender ones, "Shall we go into the church?"

As he nodded his assent Kathleen stood up, picked up his handkerchief, shook it and handed it back to him. Taking up her handbag and parasol she walked towards the open door of the small sanctuary where she had worshipped as a child. Garth followed closely, hearing the catch in her breath as the familiar interior of the empty church brought the memories of long ago, flooding back. Walking down the aisle to a front pew, they knelt together in silent prayer.

Walking out of the church into the bright sunshine Kathleen said, "I feel like a stranger in my own village."

"That is not surprising after almost twenty years, especially as you haven't written to anyone. So where shall we go now?"

"How about one of the bars, see if we can find anyone I know?"

"That's fine by me," he agreed.

They walked back through the village and into McCarthy's Bar. It was a quarter past noon and six pairs of eyes turned as they walked through the door. The middle-aged landlord stood behind the bar, five older men sat on bar stools, all of them with pint glasses of Guinness in front of them. There was a wooden bench at the back of the room and Kathleen sat down.

"A glass of sweet sherry and a Bushmills whisky please," Garth requested.

Kathleen recognized familiar faces but she was unable to put a name to them, then she looked again at the landlord, yes it must be - it's Patrick McCarthy. She stood up again to reach for the sherry, as she did he looked at her and smiled.

She returned the smile saying, "It's Paddy McCarthy isn't it?"

"Yes," he looked puzzled.

"Don't you remember me Paddy, I'm Kathleen O Sullivan?"

"To be sure, I don't believe it – not Kathleen O Sullivan?"

"To be sure, it's me, in the flesh, and this man is my husband, Garth Armstrong."

Garth shook hands with the landlord across the bar. "Very pleased to meet you Mr. Armstrong I'm sure."

As Garth exchanged formalities with the landlord, the other men were listening and one of them approached

Kathleen who had remained standing beside Garth.

"I know you, you're Daniel O Sullivan's lass, I remember when you went to England." He held out a dirty hand, then wiped it on his equally dirty trousers and offered it again.

Kathleen accepted his firm handshake with a surge of elation, she recognized him to be Brendan O Connor, the father of Tom who had driven them to Killarney on that rainy day so long ago. "How is your Uncle Dennis?" he asked. "Me and him used to be good pals when we were lads."

"He hasn't been well for some time, he suffers from bronchitis, but everyone else is fine, Seamus and Maureen – do you remember them?" Kathleen wanted to know.

"Yes of course we do," he said. He laughed with the others who were getting into a jovial mood, they nodded and agreed, they too remembered. "You tell Dennis he should come back to Kilgarvan away from them smoky chimneys, he won't get no bronchitis here."

"I suppose you're right about that," Kathleen said as she climbed up on to a barstool. "My young cousin Thomas is now a clerk in the railway booking office where my Uncle Dennis used to work."

"Is he now?" the landlord interjected. "'Tis good jobs you be 'avin over there an' you be not doin' too bad for yourselves, you bein' all dressed up. We don't be seein' the like o' that too often here abouts." He had been talking to Garth who hardly understood a word that was said.

Garth kept nodding and laughing as he gathered up the gist of the conversation, more from the expressions on everyone's faces rather than from what was actually said. He could pick out certain words and he worked from there. Even Kathleen was having difficulty recalling her native dialect. She was thrilled when Paddy McCarthy called into the back room for his wife.

"Here Maggie, look who's here, 'tis Kathleen O

Sullivan come back to see us."

A woman with a lovely rosy oval face came into the bar, "Oh no, God bless us, it is an' all," she beamed her welcome.

In a fleeting thought, Kathleen remembered how lovely Maggie had looked as a bride. Maggie took Kathleen's hand in both of hers as she said, "You look like your own mother Bridget, she was a beautiful woman and that was a dreadful time that was. Times are better now thank the Lord."

Maggie says I look like my mother," Kathleen said to Garth.

"Yes I heard. Your mother was your age when she died wasn't she?"

"Yes she was.

After shaking hands with Kathleen and Garth, two of the men left McCarthy's bar and shortly afterwards it all began to happen. The word was spreading around the village like wildfire and over to the outlying cottages and farms like a rabbit on the run.

"She's here, Kathleen O Sullivan's come home, she's in Paddy McCarthy's bar."

One by one and two by two they came to greet the long lost child of Kilgarvan - to drink her health and to wish her and the handsome man himself, 'Cead Mile Failte'. "Tis a thousand welcomes we'll be giving you Kathleen, and your man."

Kathleen was delighted to talk to some of the women who had written and received letters from Eileen and Sheelagh. She was very eager to exchange news concerning her sisters and others, who had left the village, sailing the great divide to settle in the New World of the Americas.

It wasn't long before the small bar became full of people. The windows were thrown open and anyone who could not get in, went to celebrate at O Donoghue's bar across the street. Other villagers milled around outside in the warm afternoon sunshine, young ones came who had not been born when Kathleen left the village. The afternoon wore on and Kathleen laughed and cried tears of joy. Garth's exuberance bubbled over as he drank with these wonderfully happy and friendly people. He drank Guinness with the best of them and was happy, more than once, to order drinks all round. Later on the singing started, the concertinas began to play and the happy couple joined in. Maggie invited them into the living room where she feasted them with sandwiches, tea and cakes.

"This welcome is going to go on all night," Maggie declared, "once they start, there's no stopping them."

"We have to go back to Killarney on the evening train," Kathleen told her.

"Now you know we won't hear of you going off leaving everyone, you just arriving, and not seeing half of them yet. We have a room and you can sleep here for this night. I must be out to help himself now and you'll be excusing me of course." She spoke in typical Irish manner without taking a breath, and hurried away to help her husband in the busy bar.

"Did you understand what she said?" Kathleen asked.

"Does she want us to stay the night?"

"Yes."

"Then I suppose we must," Garth agreed with a smile.

"Are you sure you don't mind darling?"

"No I don't mind at all, I haven't enjoyed myself so much for years."

They had the opportunity to wash and to rest, and later they went back into the bar. It was a lovely evening and after enjoying a drink, they walked around the village, talking to the people and stopping at the other two bars.

It was ten thirty when Garth inquired, "What time do they close?"

"Close!" Kathleen laughed, "They don't close, they carry on all night."

"All night?"

"Yes all night, it's like Maggie said, once they start there's no stopping them, they carry on all night. They'll be bringing out the poteen soon."

"Oh yes well," Garth grinned, "I wouldn't mind a wee drop of that for a change. But what about the children?" Garth was concerned. "What time will they go to bed?"

"Don't you be worrying about them darling, they're all right." Kathleen found herself speaking with the pronounced accent of her native Irish brogue.

Midnight saw them joining in the Irish dancing in the street and it was after two o'clock before they could drag themselves away. They climbed on to the large creaky iron bedstead whilst the revelling continued outside in the street and the bar below. They were tired but very happy and slept until ten in the morning.

They had breakfast with Paddy and Maggie, said goodbye to their newfound friends, and promised to return again to Kilgarvan. The absence of a telephone in the village was sufficient reason for not informing the Killarney Great Southern Hotel, of their absence the previous night.

The manager was quick to assure them, "That's fine sir, no problem."

The remainder of their Killarney holiday passed off quietly by comparison. They drove to the Gap of Dunloe by jaunting car, and to the high vantage-point above the lakes named Ladies View, by Queen Victoria's Ladies in Waiting. They enjoyed a visit to Kenmare, Killorglin, Caher Daniel and many other places around the famous Ring of Kerry.

Kathleen made out a list of people to whom they sent picture postcards it included; Bessy and the children at 'Arbour Lea', William and Gertrude Armstrong at 'The Gables', Garth's cousin Richard and his Aunt Deidre, Uncle Dennis and Auntie Nellie at Preston, Eileen and Sheelagh and their husbands in America, Uncle Seamus and Aunt Maureen and Cousin Oonagh and her husband, The Reverend John Emerson and his wife at Radcliffe, Mr. and Mrs. Kirkman, Bob Howarth and the office staff at the Mill, Miss Duckett and her sister at Garden Street, the Miss Johnsons' in Princess Street, Bury, Bill Wolstenholme and the staff at the Derby Hotel, the staff at Bealey's Maternity Home and Marie and Albert at Alderley Park. Kathleen worried in case they had forgotten anyone and keeping to the good old Lancashire custom, they bought many presents to take home for their loved ones and friends.

If Kathleen had been eager to see Kilgarvan again, her desire to see Bantry again was even stronger, and the bay was more beautiful than she had remembered. They stayed at the grand, but intimately small and cosy, Bantry Bay Hotel.

The weather was hot and they thoroughly enjoyed visiting Glengarriff, walking the hills above Bantry town and riding out along the coast road of the Beara Peninsula. It was all so unbelievably quiet and peaceful. They could ride or walk for miles whilst never meeting with a single human soul. They would meet with wild donkeys wandering in pairs over the fields and along the dirt track roads, and watch fascinated as the pheasants soared and the deer came out of the forests with their young.

On Wednesday, Garth hired a pony and trap. The landlady packed a picnic basket and they rode down through Durrus to Mizen Head and Barley Cove.

The lovely cove was completely deserted on this hot August day. The couple sat on the golden sands eating their packed lunch, they watched as the seagulls soared and dipped anticipating a morsel from their delicious meal, and then swept up over the sparkling clear blue sea and the bright green hills surrounding the cove.

They rested after the meal, then getting up from the

sand Garth said, "This is no good, that water's too tempting, I'm going in." He undressed quickly down to his underpants and ran into the sea.

Kathleen sat close to a sand dune in a vain attempt to shelter from the hot sun, she watched enviously as Garth swam and the gentle waves swished and lapped on the shore.

Soon he came out of the water to plead with her. "Darling it's great, you must come in. Come on, I've never seen you swimming, come on." He took hold of her with his wet hands and pulled her up from the sand, he combed his fingers through his wet blond hair and pulled her towards the waves. "Come on," he begged.

"How can I, you silly man?"

"Just take off your dress."

"I can't do that, somebody might see me."

"There's no one here only me."

"Garth, you know what I mean, I can't. It's just not done."

"I dare you," he challenged.

"Darling please!"

"Come on, take it off, I'll race you into the sea."

"I am tempted," she said, gazing longingly at the lovely blue water.

"Take if off," he repeated, taking hold of the skirt of her frilly white dress. "We've got the whole bay to ourselves, no one will see us only the gulls."

Reaching down for the hem of her skirt she pulled the dress over her head, and throwing it aside she hesitated, standing in her white tight-waisted camisole which extended from barely above her bust down to her frilly knickerbockers, ending a little below her knees.

"Come on, I'll race you," Garth grasped her hand and they dashed together into the sea. Laughing and gasping they waded out until the water was deep enough for them to swim. Kathleen thrilled as the deliciously cool salt water seeped

194

through her tight cotton underwear, creeping into the crevices of her perspiring flesh. She swam a strong breaststroke with Garth slightly ahead, then she turned to swim on her back and her eyes scanned the luscious green hills, encircling the cove to see if any human eyes were watching their escapade but there was no one in sight.

"I'll race you to that rock," Garth challenged as he struck out, swimming overarm stroke, into the calm Atlantic swell.

Kathleen followed close behind, whilst Garth kept looking back until they reached the smooth rock on which he climbed and pulled her up, as they laughed together breathlessly.

He placed an arm round her shoulders and kissed her cheek. "You're a great swimmer, where did you learn?"

"Bury Baths" she answered.

"I used to go there at least twice a week."

"Did you" she said, "I could only go with the girls on ladies day, James could only go with us if we all went for mixed bathing at seven o'clock on Sunday mornings. Look, she exclaimed, "there's something in the water, I saw its head, it's swimming. Look, there it is now!"

"Hush," he whispered, tightening his grip on her shoulder as the animal surfaced less than four yards away. "It's a seal."

"A seal," Kathleen held her breath with excitement.

They watched in wonder as the lovely animal with the shiny black coat dived and surfaced, obviously oblivious to their presence. The hot sun blazed down and they watched with their feet dangling in the water until another seal came into view, the two animals played together, then swam out to deeper waters.

"Race you back," Kathleen shouted, plunging back into the sea and swimming to the golden shore.

Garth allowed her a good start then dived in after her,

swimming the two hundred yards to the deserted beach. Running the last few yards with their soaking wet clothing clinging to their bodies, exhilarated, they fell down on to the hot sand and laughingly embraced.

Garth's fingers fondling through her wet hair, he kissed her for a long time, full on her lips. "I love you darling," he spoke softly, "and I love you even more for bringing me to this fantastic place, this beautiful emerald isle. I would love to come back here every year for a holiday and someday buy a house here."

"A house at Bantry?" Kathleen gasped.

"Anywhere near here where we can find a suitable house?"

"That would be wonderful," Kathleen enthused.

"It won't be for a while yet but I know it will happen one day," Garth said, sealing the promise with a fervent embrace.

The next three years were undoubtedly happy ones for the Armstrong family. Pearl Mavourneen was born in the April following their first holiday in Ireland. Garth kept his promise and they returned to Ireland for the month of August every year, always spending one or two nights at the Gresham Hotel, Dublin on arrival and departure.

Pearl was two months old when her father took delivery of his first horseless carriage. It was a Daimler, which he was, to say the least, delighted to possess. Kathleen was rather dubious as to her approval of the noisy machine, preferring the more conventional and graceful horse and carriage.

James left for his first term at Cambridge at the end of September, his mother was immensely impressed with the illustrious university. The superb architecture of the colleges and chapels, the graceful Backs along the River Cam, and the replica of the famous Bridge of Sighs, were a delight to behold. Garth and Kathleen were happy to spend two weeks holiday there with Bessy and the children in May 1903.

It was blowing a gale in September of the same year when Elizabeth met Peter on Blackpool promenade. A mighty gust of wind dislodged her bonnet and Peter retrieved it from underneath a horse drawn tram. He was staying with his family on holiday at the Imperial Hotel. Liz was charmed with his handsome clear cut features and his wavy red hair. He took Liz and her friend in the lift to the top of the Tower, and later they danced in the magnificent Tower Ballroom. Peter lived at the village of Hornby near Lancaster, and after his holiday they began to write to each other. Becoming engaged the following Easter, the wedding was arranged for October 1904. Kathleen was very pleased to give her consent to the marriage, Peter, having three sisters, was the only son of a linoleum manufacturer.

Rosie was thrilled to have the opportunity to design her sister's bridal gown and five dresses for the bridesmaids. David was to be pageboy and the bridegroom's niece Jane, who was also four years old, was chosen to accompany him in the bridal procession.

"Do you think they'll be coming?" Elizabeth asked as she sat with her mother in the gazebo writing out wedding invitations.

"Who?" Kathleen inquired.

"Our American Aunts," Elizabeth replied. "When do you think we'll get a reply to the invitation?"

"We should hear from them fairly soon. Just think, it will be twenty-three years, almost to the day since I left them in Kilgarvan. Perhaps they may not be able to come, so I'm not going to build up my hopes. I don't want to be disappointed."

It was the second week in August before the letter, post marked Portsmouth, Virginia, U.S.A., dropped through the letter box at 'Arbour Lea'. Kathleen opened it apprehensively. It read:

My Dear Kathleen,
 Sheelagh and I were delighted to receive the invitation to our niece Elizabeth's Wedding to Mr. Peter Gordon Lambe, on Saturday October 6th at 3.00 p.m. at Saint Mary's Parish Church, Bury, and afterwards for the reception at the Derby Hall.
 After careful deliberations and consultations with our families, we are very pleased to say yes, dear Kathleen. We gratefully accept.
 Sheelagh's mother in law, Mrs. Zaltowski, has offered to care for all the children, including my four boys whilst my Patrick is at work. Sheelagh's husband Alexander will be busy with the harvesting and the children will help him of course.
 The Lord willing, we will sail from New York on the **'S.S.George Washington'** *which is due to arrive at Southampton on Monday October 1st. We hope to telephone you, as you suggest, when we arrive in England. Please do not worry about having anyone to meet the boat, as we will make our own way to Manchester on the train, so you can meet us there. Please let us know the name of the railway station we should arrive at?*
 As we are sure you already know dear Kathleen, we just cannot wait for the day to arrive when we can be with you again after all these years. We are looking forward very much to meeting your children and we wish to thank our dear brother in law Garth, for the invitation to stay at your home.
 The ship leaves Southampton for the return voyage on Saturday, October 13th. We are hoping that it might dock at Cork so that we may have a glimpse of the dear old Emerald

Isle. We would love to see Kilgarvan again as you and Garth have done. My Patrick tells me he is saving his dollars, he hopes to buy a shop or a bar some day, back in the old country.

Please give our fondest love to Uncle Seamus and Aunt Maureen and our dear Irish Cousins, tell them we are looking forward so much to meeting them again. I am pleased to tell you that Mary and Michael McCarthy are both well, they send greetings to you and yours. I will not write again before we leave. Sheelagh is here beside me and wishes me to say she is over the moon with excitement at the thought of seeing you again.

In the meantime, dear sister, we send our fondest love.

> *Your Loving Sister,*
> *Eileen Finnerty.*

Kathleen went upstairs to her room with the letter in her hand and wept with joy. Pearl ran into the room, with Bessy following close behind.

"Is it bad news?" Bessy asked.

"No, it's so good I'm crying buckets."

"Well now lass, those are the very best kind of tears," Bessy said, as she sat on the bottom of the bed and Pearl toddled around the room.

"It's a letter from Eileen," Kathleen explained.

"Yes I guessed as much. Are they coming?"

"Yes they are. Oh Bessy I'm so happy, whatever did I do to deserve so much good fortune, I seem to have everything a woman could wish for."

"I'll tell you what you did my lass," Bessy answered as she wagged a forefinger, "You had one great big load of trouble before all this good fortune, and no one deserves to be happy more than you."

"Perhaps you're right Bessy," Kathleen replied; then

thoughtfully she questioned her friend, "But Bessy, what about you, you must have been very happy when your Tom was with you?"

"Yes I was love, but time is a great healer and I can't complain, I have a wonderful life here with you and the children and err…"

"And what Bessy – tell me – what are you hiding?"

"No, it's nothing," Bessy dismissed the question, pulling Pearl up on to her knee.

"Bessy, tell me," Kathleen insisted, "I know there's something you're not saying."

"It's nothing I tell you, nothing at all. Oh God forgive me for telling such lies, you might as well know, it's Arthur Carrington, the milkman."

"You mean farmer Carrington?"

"Yes, that's him, from Willow Farm, I didn't want to tell you."

"And why did you not want to be telling me Bessy Hargreaves?" Kathleen chided, laughing at her friend.

"Well, I wouldn't want to be leaving you would I?"

"So that's why you've been going off to the Hippodrome and Radcliffe Coliseum, now I understand. Is he a widower?"

"Yes, his wife died five years ago."

"Now you listen here to me," Kathleen sat up straight on the side of the bed, "I won't be having you sacrificing your happiness on my account. I know you're thinking we can't manage without you, of course we can. Can't we Pearl?" She took her child from off Bessy's knee to her own.

"But," Bessy protested.

"Does he want to marry you?" Kathleen asked.

"Yes, he has asked me."

"And what did you say?"

"I said I wanted to stay with you."

"Bessy how could you? He's such a fine man I won't

hear of you turning down such a good man for me. You have to think of yourself and your own happiness. When will you see him again?"

"About a quarter past ten this morning, when he brings the milk."

"Bessy really, I'm so happy for you, what a day this is, first the letter from Eileen and now you telling me this. Will you promise me you'll accept his proposal and will you ask him to come with you to Liz's wedding?"

"Yes all right, I promise," Bessy grinned. "I love his bald head and red face and he's always making me laugh."

"It will be your wedding next we'll be going to," Kathleen kissed her on her cheek.

"Do you think I'll make a good farmers wife?" Bessy asked, amused at the thought.

"Well if it's milking lessons you're looking for, you've come to the right person in Kathleen O Sullivan." The two friends laughed hilariously as they hugged each other.

The next few weeks passed all too quickly, there was so much to do. Peter came from Lancaster to stay at 'Arbour Lea' every weekend. He worked with his father in the linoleum business, and he often combined business with pleasure, calling at the Radcliffe Paper Mills to negotiate the purchase of paper board.

The evening of Tuesday October 2nd was a typically Lancashire one. "It always rains in Manchester," Garth remarked as they rode in the carriage to London Road Station, for it was indeed pouring heavens hard.

"It was like this when I left them in Kilgarvan," Kathleen recalled, "we were soaked in that box car going to Killarney."

"Were you dear?" Garth answered as though she had never told him dozens of times before.

They arrived at the station ten minutes after the train from London Euston. The two American travellers were waiting in the entrance looking rather lost. Kathleen alighted from the carriage assisted by Garth. Then she saw them standing by their luggage. She fled from her husband, running as fast as her ankle length skirts would allow, whilst she held on to her enormous hat.

"Eileen," she called, "Sheelagh, which of you is which? Oh love, oh my love, it's been such a long time."

"Kathleen," they cried, "Kathleen," then words failed them whilst the tears rolled down, just as they had done so long ago, when they had said goodbye in Kilgarvan.

Garth hung in the background, barely able to hold back the tears himself, knowing full well what this moment meant to his dear wife.

She turned and held her hand outstretched towards him. "This is Eileen darling and Sheelagh, I didn't know them, they're so grown up now." They all laughed excitedly through their tears. "Do you have a handkerchief darling?"

Garth shook hands and kissed his newly found sisters-in-law, "Here Kathleen," offering her his big white handkerchief. "I can see I should have brought more handkerchiefs," he announced as the women continued to laugh and cry at the same time, whilst he called a porter to help with the luggage.

"You're taller than Eileen now Sheelagh," Kathleen said, "and you look so much like Grandma O Sullivan."

"You look so much like Mammy," Eileen answered.

"Wait till you see Elizabeth, she looks more like Mammy than I do, and James is the image of Daddy."

The sisters both had mid brown hair like their father, Eileen's face was lean as their father's had been, but Sheelagh's face was round, she appeared to be happier and more relaxed than her older sister who seemed to be slightly tense and nervous. The journey back to Whitefield passed with animated conversation.

"It rains here like it does in Ireland," Sheelagh joked.

"Exactly, so it does, England's green and pleasant land and Eireann's green isle, we have this rain to thank for the green," Kathleen mused.

The three sisters chatted away constantly, as they each made an impossible attempt to convey the experiences and the joys and sorrows of the past twenty-three years, into the next hour. Garth listened in silence to the breathless women, nodding occasionally to confirm his wife's remarks, or he would ask some question as to their voyage from America. The sisters were so happy to be re-united and the visitors were delighted with their fine handsome brother-in-law.

Arriving at Whitefield, they were totally enchanted with 'Arbour Lea'. Even in the fading October light they needed only one glance at the lovely house, the well kept lawns surrounded by the stately oaks, elms and sycamores, to tell them how rich their once poor sister had become.

The following morning the family all ate breakfast together seated around the large dining table. David amused everyone by taking a spoonful of grapefruit without honey. He pulled a very wry face and wept when everyone laughed at him.

Garth kissed Kathleen and his beloved Pearl. Saying goodbye to everyone he shouted upstairs for Rosie to hurry, or they would be late for work. James, who was now almost as tall as Garth, kissed his mother goodbye. He was at the end of a second summer vacation working with his stepfather, learning the business of running a large cotton mill. He was a great favourite of his 'grandfather' William Armstrong, and everyone hoped he would eventually become a director of the Company.

After Garth, James and Rosie had left home to go to work, the three sisters with Bessy, Elizabeth and the two young children, remained in the dining room chatting together. Later, Eileen and Sheelagh said they wished to spend the morning unpacking their luggage, but first of all, they wanted Elizabeth to see the wedding presents they had brought.

"Wait about ten minutes and then come up to our room will you dear?" Eileen requested.

"All right, thank you Auntie," Elizabeth agreed in happy anticipation of the gifts. Fifteen minutes later, she tapped on their bedroom door.

"Come in Elizabeth" her Aunt Sheelagh called, "we're ready." Taking hold of Elizabeth's hand she led her over to her own single bed. There, laid out, were four pairs of beautifully embroidered real Irish linen white pillowcases, plus two of the most exquisite lace table cloths Elizabeth had ever seen.

Elizabeth gasped.

"Do you like them?" Sheelagh asked.

"Oh, how lovely," Elizabeth exclaimed! "Did you do the embroidery?"

"Yes we did," Eileen answered, "and we hope you will be very happy using them; there's something else here," she said, taking a white box, with a green ribbon tied in a bow around it, from off the end of the dressing table.

She handed it to her niece who untied the ribbon excitedly but before she could remove the lid, Eileen placed a hand on hers. "This box holds everything to make your life a happy one Elizabeth," she announced, speaking with solemn emphasis, then she nodded her assent for Elizabeth to open it.

Elizabeth was very surprised to find the box contained rosary beads and a Roman Catholic prayer book. Quietly she examined the beads and the black leather-bound book whilst her aunts looked on, then looking up she said very slowly "Thank you so very much, they are lovely, but…"

"Yes dear?" Eileen inquired.

"Well, they are lovely," Elizabeth attempted again "but…"

"But what?" Sheelagh asked.

"We are Church of England and we don't use the beads."

"Eileen gasped, "Oh dear God no!" she ejaculated as one hand went to her throat and the other one covered her mouth. The three remained silent before Eileen exclaimed to her sister. "That's why there's no crucifix and holy water in the house!"

"I see," Sheelagh answered, then looking directly at her niece she queried, "So your mother must have changed her religion when she married your stepfather, is that right?"

"No," Elizabeth replied emphatically, "my mother left the Catholic Church when I was a child."

"But why?" Eileen asked. "Your father was a good Catholic Irishman."

"My father was a drunken Irishman," Elizabeth defended her mother.

"Your father drank?" Sheelagh questioned.

"Yes he did."

"That was no reason for your mother to leave the faith," Eileen spoke scornfully.

Elizabeth felt cornered and embarrassed by these two women with their strange accents, who had suddenly invaded her peaceful life, especially the aggressive, lean faced Aunt Eileen. She attempted to explain, "My mother asked the Priest to help her and he refused."

"Don't say any more child," Eileen interrupted, "your mother has sold her soul to the Devil, and for that there is no excuse, it's not your fault, heaven forbid we should have travelled all this way to come to this."

Sheelagh protested, "Eileen please, you're forgetting yourself, we are guests in this house for a happy occasion."

"A Church of England wedding I suppose," Eileen interrupted again with an inquiring scowl at her niece.

"Bury Parish Church," Elizabeth replied as her little step sister came running through the bedroom door, which had been left ajar.

Kathleen was pretending to chase her little one and Pearl's childish laughter contrasted sharply with the silence and sober expressions of those who were conversing. Kathleen immediately sensed the tension between them.

"But the invitation says Saint MARY'S Church?" Eileen continued to question in spite of her sister's appearance.

"Yes it is, The Parish Church of Saint Mary the Virgin," Elizabeth emphasized each word.

Still with a smile on her face, her mother inquired, "Is there something wrong?"

An uncomfortable silence followed whilst Pearl looked with childish innocence from one adult face to the other.

Then Eileen took up the rosary beads, holding them up between her fingers. "It's our present," she spoke with sarcasm. "It appears not to be needed in this house. You could have informed us Kathleen before we came."

"Oh I see," Kathleen replied, "I'm very sorry if it upsets you."

"How you can possibly consider going back to live in Ireland when you've left the true faith, I really cannot imagine."

Sheelagh sat on the side of her bed humiliated, as her sister ranted on.

Changing her scornful attitude to pleading tearfulness, Eileen approached her sister, "Kathleen please, we can't bear to think of you being condemned to hell and damnation, tell me it's not true, please Kathleen?" she pleaded.

"I'm sorry it's come as such a shock to you," Kathleen apologized again, "I should have told you."

"I tried to explain mother," Elizabeth said.

"Thank you love," her mother said gently, "it isn't easy to explain, but I did have my reasons Eileen." She paused and took a deep breath, "My husband was drinking heavily and spending most of the housekeeping money. When I asked the priest to talk to him he said that a man was entitled to his pleasure and I became angry. I threatened to poss the priest in the dolly tub."

"Holy Mary and Jesus save us," Eileen intervened whilst crossing herself dramatically, "you didn't – you couldn't commit such a mortal sin," she cried out in disbelief.

"I did just that I'm afraid," Kathleen answered quietly, "mortal sin or not."

As a distraction and diversion from her sister's hostile attitude she picked up Pearl in her arms, then abruptly changing the subject she said. "What beautiful table cloths!"

"Yes aren't they lovely," Sheelagh was relieved to agree.

Then turning back to Eileen Kathleen said, "I am sorry Eileen, I should have told you, but I would like to say this, then I hope we can drop the subject. You may not realize, but there is actually very little basic difference in the doctrines of Roman Catholicism and the Church of England, so I fail to see what all the fuss is about?"

"So do I," Sheelagh said, standing up and moving towards Kathleen, "You're still my sister and I love you, no matter what," she kissed her cheek and hugged her tightly.

"Thank you Sheelagh," Kathleen returned the kiss as her eyes filled with tears.

Eileen turned away remaining silent.

Elizabeth picked up the pillowcases and the tablecloths, "Thank you very much for the lovely presents,

Peter and I are very grateful," she said and walked out of the room.

Kathleen spoke quietly, "I'll leave you now to finish your unpacking. Do you have everything you need?"

"Yes we do, thank you," Sheelagh smiled reassuringly.

"Lunch will be ready at 12.30, let me know if you need anything before then won't you?" Kathleen said before closing the bedroom door behind her.

The wedding of Mr. Peter Gordon Lambe and Miss Elizabeth Duffy, at the Parish Church of Saint Mary the Virgin was a very fashionable affair. It was a day for the re-union of long lost cousins. James, and his cousin Thomas O Sullivan began a friendship which was to last a lifetime. Peggy O Sullivan, who was still unmarried at the age of thirty-two, and her sister Kathleen, were invited to America by their cousins where they were to eventually marry and settle down.

Peter and Liz, he never called her Elizabeth, spent their wedding night at the Derby Hotel. The following day they travelled by train to Keswick for their honeymoon in the Lake District. Peter had purchased a four-bedroomed country house close to the village of Tatham, North Lancashire. Kathleen was very happy in the knowledge that her daughter's future seemed to be so secure. Peter, she was sure, would prove to be a very loving husband.

On the Thursday, after the wedding, Garth and Kathleen travelled with Eileen and Sheelagh to say goodbye to them at Southampton. Although nothing further had been said concerning religion after the initial hard words, there remained a feeling of uneasiness between Kathleen and

Eileen, spoiling the whole visit, which should have been such a joyful one. Kathleen did her best to overcome the tension between them but her efforts did not succeed.

"You will come over to Virginia won't you?" Sheelagh asked before they said goodbye in the cabin on the ship.

"Yes we will, when the children are older and James can help my father at the mill," Garth promised. "We'll come for three months, O.K. as the Yankees say," he joked.

"O.K." Sheelagh kissed her brother in law, "I'll hold you to that promise."

Three weeks before Bessy's wedding at Stand Church Whitefield, Kathleen engaged a new Nanny for the children. She was a dark haired, brown eyed, homely young woman of Irish descent named Mary McCoy. David and Pearl took to her immediately. She taught David the alphabet and numbers, and Kathleen and Garth were delighted with his progress.

Although they still continued to see each other quite regularly after her marriage, Bessy was much missed by Kathleen. She had been a very dear close friend for ten years and her absence inspired Kathleen to write a short verse entitled 'Absent Friends':

As through the lanes I wander
The birds for company,
On absent friends I ponder
And bygone jollity,
Some o'er the world are roaming
Some ne'er will come again
So a little prayer I'm breathing
As I wander down the lane.

It was 1906 when James brought Sarah home for the summer vacation. She was a very pretty blonde girl from Devonshire who was reading geography at Newnham College, Cambridge. It was obvious that James, who had known her only three months, was totally smitten.

One morning when Sarah was washing her hair, Kathleen and James were out together in the garden.

"Sarah's a lovely girl James."

"I'm glad you like her Mam."

"Yes I do, very much. Are you hoping to marry her?"

"If she'll have me." The colour rose in his cheeks.

"I would love to have her as a daughter in law." Kathleen continued to twist the dead heads off an early yellow rose bush, looking thoughtful, she hesitated before asking, "It wouldn't be possible for you to marry until later next year after you both graduate would it?"

"No, I don't suppose it would," James answered. "We'll just have to wait."

"Mm I suppose you will, eighteen months is rather a long time to wait, don't you think?"

"What's bothering you Mam, something on your mind?"

Kathleen turned to face him and taking a deep breath she said, "I suppose I should leave this to Garth but..."

"Leave what to Garth?" James asked getting exasperated.

"To talk to you, man to man."

"The realization dawned on him and he laughed nervously, "Mother I DO know, about the birds and the bees, I'm not a child." He spoke softly, smiling at her with sympathy.

"Yes I expect you do James, but how do you feel about being chaperoned?" James remained silent so Kathleen continued, "You know what happened when Garth went to South Africa and what my foolishness led to, the future

210

happiness for you and Sarah depends on your self control James."

'I could not love thee dear so much loved I not honour more', James quoted. "That's what you mean isn't it Mam?"

"Yes it is. It's a matter of great concern James, especially in these modern times when there are so many outrageous ideas being bandied about."

"You need not worry, I promise you, I will have the greatest respect for Sarah's virginity." He bent to kiss her on her cheek, and turning on his heels, he walked with determined strides to his beloved in the house.

Kathleen sighed with relief, she knew her son and her son would keep his word. She could not bear to think of Sarah having to endure the agony and shame of unmarried pregnancy that she herself had borne.

James and Sarah both graduated with honours in 1907. The wedding took place in September at the tiny church in the hamlet of Taddiport, Torrington, North Devon. Mr. and Mrs. Kirkman were the guests of honour. The groom was very happy to take his virgin bride on honeymoon to Falmouth. Later he rejoiced when he was offered a directorship at William Armstrong's cotton mill, the place he had tried, so many years ago, to persuade his mother to avoid like the plague. He bought a house on Walmersley Road, Bury, so he and Sarah could live close to his elderly benefactors.

It was May 1908 and Rosie was almost twenty years old when Garth asked her if she had noticed the empty shop on Silver Street, Bury? They were alone together in the drawing room at 'Arbour Lea'.

"Yes I've seen it, but it's way beyond my reach."

"You're working most days for twelve hours a day, and yet you still can't afford your own shop?"

"No I can't, I'm saving every penny I can, at this rate it will be at least another fifteen years," she sighed! "Well I suppose one day, maybe."

"Your mother and I are hoping to buy a house soon at Bantry, why don't you come over there with us?"

Rosie shook her head, "No thank you, I'd rather stay here working in Bury, thank you for asking me."

"Do you remember when we drank to Miss Rosie's Gown Shop when you lived in Garden Street?"

"Yes I remember," she said dolefully. Then jokingly she said, "I was living in cloud cuckoo land then wasn't I?"

"Are you good at popping champagne corks?" Garth asked.

Unsuspectingly she answered, "No, I'm only good at drinking it. What are we celebrating?"

"You need to do something before I can answer that question."

"Me, what do I have to do?"

"Taking a fountain pen from his top pocket, Garth moved over to the small mahogany table. "You need to sign this document, on the dotted line, it's been drawn up by my solicitor." Holding out the pen towards her he asked with a smile, "Can you sign your name?"

"What is it?" she queried, walking over to the table and closely examining the form. Staring at the paper, Rosie read enough to realize that if she signed it, she would be the proud owner of a twenty-five year lease for the large empty shop in Silver Street. She looked at Garth and opened her mouth to speak – "This is too good – but the stock – I don't have..."

"This cheque for £500, goes with the lease. It's from your 'Grandmother' Armstrong. It's a loan, to be paid back as and when you're able. Now will you sign?"

She took the pen from him, placed it down on the table and throwing her arms around his neck, she hugged him.

He laughed, "Hurry up, the champagne's waiting," he smiled at her.

"Where do I sign?" she asked.

Garth pointed to the dotted line and she signed Rosemary Duffy.

He took the pen from her and walking over to the door, he opened it and called out, "Kathleen." His wife appeared in time to see the champagne overflow from the bottle.

Kathleen held out a glass for Garth to fill and then drank with joy to her daughter's good fortune. "To Miss Rosemary's Gowns," she toasted, then she hugged her daughter with glee.

CHAPTER 5
THE LIVING AND THE DEAD

Seafield House was situated high above Bantry town with incredible views of the bay.

"This is what we've been looking for darling," Garth said as they approached the house where they had an appointment to view with the owner-occupiers.

It was a beautifully appointed Georgian house surrounded by very attractive gardens, with two adjoining cottages. Kathleen particularly liked the large drawing room with the high double French windows leading out to the garden. The spacious dining room had a very large mirror above the fireplace, the windows with mullioned fanlights, extended up to the high, embossed ceiling.

There were eight bedrooms, servants quarters, stables and the usual offices. The price included the fine deep embroidered pelmets, the curtains, the Indian carpets and many lovely pieces of mahogany furniture. The owners were moving to Rhodesia the following spring, and wished to take with them only their personal effects, together with items of special value.

Kathleen was in raptures when Garth was ready to agree the sale. "Do you like it Kathleen?" he asked.

Smiling broadly at him she answered, "Yes I do Garth." At the same time she was thinking, 'Yes indeed, I do like it, it's so wonderful.

"It would suit us to take over on April 1st after you leave," Garth told the young John Courtney. "Our son James," he continued, "graduated last year and he is shouldering some of the work for me at the mill, so next year would be ideal for us to move."

"That would be fine for us," John Courtney agreed. "I'll have all the necessary documents drawn up before the end of your holiday."

"Would you care to stay for afternoon tea," Margaret Courtney invited, "we're having it out on the terrace."

"Yes, that would be lovely, thank you very much," Garth and Kathleen were happy to accept.

"Do you visit Bantry often?" John asked when they were having tea.

"This is the eighth year," Kathleen replied. "We first came in 1901."

"Have you met the Whites, from Bantry House?"
"No," Garth said. "We've often seen them, but we have never been formally introduced, have we darling?"

Kathleen shook her head in agreement.

"Edward and Arethusa are a charming couple. They have two little girls, the youngest Rachel, was born at the same time as our son," Margaret said.

"If Mr. and Mrs. Armstrong are going to live here, it would be good for them to meet the Whites, wouldn't it darling?" John asked.

"Yes, I was thinking that myself. Isn't there a concert next Wednesday, at Bantry House?"

"There is," John replied. "Dame Agnes Spencer is giving a recital with Carl Messener at the piano. Would you care to be our guests?"

"Yes, we would love to go, wouldn't we Kathleen?"

"Very kind of you to ask," Kathleen agreed.

"What part of Ireland are you from?" John addressed his question to Kathleen.

"Kilgarvan," she replied.

"Oh, not very far from here."

Wishing to divert the questioning Garth interceded, "My wife was an O Sullivan and I am one of the Armstrongs

215

of Westmorland. Neither of us can lay claim to the aristocracy I'm afraid."

Garth's remarks were passed off with good humour by the Courtneys, as they were obviously anxious to please the wealthy prospective purchasers of Seafield House, aristocratic or not.

It was six thirty on Wednesday evening when the Courtneys called for Kathleen and Garth at their hotel in Wolfe Tone Square. Seated in the brougham, they travelled the short distance around the corner, the bay horse swung left at the coachman's bidding, entering the grounds of Bantry House under the archway of the lodge gatehouse. They ascended the winding narrow road through parkland to the ancestral home of the White family, who were descended from the former Earls of Bantry.

The Majestic Stately Home situated with a hill backdrop, and breathtaking vistas across to the Caha Mountains, had been occupied by the same family since 1750. From the commanding demesne, the bay appeared to be like a private lake. The Hog, Rabbit, Horse and Lousy Castle islands, protruded like emeralds from the sapphire sea, as the evening sun spread a light gold mantle across the bay, sparkling on the gently dancing waves.

The concert wasn't due to begin until seven thirty, so the Courtneys suggested that they walk around the grounds. They strolled leisurely down the terraced garden, between the statues, to the low white stone sweeping ornamental balustrade.

Kathleen held Garth's arm as she looked down on the shore where she had once run bare foot with her brother James. "Who would ever have believed that one day I would be up here, what would my Mammy and Daddy say if they could see me now?" Kathleen wondered.

Later, as they entered the lovely house, the Armstrongs were introduced to Edward, and his wife, the exquisitely fair Arethusa Leigh-White, who were delighted to welcome them to Bantry House. The very enjoyable concert was held in the long library at the back of the house. The guests numbered no more than eighteen and after the concert their hosts provided refreshments.

Before the evening ended, they had the pleasure of being shown around the house containing innumerable treasures and objet d'art. In the Rose Drawing Room they were shown the Aubusson Royal Tapestry of four panels, made for Marie Antoinette on her marriage to the Dauphine, who later became Louis XVI. The magnificent rooms contained superbly woven carpets and tapestries, regency tables, hand painted tables, exquisitely decorated cabinets, chandelier and candelabra, prints in silk and gold thread, portraits, wax models, alabaster vases, mirrors, bureaux, chippendale chairs, wine bins, teapoy, wall lights, pianoforte, urns, work boxes and oriental screens.

Kathleen had seen similar things at Muxnaw Lodge and Lord Stanley's home at Alderley Park, but never had she seen so many beautiful objects in such a magnificent setting as Bantry House.

Kathleen and Garth were invited to lunch the following Wednesday with the Whites, and so began a friendship between the two women which was to last for many years to come. There was an affinity between them, a strong mutual desire to get to know each other better.

Having completed all the legal arrangements for the

purchase of Seafield House, they returned home after their holiday to 'Arbour Lea'. One evening Garth stood with his back to the fire whilst Kathleen sat knitting.

"Are we going to put dust sheets over everything here when we move to Ireland?" she asked.

"I've been thinking of asking James and Sarah to take the house on lease. James is doing well at the Mill but my father isn't getting any younger, if anything was to happen to him, I would need to spend more time in Bury."

"But if James and Sarah moved in here, they probably wouldn't want to move out," Kathleen reasoned.

"No, I suppose you're right darling but don't you think there's enough room for all of us here?"

"We could stay here as a temporary arrangement," Kathleen agreed, "but not permanently. Two mistresses in one house would be one too many, I'm afraid."

Changing the subject Garth asked, "Did I tell you, James has asked Cousin Thomas O'Sullivan to take on the job as assistant manager?"

"Thomas, what does he know about cotton mills?"

"Not much I suppose, but the job is concerned more with accounts and wages, and he knows quite a lot about that, I think he could do very well."

"I am surprised, but I'm pleased for Thomas," Kathleen said.

"What do you think about Mary staying on as governess?" Garth asked.

"I think she should stay with us, don't you darling? She is very intelligent and she has a wonderful way with the children. They accept lessons from her as a pleasure, if we take on someone else they could adopt a different attitude. I am sure Mary would love to go with us to Ireland. Of course darling," she added with wifely diplomacy, "the final decision rests with you."

"No, I believe you're right Kathleen, Mary's doing a

very good job, so I think we should let her carry on."

"There's one more thing darling."

"What is that?"

"I feel awful every time I see Aunt Maureen."

"Maureen, whatever for?

"Every time I see her I keep talking about Ireland and she has never been back there for twenty-seven years."

Garth was silent and then he asked, "Does Uncle Seamus know about caring for sheep and cattle?"

"Yes he does, at least he did when we lived in Kilgarvan. Why?"

"I want to start farming in Bantry, in a small way at first of course."

"I began life as a farmer's daughter, and now you want me to end it as a farmer's wife," she laughed.

"Yes, that's the idea Miss O Sullivan. Do you think Seamus and Maureen would like to go back to Ireland?"

"I'm sure they would, but they can't afford a week at Blackpool, never mind a holiday in Ireland."

"I don't mean for a holiday, I mean to live. They could have one of the cottages and work for us."

"That's a wonderful idea darling," Kathleen enthused, "I'm sure they would love it, that's if they didn't mind leaving the family in Preston."

"Peggy and Kathleen are living in the States and Oonagh and Thomas are married so why not?" Shall we go over to Preston to ask them?"

"Yes please. When shall we go?"

"We could go this week-end. How old is Seamus now?"

"Kathleen thought for a moment, I think he must be fifty-five now."

"Is he really, he doesn't look it?"

"No he doesn't, but he must be tired of stoking coal on railway engines after all these years."

"Yes, I expect he is," Garth agreed.

The Armstrong's took up residence at Seafield House, Bantry, in the spring of 1909, taking David and Pearl and their Nanny/Governess with them. Seamus and Maureen were delighted to leave Preston to live in the rent-free cottage. Garth gave them wages for working in the vegetable garden and caring for the animals.

Kathleen found no small satisfaction in returning the small black marble clock, which she had always called her mother's, back to Ireland. It was still ticking away merrily after twenty-eight years; the clock face had yellowed with age but it remained Kathleen's most treasured possession.

Rosie's gown shop was flourishing and she went to live with William and Gertrude Armstrong, at 'The Gables'. James and Sarah moved from Walmersley Road to 'Arbour Lea'. Sarah was expecting her first child in August, at the same time as her sister in law Liz, who was living happily at Oakland House, Tatham.

Garth and Kathleen intended to live for ten months each year in Ireland, returning to England, usually in the spring and autumn.

Shortly after moving to Bantry, they were instrumental in helping Eileen and John Finnerty and their four sons to move back to Ireland from America. They took over a bar and guesthouse at Glengarriff, situated along the coast, a few miles from Bantry.

"I wish it could have been Sheelagh instead of Eileen," Kathleen lamented.

It was the summer of 1910. The weather had been very hot and very dry for a long spell and now it had begun to rain. Garth knew the road was greasy as he drove his Ford car home from an enjoyable day out at Barley Cove. The road was rutted and uneven.

Disgruntled, Garth muttered to himself.

Kathleen sat beside him, David and Pearl seated in the back, were chattering away to each other. Suddenly the car skidded into the side of the road coming to an abrupt halt.

Kathleen cried out as she was thrown against the celluloid windscreen.

"Damn, Oh I'm sorry darling, are you all right, good thing I was only doing twenty, it could have been nasty." Quick to apologize for his bad language, Garth prattled on nervously. "Are you sure you're not hurt darling?"

"No I'm not hurt, at least I don't think so. What's happened," she asked with consternation as Garth opened the driver's door and looked out?

"We're stuck in a rut," he said.

"That's all we needed," Kathleen breathed.

The children giggled nervously.

"Be quiet children, it's not amusing, we're stuck in the middle of nowhere.

Garth walked round to the back of the car, making a vain attempt to dislodge the solid tyres from the equally solid sun-baked ruts of mud. David strutted round to join his father and kicked with the toe of his shoe at the caked mud and pushed, attempting to free the vehicle.

The rain started to come down more heavily, father and son dived back into the car as the water beat down on the canvas roof.

"It's no use, we can't move it, we'll just have to wait."

"But darling," Kathleen protested, we could be here for hours and we're going to the dance at Bantry House tonight."

A dance was being held for the visiting naval officers from the two British Navy frigates, anchored in Bantry Bay.

"We must be about three miles from Durrus," Garth estimated, "there's sure to be someone coming along soon."

They all sat for the next half an hour playing I spy whilst the rain poured intermittently. Two wild donkeys ambled past but not a human soul came into view.

Kathleen was just about to expound the virtues of the horse drawn carriage as opposed to the unreliable automobile, when a passing carriage halted, a man jumped down and tapped on the window beside Kathleen. She opened the door.

"Can we help old boy?" The man addressed Garth who got out again and the two men walked round the vehicle, studying the situation together.

Garth came round to the passenger side, "Come on darling, we've been offered a lift. "Get out children, don't forget anything."

"What about the car?" Kathleen asked.

"That isn't a problem, the chap at the garage will come out for it. Come along now, we mustn't keep these kind people waiting."

They climbed into the luxurious carriage, sitting with the children between them, opposite a frail looking well-dressed woman and the tall, dark, handsome man who had offered them the lift. They rode to Bantry, along the Durrus Road, the women and children listened whilst the two men expounded their views on the horseless carriage. The man had a fine deep voice and spoke very good English. They had been riding along for some time when the woman touched the man lightly on his arm and she nodded towards their guests.

"Oh good heavens. Do forgive me, we haven't introduced ourselves. Rothmere's the name, Simon Rothmere, and my wife Isabella. And you are?"

"Armstrong, Garth Armstrong, my wife Kathleen and our children David and Pearl."

Kathleen caught her breath at the mention of the name, Rothmere. The woman smiled at her and she smiled back automatically. Garth continued to talk to the man about cars and Kathleen clasped her hands tightly on her knee.

"Rothmere indeed! Does he not realize who he's talking to like some long lost friend."

The coach rolled and swayed on well-sprung suspension and she was overcome with a feeling of passionate fury. She felt as though she was on the outside of the coach looking in. Closing her eyes, she was back again in the blacked out cottage, listening to the terrifying thud of the ramming pole as it thundered against the wall of her home – she watched as her father wept uncontrollably in her mother's arms. She heard again the voice of Father Murphy telling her of her father's death and smelled again the sick room, seeing her mother and the little Molly as they writhed with the typhoid fever.

"Kathleen darling," she heard Garth speaking insistently and felt Pearl shaking her arm. "Kathleen, are you unwell?" Garth pleaded.

She looked around the coach at the five pairs of eyes staring at her with puzzled expressions.

"Darling, the Rothmeres are going to Bantry House tonight, isn't that fine?"

"Yes, forgive me, I'm sorry Garth, yes. Lord and Lady Rothmere isn't it?" she asked.

The couple nodded, the extremely good looking man, who was about ten years younger than herself, eyed her with concern.

Garth continued talking exuberantly, and as Kathleen watched the rain streaming down the coach window, she fumed inwardly at his failure to remember the name of her family's persecutor.

"How could he possibly forget," she wondered, "how could he?"

They halted at the Bantry garage as Garth instructed the man to collect the stranded car, then they drove up to

Seafield House.

"You will have a drink with us won't you" Garth insisted.

"Yes thank you, but we mustn't stay long or we'll never make it back from Kenmare in time for the dance," they said.

Isabella drank neat brandy, surprising Kathleen. She had no doubt once been beautiful, but she was now very pale and thin. Kathleen wondered what she was suffering from?

"I'm surprised we haven't met before at Bantry House," Garth said.

"We haven't spent much time in Ireland during the last two years. Isabella is often unwell and takes the spa waters," Lord Simon informed them.

The Rothmeres did not stay long but before they left, Garth had happily accepted their invitation to dine with them the following week at the Manor House, Kenmare.

Their coach was hardly out of sight before Kathleen turned on Garth, "Don't you realize who those people are?" she demanded whilst quickly pouring herself another sherry.

"Yes I do, I knew as soon as he mentioned the name, but it was too late then."

"Too late, what do you mean too late?" Kathleen glared at him angrily.

"Darling, do be reasonable, it is thirty years since the eviction."

"Well it seems like yesterday to me, surely you're not trying to excuse that monstrous family?"

"Of course I'm not, but it wasn't him, it was his father, Cecil Rothmere," Garth reasoned.

"And how do you know Cecil Rothmere won't be dining with us next week at Kenmare, that's assuming I go of course, which is most unlikely."

"Lord Cecil died, four years ago."

"Who told you that?" Kathleen gasped.

"I read the obituary in *'The Times'*."

"Why didn't you tell me the good news?" she asked with scathing sarcasm.

"I didn't tell you," he answered slowly, "because I didn't want to stir up bad memories, and it seems I was justified."

"You wouldn't expect me to be delirious hearing that despicable name would you?"

"No of course not," he said, "but Kathleen please, it isn't like you to behave like this." Taking hold of her gently by the shoulders he asked, "Doesn't the good book say *'render unto no man evil for evil but keep conquering'*..."

"The evil with the good," Kathleen interposed as she lowered her eyes, "yes I suppose it does."

"Love builds up and heals the wounds but hatred destroys, wouldn't you say?"

She nodded slowly, "Yes, you're right," her eyes met his gaze, "I'm sorry," she said "I was furious, I could have strangled him with my bare hands when I knew who he was."

"And that isn't Christian, is it?" he asked with gentle reproach.

She sighed, "No darling, it isn't Christian. I'm sorry I was so nasty to you." She rested her head against his shoulder and he wrapped his arms around her.

"You like him don't you?" she whispered.

"Yes I do, I'm looking forward to tonight. What will you do if he asks you to dance with him?"

She sighed again and replied, "I will have to accept graciously, I suppose."

"Will you promise me something darling?"

"What?"

"Will you promise me you won't mention the past. What possible good could it do now? The past is the past and nothing can change it."

"Of course, I promise," she smiled up at him and they

kissed.

"We must hurry and dress for the dance. What are you going to wear?"

"The emerald green off the shoulder gown we bought in Cork."

"Good, you look ravishing in that."

Bantry house seemed more magnificent than ever that night, and Lord Simon Rothmere was devastatingly charming. The more distant Kathleen behaved towards him, the more his eyes expressed his admiration for her.

As they danced together in the long library, he complimented, "Your husband is a very fortunate man, Mrs. Armstrong. May I call you Kathleen?"

"You may," she smiled at him then quipped back, "I'm a very fortunate woman to have such a fine husband Simon."

And so it was that the Armstrongs and the Rothmeres became firm friends.

By August 1911, Kathleen had been proudly presented with five grandchildren - a son and a daughter, born to James and Sarah, and three daughters to Peter and Elizabeth. The five were to be the first of many, and Seafield House, especially in the summer time, resounded to the happy cries of the young ones.

Kathleen's American born teenage nephews, Patrick, Seamus, Eamonn and Sean, also visited regularly from nearby Glengarriff. The youngest, thirteen year old Sean, was her firm favourite.

Lord Simon and Lady Isabella Rothmere would always spend a great deal of time with the Armstrongs, whenever they were in Ireland to the never-ending indignant disgust, and disapproval, of Kathleen's sister Eileen.

The governess, Mary McCoy, began courting with John O Mahony, a native of Bantry town. Pearl doted on her pony; she and her mother would spend many happy hours riding out over the hills. David wasn't keen on horses but he enjoyed fishing, he often brought home salmon and trout to help fill the larder. Seamus and Maureen loved their cottage, they continued to work, and to enjoy themselves with a will.

When the time approached for the long promised visit to Sheelagh in America, it was decided that Aunt Maureen and also Eileen should accompany them, as well as David and Pearl. Everyone was overjoyed when Garth arranged to book their passage on the beautiful new ship, the *'R.M..S.Titanic'*, due to sail from Southampton on her maiden voyage, on Wednesday April 10th 1912.

"Everyone's talking about her darling, she's a wonderful ship, absolutely unsinkable," Garth enthused.

"Will we have to travel to Southampton?" Kathleen queried.

"No, that's the beauty of it, she's calling at Queenstown, so we can travel from Bantry to Cork, then Portsmouth, Virginia, U.S.A. here we come! I've booked one of the largest cabins, so who knows, we may even dine with the Captain."

"Sounds wonderful darling."

"Where will Aunt Maureen and Aunt Eileen sleep?" David wanted to know.

"They will have a cabin quite near to us," his father reassured him.

"What will we do on that big ship?"

"We'll play games on the deck, there'll be concerts

and shops, and lots of things to do," Kathleen informed him.

"David will be seasick," Pearl chirped in, "he's always sick when we sail to England."

"I won't be sick on a big ship like the Titanic, it won't toss about like the little ones."

"You'll get sick just the same, I know you will. You even get sick in the car."

"Now Pearl be quiet. David can't help being sick, go and play with your dolls," Kathleen scolded.

When they were both out of earshot Garth asked, "Pearl won't be seasick will she darling?"

"She never has been, why do you say that?" Kathleen queried.

"She was probably conceived when we were crossing the Irish Sea, that's why I chose Pearl for her name."

Kathleen laughed, "I don't imagine there are oysters in the Irish Sea Garth."

"You were the oyster darling, and a very tasty morsel too, if I may say so."

"Really Garth," Kathleen chided humorously, "I've been called many things in my time, but never an oyster. I suppose you chose Mavourneen because we were coming back to Ireland, but Pearl; if she'd been a boy I suppose you would have named him Jolly Jack Tar."

Garth took her in his arms, "I love you so much my sweet, I love you more as each year goes by. Why don't we go up to Dublin to do some shopping, it's ages since we stayed alone at the Gresham."

"That's a good idea, when shall we go?"

"How about next week?"

"Yes why not," Kathleen agreed.

"I'll phone the hotel now," Garth said, "I hope I can get through to Dublin, sometimes it takes ages."

"Yes, you do that darling and I'll write to Sheelagh. She'll be thrilled when she knows we've booked on the

'Titanic'."

Garth and Kathleen spent a few happy days together at Dublin. They told everyone they met how much they looked forward to sailing to America on the great new ship.

When the daffodils tossed their sprightly heads in March, the atmosphere and excitement at Seafield House was electric.

"I wish Aunt Eileen wasn't coming with us," Pearl remarked one day. "She'll be bossing me all the time, I know she will."

"You mustn't talk about your aunt in that manner," her father scolded. "She wishes to see your Aunt Sheelagh again and she'll be company for Aunt Maureen."

"Have you decided to take the car?" Kathleen asked.

"No, we should be able to hire one over there, that's if I can persuade myself to drive on the wrong side of the road for three months. Did I tell you, I'm ordering a new car for when we return?"

"What is it like Daddy, can I see a picture?" David asked eagerly.

"Yes, there's one in the *'Cork Examiner'*, I'll get it for you."

Garth went into his study to get the newspaper. He picked it up and looked at the date which was Wednesday April 3rd 1912, the thought flashed through his mind, "This time next week, we'll be waiting in Cork for one fantastic ocean liner."

Walking back into the drawing room he glanced through the window as he saw a telegraph boy easily recognized by his navy blue uniform and red pill box hat, cycling down the driveway towards the front door. A few seconds later, the doorbell clanged and Garth hurried to answer.

He met the maid in the hallway, "It's all right Sally, I'll see to it."

He opened the solid oak door, "Telegram sir, for Mr. Garth Armstrong."

"Thank you" Garth said, taking a threepenny bit from his pocket as a tip for the boy as he handed him a small buff coloured envelope. Tearing open the telegram from Bury he read: *"Father very ill. Please come at once. Mother."* His left hand went up to his forehead as he stared at the words.

"Bad news sir?" the boy inquired.

"Yes, it's bad news," Garth responded slowly, "very bad."

"Is there a reply sir?"

"Err no, no thank you, no reply," Garth stammered.

The boy continued to stand in the doorway, then he coughed loudly.

"Oh yes, there you are," Garth handed him the coin and Kathleen came into the hall.

"What is it darling, a telegram?"

"Yes it's Dad," he answered.

She took the paper from him as he sat down heavily by the hall table.

Kathleen let out a cry, "Oh no, he can't be, not when we're goin to Am...." Seeing Garth's shocked expression she cut short the inopportune remark. Standing by him, she took his head in her hands, he put his arms around her and began to weep quietly.

Sally came out into the hall again, Kathleen shook her head and the maid quickly returned to the scullery.

Ten minutes later, they sat together in the drawing room. Garth had composed himself and was attempting to take control of the situation.

Forgetting about the picture of the car, David had gone out to the garden.

"We'll collect Maureen from the cottage and take her to see Eileen," Garth said. "They're both going to be dreadfully disappointed to say the least."

Half an hour later, Garth, Kathleen and Aunt Maureen drove along the Bantry Bay coast road to Glengarriff. Arriving at the small hotel where Patrick, Eileen's oldest son was serving in the bar Garth asked, "Is your mother at home Patrick?"

"Yes she is." Puzzled to see the three sad faces he requested, "Will you go through to the living room?"

Enjoying their usual quiet elevenses, Eileen and her tall, sandy haired husband were very surprised to see the unexpected visitors. Patrick stood up as the women entered the room.

"Hello," Eileen greeted. Her face paled when no one answered. "Whatever's the matter?"

The women sat down but Garth remained standing. "I'm afraid it's bad news," he held out the telegram to Eileen. After reading she remained silent for a few moments, then with all eyes looking upon her she said, "I'm very sorry Garth, it must be very serious for your mother to send for you, especially when she knows you're due to sail next week. I hope your father will recover soon." She continued in a subdued tone, "I had a premonition that something was going to go wrong. It all seemed too good to be true, poor Sheelagh, she'll be so disappointed."

"Yes she will," Garth agreed. "Whilst my father is sick I won't be able to go in the near future, we can't expect James to carry all the responsibility at the Mill. But….," he paused before continuing, "We've been wondering, there's no reason why you and Maureen shouldn't go next week as we planned."

Eileen did not answer but Maureen said, "We left the children in tears, they've been looking forward to the holiday so much."

Eileen responded, "If we are going, surely they could come with us, they would love it on the farm with Sheelagh's children and" she paused thoughtfully, "it would give you and

Kathleen more freedom to help your parents."

Garth looked at Kathleen as the thought flashed through her mind what Pearl had said about her bossy Aunt Eileen and David being sea sick. "I don't know," she hesitated, "We've never been separated from them for so long."

"They'll be all right with us," Maureen said as she extended a comforting hand towards Kathleen. "We'll look after them, they're growing up now, David's eleven now and Pearl is nearly ten."

Kathleen smiled sadly at her aunt, "Yes I know you'd look after them but..."

"Would you be able to take them all to the ship at Queenstown, Patrick?" Garth intervened as though he had already made up his mind and the matter was settled.

"Yes of course, no problem," Patrick agreed. "What a dreadful shame you can't go, you've waited so long."

"Thank you Patrick, I can hardly believe we're not going. We'll have to go to the shipping office in Liverpool tomorrow," Garth continued, "I'll show them the telegram and cancel the two-berth cabin and then," addressing the two women, "the four of you can be together in ours."

"That's very generous of you Garth," Eileen said. "Have you time for a drink, then you can go and give the children the good news."

"Yes, just a quick one," Garth replied, "then we must get back, we've such a lot to do."

Arriving back at Seafield, he decided to have a quiet word with Kathleen. "Darling why don't you go with them, then perhaps I might be able to come over for a couple of weeks in June, when dad's feeling better. You know how

232

devastated Sheelagh will be if you don't go."

"Do you really want us to be separated for three months?"

"No, you know I don't but…"

"That settles it then, I'm staying with you where I belong. All right?"

"He kissed her and agreed, "Yes love, all right, but we must hurry with the packing, it's a long ride to Dublin. I hate travelling at night but this time it can't be avoided."

Before leaving, Kathleen quickly telephoned her friend Arethusa, at Bantry House, with the news about Garth's father. They would not be sailing on the Titanic after all!

Seventy-year old William Armstrong was in a private ward at Bury Infirmary, and was not expected to live much longer. His lungs, having been weakened over the years by his constant cigar smoking habit, were ceasing to function. Arriving at the hospital, Kathleen and Garth found Gertrude and Rosie, the two women who enjoyed such a close relationship, sitting by his bedside. He hardly recognized Garth, and in his lucid moments, he kept asking his wife for his hat and coat, so he could go to the Mill.

He died on the following Wednesday, when Garth was sitting with him at 2.30 in the morning. It was the dawn of the day when the mighty *'Titanic'* was due to sail, amidst a thousand cheers, from Southampton to New York. His two beloved grandchildren were being taken to Cork City to board the magnificent liner when she reached the shores of southern Ireland.

The cotton mill was closed on Monday April 15th the day of the funeral. William had been born in the village of Ainsworth and that was where he had requested to be buried.

The clock on the square church tower pointed to the hour of three p.m. The funeral cortege, and the very large gathering of mourners, filed into the church for the service.

As is the custom in the north of England, the chief mourners, many of whom had travelled a considerable distance, were accorded hospitality, usually at a hotel or restaurant immediately following the burial. The funeral of William Armstrong was no exception, a very substantial meal was provided in the upstairs function room at the Royal Hotel, Silver Street, Bury.

It was 5.30 p.m. when the mourners, who were still seated around the long tables after the meal, were chatting away quite cheerfully. Only the elderly widow sat quietly sipping tea watching the others whilst lost in her own thoughts. One or two of the men had drifted down to the ground floor bar to enjoy a pint of the best Bury Brewery beer, the main topic of conversation being the estimated amount the old man had left in his will, and the beneficiaries.

Their interest in this subject changed dramatically however as the cry of a news boy drifted in from the street outside. "Extra, extra read all about it – Titanic hits iceberg – read all about it." He pushed his way with his arms full of newspapers through the revolving doors and into the bar, "*Evening Chronicle* sir?"

"Yes lad" the man said, taking the paper, "What's all t' shoutin' about?"

"Titanic mister, she's down," the unkempt boy replied.

"Nay lad, don't be daft, Titanic? It's unsinkable!"

"It was, but it's not any more, look what paper says." He held up the Manchester newspaper with the glaring black headlines for everyone to see '**TITANIC HITS ICEBERG – MANY LIVES FEARED LOST**'.

Unable to believe their eyes, the men handed over the coppers to the boy and began to read.

"There's a funeral party going on upstairs lad," the barman said, "you'd better take some up there."

The boy quickly mounted the stairs with his arms full of the dreaded news.

Kathleen was chatting away to Sarah about the antics of her grandchildren when the bold type headlines screamed at her as the boy held up the papers.

Clutching Sarah's arm and dropping her glass on the table she shouted "DEAR GOD NO –IT CAN'T BE, NO! Jumping up from her chair she rushed round the table and grabbed at a paper. The room swirled around she slumped against the table, and collapsed in a heap on the floor.

Most of the mourners knew that the two grandchildren of the late William Armstrong had sailed on the 'Titanic'. Garth was in the gentlemen's room when the papers were brought up. Walking back into the dining room he could not understand the screams and cries of the women, the rustle of newspapers and the silence of the men.

Then he saw the reason for himself, and he shouted "OH GOD, OH MY GOD, NO IT CAN'T BE." Grabbing at a paper the awful words floated before his eyes, just as the flotsam from that mighty ship was floating in the icy cold waters of the north Atlantic Ocean, including his own child's favourite doll. Not realizing that Kathleen had fainted, he sat stunned, trying to read the smaller print but the words kept swimming together.

Thomas O Sullivan sat with his head in his hands. "Please God keep my Mammy safe," he prayed. "Please God keep her safe, please God," then he started to sob and his wife tried to comfort him.

Scarcely knowing what he was doing, Garth poured a glass of brandy for Kathleen, before he discovered that Liz was supporting her mother as she lay on the floor.

"Don't worry," Peter said, in an attempt to console his inconsolable mother in law, "There are plenty of lifeboats, they'll be all right."

"I should have gone with my babies," Kathleen sobbed, "I should have gone with them."

"I'm glad you didn't," cried the weeping Liz as she held her sobbing mother in her arms.

They were staying with Garth's mother and Rosie at 'The Gables'. Garth tried his best, with the help of the Bury Police and the 'News Chronicle', to find out the fate of their loved ones.

Frantic telephone calls were coming through from a distraught Patrick and Seamus in Ireland. Hundreds of lives had been lost, that was all they knew. They could only endure in agony and pray. Kathleen had never lived through such dreadful hours. Garth kept dosing her with brandy to try to get her to sleep. The hours extended to days whilst they hoped for news.

Garth had been sitting for interminable hours in the 'News Chronicle' office, when at last the names of survivors began to come through from New York to London and then to Manchester. He stared for hours with aching eyes as the lists of survivors appeared with other news on the teleprinter. Then he saw the four precious names he had waited for – Eileen Finnerty, Maureen O Sullivan, David Armstrong, Pearl Armstrong.

"Thank God, thank God," he muttered to himself. Jumping up, he hurried to the nearest telephone, having to wait impatiently, in the large newspaper office until there was a telephone free. His voice choked as he finally begged the operator to connect him to Bury 324. He held back tears whilst he waited for the answering click and Kathleen's anxious response.

"Hello," she said.

"They're safe Kathleen, they're safe!"

Kathleen did not answer, whilst he waited. "Kathleen, are you there?"

"Yes," she sobbed down the telephone, trying her best to control herself. "Are you sure, are they safe?"

"Yes, I've seen all their names, they're safe." The tears of relief rolled down his face.

"Come home now darling," she sobbed with tears of gratitude.

"I'm coming, I'll be back as soon as I can," he assured her as he hung up the receiver.

The news of the dreadful disaster continued in the papers each day, the awful truth emerging that more than fifteen hundred people had perished. There had been a shortage of lifeboats and yet some of them had even left the ship half-empty. The rule of women and children first had torn so many husbands away from their weeping wives, the wives being condemned to sail away from the ship in the lifeboats whilst their beloved ones were sucked down into that icy tomb.

Kathleen and Garth learned to love each other more than ever during those following days, not daring to think of what might have been.

The summer of 1914 was gloriously hot. Rosie married her policeman, Edward Ramsbottom, on August 1st and war was declared on the 4th. David followed in James's footsteps attending Bury Grammar School and Pearl began to attend Liz's old school for young ladies at St.Anne's-on-Sea.

The time that Garth and Kathleen were able to spend in Ireland became more and more reduced and the possibility of a visit to America, during wartime, was out of the question. James had made some remarkable improvements at the Mill. He had installed a first aid room, extractor fans and adequate heating and ventilation. Weavers with babies, under twelve months old, were no longer allowed to start work before 8.00 a.m. Consequently, Armstrong's Mill became noted as one of the most advanced in the north of England. The weaving of mattress covers was soon converted to fulfil Admiralty orders for navy blue cloth, to make naval uniforms. Everyone hoped the war would be over by Christmas, but the end of 1914 came and went, and the fighting continued on.

Gertrude Armstrong died in February 1915. 'The Gables' was left in her will to Garth, and a very generous sum of money was left to Rosie, which she used to purchase a fine house for herself and Edward at Holcombe village.

The young men of Europe were slaughtering and maiming each other in bloody combat. "What good can all this fighting possibly do?" Kathleen grieved. She read the newspapers each day, spending more and more of her time knitting balaclava helmets, scarves and socks for the soldiers suffering in the mud and flea ridden trenches in France.

Peter Lambe joined the Royal Flying Corps, leaving his beloved Liz to cope with her four daughters and another one soon to be born.

Ireland was in turmoil like a cauldron on the boil. For hundreds of years she had suffered under the despicable cruelty of British Protestant rule. Now the fuse, for the Southern Catholic rebellion had been lit by the rising of Protestant Orangemen, under Sir Edward Carson, in the North.

British and Irish soldiers, fighting the Germans side by side in Europe, sang together the rousing marching song *'It's a long way to Tipperary, It's a long way to go'*.

"Yes it is a long way to Tipperary," Kathleen mused. "How many British people even know where Tipperary is?"she wondered. "They probably think it's in Africa or somewhere else, anywhere but Ireland. Irish blood is being shed for the land of hope and glory, whilst the Irish are rebelling at home against their Imperial masters."

Kathleen turned these thoughts over in her mind as she pondered the plight of her countrymen. Refusing to change their religion, their culture and their language had meant the denial, not only of material progress, but their basic human rights as well. No Catholic Irishman had been allowed to practice his religion, to hold any position such as a doctor, lawyer, politician or teacher. Men would risk their lives in order to teach the children, hidden away in the corners of fields known as hedge schools, receiving payment from the impoverished villagers of food instead of money. Of course, should they decide to change their religion, then that would be another story. 'All part of man's inhumanity to man' as Garth would tell her.

One day, shortly after the Easter rising in Dublin in April 1916, James invited his mother to have lunch with him at the Boar's Head Hotel, saying he wished to discuss something with her. They had almost finished a good wartime meal when he broached the subject uppermost in his mind, "Do you think we'll be eating many more meals like this?" he asked.

"I hope so," Kathleen replied, "Why do you ask?"

"I ask because the Germans are sinking hundreds of tons of merchant shipping every month."

"Is this why you asked me to dine with you, warning me it's almost my last meal?" she teased.

"No it isn't, but I do want to help the war effort. I've been here in Bury long enough."

"What are you saying James? Do you want to go sticking cold steel into German bellies?"

James took up his glass, frowning at his mother and taking a good drink from his scotch and soda he said, "Don't speak like that mother, it's vulgar."

"All right James, what shall I speak like then?" she asked scathingly.

"I'm thirty-two, I should be at the front line in France with all the rest," he protested.

"You're not the only one exempt from military service, you work very hard making cloth for naval uniforms. Someone has to do your job."

"Oh yes," he scoffed, "amongst a lot of women and a few old men." Changing his tone he continued, "I was thinking of joining the Royal Flying Corps like Peter, since Mr. and Mrs. Kirkman died I feel more free to go."

"What about Sarah and the children?" Kathleen asked.

"Sarah seems to think I should go, her parents keep hinting in their letters, her brother's a naval lieutenant you know."

"Yes, I know, but what about Garth's attacks of malaria, what would happen at the Mill if he couldn't work?"

"Then you would have to step in to run things."

"Me?"

"Yes mother. Other women are working on munitions, so why shouldn't you be running the Mill?"

Silence fell between the two as the waitress came with the bill and James paid for the meal. Kathleen sat looking solemn with her hands clasped in her lap. James went out to the gents and when he returned to the table, he sat down again to finish his drink.

"Do you remember when Garth came back from South Africa and we were drinking champagne?" Kathleen asked.

James nodded, "Yes I do, what about it?"

"I distinctly remember Garth saying that war is a filthy business, and asking you to keep out of it. This war is far worse than the Boer War James."

"This is a holy war the British are fighting mother."

"Holy means clean James, there's nothing clean about muddy battlefields and fly infested corpses. War is God dishonouring and despicably filthy."

"But if none of us went to fight, we'd be over run."

"No James you're wrong, if no one fought, there would be no wars, and all those dead bodies wouldn't be piling up at Verdun."

"But Mam," he protested, "the Prussians started it."

"Yes they did, and no doubt intended to contain it, but it grew too big for everyone, and now look where we are, in the middle of a World War." Kathleen spoke quietly but her indignation brought the colour to her face. "There's something else as well," she continued.

"What's that?"

"Your Finnerty cousins will probably be fighting in Ireland against the British."

"That's not surprising. They were reared on hatred for the British."

"So if you joined the British Army, you could end up killing your own Irish cousins."

"Heaven forbid! Could be Thomas O Sullivan himself I'd be fighting," he joked.

"It's nothing to joke about James. If England was at war with America, you'd be killing your Zaltowski cousins, or it could be their cousins, if England was fighting the Russians. It's just a sickening merry go round, absolutely preposterous."

"All right mother, I understand your argument, but time is getting on, I have an appointment at two."

"You wanted my opinion James, so what do you think

about it?" Kathleen persisted.

"I'm going to think about it, I'll let you know."

"I'll pray about your decision James."

"You do that Mam," he answered as he helped her on with her coat.

James's ultimate resolve to avoid the war if at all possible was followed by devastating news. Liz's husband Peter lay seriously wounded in St.Dunstan's Eye Hospital. Liz travelled down on a crowded train with her mother and Garth. Arriving at the hospital, overflowing with wounded, they found that Peter had lost the sight of both eyes. His bright red wavy hair hung over the white, blood stained bandages swathed around his head, as he groped for Liz's hand.

Kathleen had never beheld a sight more devastating as all those pitiable young men in the ward, every one now unable to see. Peter's face had been so handsome, his eyes so beautifully big and blue. He had never seen his fifth daughter and now he never would, Liz shed bitter tears at the abominable realization that her Peter would never be able to see her again. Kathleen and Garth sat waiting at the entrance to the ward whilst the tragic young couple tried to build some semblance of hope from their shattered lives. Whilst she waited, Kathleen scribbled one of her little poems:

> *"Oh War! Oh evil monster which*
> *Hath o'er the world,*
> *The crimson flag*
> *Of wrath unfurled,*
> *Till nought is ours*
> *Which yet imparts*
> *The sting, of thine impassioned darts,*
> *Impoverished, Wordless, Hypocrisy,*
> *Thy stain imposéd ruthlessly,*
> *Stung to retort in calumny*
> *As woman, deserted, wantonly!"*

Kathleen took on the task, for the next three months, of caring for her grand daughters. Liz stayed close to the hospital to encourage Peter every day.

It was May 1917 when the Armstrong family attended the funeral in Sussex of Lady Isabella Rothmere. Lord Simon, a Brigadier in the Royal Sussex Regiment had twice been to the war front in Belgium, but most of the time he was able to keep an eagle eye on the prosperity of his vast estate at Brindle. After the death of the Lady Isabella, David and Pearl began to spend many enjoyable vacations in the company of His Lordship at Brindle Hall.

James had received two white feathers and the contempt of former friends, before his call-up papers dropped through the letterbox at 'Arbour Lea' in the spring of 1918.
Garth came home from the Mill with the news, "James's exemption is cancelled, his call-up papers arrived this morning."

"What did James say?" Kathleen asked.

"What can he say, he'll have to go. This war is a monster with a voracious appetite. It won't be satisfied till it's sucked all the young men down it's greedy throttle."

Whilst listening to Garth, Kathleen was sitting at the bureau writing to Seamus and Maureen. Putting down the pen, she went out into the hall where she picked up the telephone. "Whitefield 370," she requested the operator.

The response came from her daughter in law.

"That you Sarah?" Kathleen asked.

"Yes Mother, I was going to ring you, I think Jane has the whooping cough."

"Oh dear that is nasty, I am sorry. Have you called the Doctor?"

"No, not yet, I'm going to call him first thing in the morning."

"How are the others?" Kathleen asked.

"They're all right yet, but I suppose they're bound to get it. Didn't you talk about burning a camphorated oil lamp for whooping cough?"

"Yes I did, put one in Jane's room, and make sure you keep all the bedroom fires going well, children need to be kept warm."

"Yes, I'll do that, I've got Nanny to help me, she's very good."

"Good, will you phone me after the Doctor's been?"

"Yes, don't you worry, I'll take good care of them."

"Yes I know you will Sarah. Is James there please?"

"Yes, I'll call him."

Kathleen waited to hear James's voice.

"Hello mother, can I help?"

"Is Sarah listening James?"

"No," he replied as he watched his wife ascending the wide staircase.

"Garth tells me you've got your military call-up papers."

"Yes I'm afraid I have."

"Burn them James."

"What mother," James asked, unable to trust his hearing. "What did you say?"

"I said burn them, in the fire, destroy them."

"You can't be serious."

"I was never more serious."

"But," he protested as Kathleen interrupted.

"Burn them, and if they send you any more, burn those as

well, then it will be too late and the war will be over."

There was a long pause, "James, are you there?"

"Yes I'm here."

"Did you hear what I said?"

"Yes I did. I was about to fill the forms up ready to post them to-morrow."

"Don't do that James, just put them on the fire. Hurry up, do it now, I'll wait on the line, go on."

"There's no need for you to wait, I promise, I'll burn them, there's a good fire in the drawing room, it will give me the greatest of pleasure."

He heard his mother's deep sigh at the other end of the line before she said, "Good night James."

"Good night Mam," he replied, "Sleep well."

Everyone went wild with joy when the armistice was declared on November 11th 1918. It was a week later when Kathleen answered the telephone at 'The Gables'. The operator requested her to stand by please for a long distance call from Paris, France.

Wondering who the caller could be, Kathleen waited patiently until the English operator announced, your caller's on the line, go ahead please."

"Hello," she responded.

"The voice of a young man with a pronounced American accent questioned, "Is that Mrs. Armstrong?"

"Yes speaking."

"Aunt Kathleen?"

"Yes, who is it please?" The two voices shouted and then receded on the atmospheric waves.

"It's Sergei and Daniel, my brother Daniel's here. We're in Paris. Can you hear me?"

Kathleen trembled slightly as she shouted back "Yes Sergie," her voice choked with emotion, "I can hear you."

"We have some furlough," he explained, "Can we come to see you?"

"Yes yes, yes of course you can. When will you come?"

"Soon Aunt Kathleen, soon. We'll phone you when we get to London, England. Is that O.K.?"

"Yes Sergei, O.K. O.K. We'll look forward to that."

"Your time is up caller," the crisp voice intervened.

Kathleen held on to the receiver, "Goodbye Sergei, Goodbye Daniel, see you soon?" The line crackled loudly but she was in raptures as she replaced the receiver.

David came to see what all the fuss was about. "Who was it Mother?" he asked.

"It's your cousins in Paris, they're coming to see us before they go home to the States."

"Two more real live Americans coming here, yippee!"

"Yes, we'll have a big party for them, we'll invite lots of friends, perhaps we may be able to take them to Ireland to meet all their relations over there. I must tell your father," she said as she picked up the receiver again to relay the good news to Garth at the Mill.

At the end of the war, the rider of the blood red war horse of the Apocalypse restrained his steed for a time. The rider of the black horse of famine followed relentlessly in his wake and the sickly pale green horse, whose rider's name is death and hades, pursued him at full gallop. So it was as a result of the pestilence of Spanish influenza, (which claimed more than twenty million lives throughout the earth), that

Edward, the beloved husband of Arethuse Leigh-White, and the owner of Bantry House and Estates, died in a London Hotel, on February 28th .1920, at the age of forty-four.

At the beginning of March, a letter addressed to Kathleen arrived at 'The Gables'. John and Sally O Brien had been left to take care of Seafield House whilst the Armstrongs were absent from Bantry. The letter read:

Dear Mrs. Armstrong,

Your Uncle Seamus has asked me to write to tell you that your Aunt Maureen is very poorly. He begs you to come home to Bantry as soon as you can. She has been ill for the past three weeks and is getting worse all the time. Everything at the house is all right except the telephone, we cannot use it because of the troubles. There is a lot of fighting and burning all over Ireland, especially in the city of Dublin, so please be careful when you come over. Times are so bad, the people hate those British Black and Tans. I am sorry to be the bearer of such bad news.

John sends kind regards to yourself and Mr. Garth.

Your very willing servant,
Sally.

Arriving in Dublin on March 7th 1920, as the Anglo-Irish War of Independence continued to rage; Kathleen and Garth were fortunate to obtain a room at the Gresham. Two of the hotels in O'Connell Street had already been destroyed, with the consequence that business at their honeymoon hotel was flourishing.

This time the journey from Dublin to Bantry was a nightmare. They were compelled to change trains repeatedly and each train travelled slower than the last. Every train crew dreaded booby traps, especially when transporting the hated Black and Tan British troops. Bridges were being blown up and houses burned throughout the country. Often two English houses would be burned for every Irish one burned, the Armstrongs dreaded what they would find on their arrival at Bantry. Would the fact that their Irish servants, John and Sally O Brien were resident at Seafield House, safeguard their Irish home?

Whilst changing trains at Mallow, they were horrified to hear sniper fire outside the station. They had left Dublin early in the morning, it was now six thirty in the evening and even a cup of tea was hard to come by. They were very weary and beginning to feel sick with hunger.

It was late evening before they were thankfully supervising the unloading of their luggage for the final time that day from a guardsvan. This time it was Bantry station. Home at last! John O Brien had been waiting for them on and off for hours. Dressed in gaiters, peaked cap and chauffeurs' uniform, he still looked very spruce.

"Have you been waiting long John?" Kathleen asked, as their luggage was loaded into the enormous boot of the gleaming Rolls Royce. "We've had a dreadful journey."

"Sorry about that Ma'am, we'll soon have you home now," John reassured them.

"How is my aunt?" Kathleen was anxious to know.

"She's very poorly I'm afraid, Doctor says 'tis cancer of the stomach."

"Oh no, not that," Kathleen groaned at the awful news. "Can we go straight to the cottage?" she pleaded with Garth.

"Yes of course darling, but I expect Sally has prepared some food for us, and we don't want anything to spoil, do we?" Garth was so hungry he felt he could eat the proverbial horse.

"If you wish, I'll bring some food to the cottage Sir?"

"That would be kind of you John, we would appreciate that. Will you drive us straight to the cottage then please?"

"Yes Sir I will," Kathleen sensed that he was very glad to have them back after their long absence.

The evening was cold and the black rain clouds scudded over Bantry bay. They entered the cottage where the sick woman lay on a bed in the corner of the downstairs living room. Seamus welcomed them in, relieved and overcome with emotion at seeing them again.

Maureen looked many years older than sixty-seven, and Kathleen's tears dropped unashamedly onto the pillow as she embraced her loved one. The woman who had come so close to replacing her mother, smiled and bravely did her best to chat to her niece.

Kathleen was determined that Maureen should have all the expert nursing care that money could buy. The following day, a bed was prepared ready for the new patient, at the Bantry hospital, situated high above Bantry town. During the journey in the ambulance, Maureen winced each time the solid tyres bumped over the ruts and potholes in the road, causing her so much more pain and discomfort.

"Hold on to me my love, we'll soon be there," Kathleen attempted to assure her.

Her Aunt lay precariously strapped to a canvas stretcher, the thick red woollen blankets seeming as though they would completely envelop the frail little woman. Arriving at the hospital, she was duly installed in a private ward. Her family would be allowed to visit as often as they wished.

Shortly after her aunt's admission to Bantry hospital, Kathleen called to commiserate with her friend Arethusa, who had also recently returned to Ireland, for the funeral of her husband in Bantry. She had been living with her two teenage daughters Clodagh and Rachel in England. The two women sat together in the beautiful Rose Drawing Room. Having been empty for some considerable time, most of the furniture in Bantry House remained under dust covers. Kathleen listened with deep sorrow as the young, premature widow, wearing full black mourning dress, related the tragic events of the past few months.

Arethusa related with pride, just how much her Edward had been loved by all and sundry in Bantry, telling Kathleen how one local man had been heard to say, "It was the grandest funeral you ever saw, every tinker in the countryside was at it."

Bravely she fought back her tears, inquiring of Kathleen, "How are you and the family, my dear?"

"Garth and the family are well, but my Aunt is dying, she is in Bantry hospital, I'm afraid."

"Oh I am sorry Kathleen."

Kathleen shook her head and placed her hand over the other woman's, "No please" she said, "I must not burden you with my troubles, you have..." she stopped mid sentence.

Arethusa, in an effort to hide her grief, turned to pull the bell sash by the side of the fireplace and drew her blue mohair shawl more tightly around her shoulders. A manservant entered the room.

"Could you please attend to the fire Michael." The conversation resumed when he had done her bidding and left the room.

"I'm so sorry Kathleen, I'm afraid I'm very worried."

Kathleen waited whilst her friend gained composure and continued, "It's this military situation, they're threatening to take over the house."

"Take over the house," Kathleen queried, "you mean this house, who is?"

"The British Army, this house has been listed for troop occupation."

"Troop occupation – Bantry House?" Kathleen was astonished. "They can't do that!"

Arethusa stood up by the 18th Century fireplace said to have come from the Petit Trianon at Versailles. Drumming her fingers nervously on the white mantelpiece she said, "I'm afraid they can and they will, unless some miracle happens to stop them."

Kathleen looked up at the Aubusson Royal Tapestry hanging above the fireplace, it was made for Marie Antoinette on her marriage to the Dauphine and its magnificence was awe-inspiring. Her thoughts went through a flight of fancy as she imagined soldiers in army boots, trampling through the stately home and across the sweeping lawns. Looking up at the Waterford crystal chandelier she said, "I can't imagine it, surely they can't just take over?"

"But that isn't the worst of it Kathleen," Arethusa continued, "If the British do occupy the house, the I.R.A. will possibly attack and no doubt burn it down."

Kathleen gasped and her eyes widened in horror. "No please, that would be sacrilege, is there nothing that can be done?"

"Nothing short of a miracle I'm afraid, I've done my best to think of a way out but I can think of nothing. The house has been left in trust for Clodagh but I am afraid there will be no house to inherit if the military have their way."

It was almost a week later when Kathleen answered the telephone call from Arethusa, whose voice was tense as she spoke, "I have found a way to save the house Kathleen."

"Have you really," Kathleen answered, "That's wonderful, but how?"

"The hospital has to be evacuated, I have asked the nuns and they have agreed to my plan."

"The hospital – you mean Bantry hospital – evacuated?" Kathleen could not believe her ears.

"Yes," Arethusa continued hastily, "we're going to move the patients over here into the library."

"The library? I'm sorry, I don't understand."

"The Hospital is to be moved to Bantry House."

"Bantry House? But my aunt, she's dying…"

"Yes, I'm sorry my dear, we will take every possible care, I promise." There was silence before Arethusa continued, "It's the only way to save the house, you remember I said only a miracle."

"Yes yes of course," Kathleen hesitated, "but I don't understand, why the hospital?"

"Because if the patients are moved to the house, the British Army will probably occupy the hospital."

"Oh I see, how ingenious."

"I'm so glad you think so Kathleen, but there's a tremendous amount of organizing to do and no time to lose. I was wondering, I know it's short notice, but would you and Garth come over this afternoon. I hate to ask, but I'm afraid we're going to need lots of willing hands, I'd be most grateful…"

Kathleen cut her friend short, "Please don't apologize, we'll do everything we can to help, anything at all. Will two o'clock be all right?"

There was a very audible sigh of relief before she replied, "Yes thank you so much that will be fine; goodbye."

"Goodbye," Kathleen replied. Replacing the receiver she hurried to tell Garth the amazing news.

A watery sun shone down on the morning when the twenty-six patients, men, women and children were being transported from the hospital to Bantry House. The Sisters of the Convent of Mercy and others had worked like trojans during the previous days. Equipment had been packed and moved, transforming the library of the stately home into a sanctuary where the sick and infirm could be nursed. A chapel was sanctified in the library.

It was indeed a motley procession of horse and cart, donkey car and motor vehicle transportation. The patients were wrapped in blankets and supported on mattresses and pillows. The nuns and other helpers walked beside, or rode with the patients, down the steep main street of the town to Wolfe Tone Square, and round to the entrance to Bantry House. The public gathered into groups on the narrow pavements, many of them making the sign of the cross as the sick ones passed by.

Within days rumours began to circulate. The despised and dreaded British Black and Tans were starting to move into the vacated hospital premises from where they would seek to combat the activities of the Irish freedom fighters.

Arethusa Leigh-White had indeed succeeded in safeguarding the future of the magnificent ancestral home for posterity!

A stiff wind was blowing from the west across the bay the night when young Sean Finnerty, a proud member of the Coomhola Company, 5th Battalion, West Cork Flying Squad, moved stealthily with his comrades into the grounds of the former hospital, high above Bantry town. Sean and his colleagues were determined they would completely destroy the premises now used to shelter the British Military.

They were well equipped to carry out the task. The paraffin rags and the brushwood torches were ignited and their hearts leapt like the flames, as they anticipated the subsequent panic and the speedy evacuation of their enemies, from their comfortable barracks.

Sean stood tall and broad shouldered, every inch the son of his Galway ancestors. His red hair matched the colour of the flames now dancing a bright reflection in his deep blue Irish eyes. He felt elated at his first encounter with the enemy. The smell of the raging fire, whipped up by the strong west wind, filled his nostrils. He listened as the glass window-panes cracked, watched as the smoke and the darting sparks shot away into the moonless midnight sky, now glowing red above the fire.

He heard the unfamiliar accents, as shouts from the enemy mingled with his commanding officer's call to withdraw, but silhouetted in the bright light from the fire, he became a prime target for an enemy bullet. His tall frame stumbled and he fell with a cry to the ground. The calf of his left leg burned as though pierced with a red-hot knife. His colleagues, who attempted to rescue him, were driven away by enemy fire.

In the affray he was left lying wounded, whilst the British soldiers forming a human chain, passed buckets of water in a vain effort to quench the roaring fire. He watched as the hundreds of sparks shot heavenwards, becoming terrified lest he should be set alight by the scattering fragments of burning red hot debris. The heat was intense and he grew ever weaker as the blood oozed out from the wound in his leg.

The blaze could be seen from as far away as Dursey Island and Mizen Head. Many residents of Bantry gazed up in fear and wonder as they watched their former hospital burn to the ground. The whole town was bathed in the awesome glow.

Unaware of the desperate plight of their nephew, Kathleen and Garth watched the fire from their bedroom window. Although on slightly higher ground, Seafield House was a mere seven hundred yards from the former building where mercy and loving kindness, had once reigned supreme.

"I definitely heard gunfire didn't you?" Garth asked as he stood in his dressing gown watching the blaze.

Kathleen had moved away from the window and was getting ready for bed. "Yes, I suppose I did, but I do wish we could have some peace, four years of fighting in Europe and now this."

":Yes, we never expected to see such sights in Bantry," Garth replied. "Just look at those flames, like Dantes inferno, not a ghost of a chance of putting it out."

"Perhaps that's how it will always be," Kathleen shuddered.

"What do you mean?"

"I mean that maybe the Irish will always be fighting the English, always fighting with no one able to put out the fire, just more and more suffering, without any hope of peace."

"I'm English and you're Irish and we don't fight," he jokingly attempted to cheer her. Then changing the subject he asked, "When is Pearl coming over from Sussex? It isn't safe travelling over here, you would think Simon would have the sense to make her stay in England."

Stifling her apprehension for her daughter's safety Kathleen replied, "No one can make Pearl do anything she doesn't want to do. I think she'll be here for the August bank holiday." Picking up Pearl's last letter from the corner of the dresser she leafed through the pages, Yes, they'll be here in a few weeks, time passes so quickly."

"Is Lord Rothmere coming too?" Garth asked.

"Yes of course," then thoughtfully she asked, "Do

you think it's right that they should spend so much time together?"

"Who Simon and Pearl? Yes of course, he's like an uncle to her. You know how much she loves the horses at Brindle."

"Well if you think it's all right darling." Kathleen shivered, "It's getting chilly in here, I hope the warming pan's still hot."

"Oh sorry my sweet, yes, you get into bed. "I'm going to carry on watching the fireworks," he said as he lifted the heavy copper warming pan, placing it between the sheets he pulled the long handle back and forth to air the bed. "That better darling?" he asked as Kathleen, in pink satin nightgown, slid down between the folds of best white Irish linen and he bent to kiss her. "Goodnight my love" he said then added, "I wonder where those soldiers will camp tonight, I don't suppose they'll get much sleep?"

"No, I don't think they will," Kathleen sighed as she snuggled down in the big four poster bed then as an after thought she added, "Just think of it, that would have been Bantry House burning now if the soldiers had been billeted there."

"Yes I suppose you're right, what a dreadful thought."

"Goodnight my love," Kathleen said. "Don't stay out of bed too long, you'll catch cold." She settled down to sleep, with a silent petition to her God to take care of her loved ones, especially those across the sea in England. She was unaware that her favourite nephew lay in desperate straits, terrified and bleeding profusely, beside the blazing fire of his own making.

The following day the town was abuzz with rumours

concerning events of the previous night. How a few of the soldiers had been injured, another killed maybe? No one knew the truth, they could only surmise. The hospitals gone, there's no doubt about that, burned to a cinder. Holy Mary what a night!

"They've taken one of them to Bantry House," one man said. "Out of his mind, howling his head off, God help him."

Kathleen drove with her Uncle Seamus through the town to Bantry House to visit Maureen whom they found in deep distress.

"It's our Sean she groaned, they brought him in last night." The tears ran down her cheeks, she pointed in her weak and feeble state towards the screen dividing off the male patients, from whence she had recognized the agonized cries and ramblings of her great nephew.

For the moment, Kathleen thought her aunt herself was delirious as she had often been during the past few days. She looked at her uncle, who thinking the same as herself, shook his head just as a tall, middle-aged nun came in through the door nearby.

"Come now Mrs. O Sullivan, you mustn't be upsetting yourself so, the young soldier is going to be all right, we're taking good care of him." She plumped up Maureen's pillows and tidied the bedside table, then turning to Kathleen she said quietly, "She's very weak Mrs. Armstrong, perhaps it would be best not to stay too long to-day."

"Yes Sister," Kathleen obediently nodded her agreement "but please Sister, could you tell me – the young man – perhaps he could be my nephew," she questioned hesitantly.

The two women had moved over by the window overlooking the one hundred stone steps, rising up through the shrubbery in the beautiful terraced garden at the back of the house.

"Your nephew?" the nun queried.

"Yes Sister."

"Why do you think he's your nephew?" she spoke slowly and deliberately, in a vain effort to disguise her weariness.

"My aunt," Kathleen gestured towards the bed where Seamus sat, attempting to console his wife.

The nun raised her eyebrows, plainly expressing the question, "How can you believe the incoherent ravings of a dying old woman?" Then thinking better of it she said, "There's a chance you may know him, so there'll be no harm if you look, he's in the first bed near the door." Pointing past the grey marble pillars she turned on her low heel shoes.

Kathleen followed her across the highly polished wooden floor, the unsolicited reflection passing through her mind, how she had danced in this room in happier days.

As the Sister held back a fold of the screen surrounding the young man's bed, Kathleen gasped her recognition of the deathly white features and the halo of copper red hair resting on the firm white pillow. "Oh no, it is – it's our Sean," Kathleen moved to the head of the bed and the Sister closed the screen.

Heavily dosed with morphine, his hair and skin damp with sweat, Sean lay in a drugged stupor.

"He had no identification," the Sister explained. "The soldiers brought him here in the middle of the night, he had a bullet in his leg, we had to operate. Christ have mercy on him." The Sister crossed herself.

"The soldiers," Kathleen queried as she remembered the two British soldiers guarding the entrance to the house as they came in. "You mean the British?"

"Tis the same," the nun whispered. "They've taken him prisoner, God help him."

Taking a face cloth from the side of the bed, Kathleen

proceeded to wipe Sean's brow, she listened as the nun continued. "He should have been taken to the British military hospital at Bandon but it was too late in the night, the soldiers needed rest themselves so they brought him here. We must thank the Lord for His mercy, we must so."

"Yes Sister, indeed we must," Kathleen agreed. "I must go to Glengarriff to tell his mother." The tears welled in her eyes as she gazed at his deathly pallor.

"I doubt if he'll be conscious at all to-day but his mother will want to see him of course," the Sister sighed, revealing her obvious tiredness. "Mother Superior will be coming down soon," she muttered as if to herself.

Moved with empathy, Kathleen pleaded, "Is there anything I can do to help?"

"No my dear, the Lord is with us. You be away on your errand of mercy, we'll see you to-morrow, God willing."

As John O Brien drove Kathleen away through the lodge gates of Bantry House they saw the two soldiers again, but this time knowing just who they were posted to guard.

"They don't need to worry," Kathleen thought, "Sean won't be going anywhere for quite some time. How would Eileen and Patrick receive the news, she dreaded having to tell them."

The two sisters had seen more of each other recently during sick visits to their aunt's bedside, than they had for many years. Travelling along the coast road, where she had first ridden so many years ago in the donkey car with James, Kathleen's thoughts dwelt on her unhappy relationship with Eileen. "We're not like sisters at all, we have so little in common. She's never forgiven me for changing my religion and associating with the Rothmeres, and now this war is making matters worse. Catholic against Protestant, just like it's always been. I'd love to talk to her but she's so disgustingly prejudiced, she won't listen. If two so-called Christian sisters can't get along together, it's no wonder there are wars."

Arriving at the quaint village of Glengarriff, a gorgeous beauty spot and tourist haunt, John parked the car on the cobblestones outside the Finnerty's Bar. All eyes turned as the fashionably dressed Mrs. Armstrong entered the bar, and one or two of the men frowned suspiciously. Her brother-in-law was serving.

"Is Eileen in Patrick?" she asked, thinking how much Sean resembled his father.

"Yes," he said, "she's in the back, is Aunt Maureen worse?"

Kathleen shook her head and whispered to him, "It's bad news Patrick, it's Sean, he's been wounded." She watched his shocked expression, "Will you tell Eileen?" she pleaded relieved that she did not have to break the devastating news to her sister herself.

She followed Patrick through to the living quarters. They could see Eileen standing in the back kitchen with her hands in the sink. Seeing her sister who so rarely entered her home, Eileen suspected bad news. Reaching for a hand towel she walked from the kitchen into the living room. "Aunt Maureen?" she questioned.

Her husband shook his head, "No, it's not Maureen, sit down here," he said, indicating the sofa.

She sat down, holding the towel between her half-dried hands, "What is it?" she asked looking from one to the other.

"Sean's been wounded," Patrick told her whilst moving to sit beside her, his arm going around her shoulders. Then realizing that was all that he knew, he turned to Kathleen for more information.

She responded quietly, "I went to see Aunt Maureen and Sean was there – a bullet wound in his leg. They took him into Bantry House in the middle of the night."

"Who did?" Patrick wanted to know.

"The British."

"God have mercy," Eileen buried her face in the towel.

"I'm afraid he's been taken prisoner. Didn't you realize there was something wrong when he didn't come home last night?"

"He hasn't been home for over a week," Patrick answered, "he's been training with the Flying Squad."

"He's very poorly," Kathleen told them, "I think he's lost a lot of blood, you must go to see him."

Eileen's hands dropped from her tear stained face to her lap, "We can't go together" she said, "One of us has to stay to look after the bar."

"I'll do that" Kathleen offered without hesitation. "I used to be a barmaid so I'll manage all right."

"That's very good of you," her sister spoke softly.

"Tis nothing at all," Kathleen chided gently and reached for her hand. They held each other tightly and wept on each other's shoulders, whilst Patrick looked on. It was the first time the sisters had loved each other since Eileen had returned from her voyage on the *'Titanic'*, but now, at last, all grievances were forgotten in their mutual anxiety for Sean.

261

Death arrived mercifully for Aunt Maureen on the last day of May at four o'clock in the afternoon. Kathleen felt as though she had lost a mother for the second time in her life. She watched as her Uncle Seamus, sitting beside his wife's bed, wept uncontrollably. He had lost his bride of forty-nine years and he was inconsolable. The ceremonial removal of the body from Bantry House to the Chapel of Rest was arranged for Friday evening. The funeral would take place on Saturday morning at St.Finbarr's Church.

An idea suddenly came to Kathleen. She discussed it with the nuns who agreed to the plan, with the approval of Father O Connor of course. Kathleen put her suggestion to the Priest privately, as they sat together in the vestry at St.Finbarr's. He chuckled and nodded as Kathleen explained her scheme and it began to take shape in his mind.

"The Lord be praised," he said, "'tis a grand idea. Don't you be worryin' now my dear, I'll make certain the biggest crowd in Bantry town will be at the removal tomorrow night, I will for sure."

Kathleen sighed with relief and thanked the Priest.

"I'm hoping to take him back with us to England," she told him. "He won't be safe here after what has happened."

"Well now, that will be up to the young man himself. Lets get him out from under the noses of them soldiers afore we talk about that now eh!"

When Friday evening came, Sean was laid fully clothed, wrapped in blankets with a pillow for his head, on a large board secured to the axle of the cart which was to bear his Great Aunt's body from Bantry House. The bier was draped with the largest green baize cloth the Priest could lay his hands on. As he had promised, the crowd was large indeed and the horse moved slowly, pulling the burden of the living and the dead, down the winding path to the lodge gates where the British soldier guards saluted, in tribute to the dead, as the coffin passed by.

When the cortege arrived at the Chapel of Rest, the tears of the Finnerty family changed to tears of joy as Sean appeared amongst them, as it seemed from nowhere.

Kathleen waited until after seven o'clock before she was able to talk to him alone. His family had gone home leaving him in the care of the Priest and his brother Patrick. He would not leave the chapel until after nightfall. After the service she approached him as he sat watching the yellow flames of the altar candles and those surrounding the coffin. He smiled at her as she sat down beside him in the shadowy pew.

Speaking softly he said, "I want to thank you Aunt Kathleen for everything you've done for me, I'll never forget your kindness."

"You're not safe yet though are you?" Kathleen whispered. "We can come back for you after dark, they'll never think of looking for you at Seafield."

"But I can't do that can I?"

"You can come back to England with us, you're Uncle Garth will find work for you and you'll be safe." Kathleen spoke with satisfaction, everything was going according to plan. "All right Sean," she said, "We'll be back for you about nine o'clock."

As Kathleen was getting up to leave, the young man placed his hand on her arm, "Aunt Kathleen" he pleaded, "I can't go with you, I'm sorry, I know you've done so much but…"

"But what, why can't you?

"I," he hesitated, "I have to stay here and carry on the fight."

"Oh no!" Kathleen gasped. "Stay and fight, your leg isn't better yet, you've still got the bandages on, you mustn't stay here," Kathleen was horrified.

He raised his head in defiance and the venomous change in his tone struck fear in her heart. "We've suffered them pompous divels far too long, we have to get them out of Ireland."

"But the British have been here for hundreds of years," Kathleen protested. "You'll never get them out of Ireland, you're trying to fight the greatest Empire this world has ever seen."

"Empire or no Empire, they'll be out of Ireland soon. Here, read that," he said as he handed her a crumpled piece of paper.

Kathleen stood up to read the scribbled verse by the light of the altar candles.

> *Forget not the Boys of Kilmichael,*
> *Those brave men so firm and so true,*
> *Who fought neath the banner of Fenian*
> *To conquer the red white and blue.*

Kathleen stared at the paper as Father O Connor approached the altar. She turned to appeal to him. "Father," thank you for helping to rescue my nephew. We want to take him to England where he'll be well cared for but..." she hesitated as out of the corner of her eye, she saw Sean, and his brother who had joined him, shaking their heads towards the Priest.

There was silence until, the Priest, addressing Kathleen said, "Wouldn't you be knowing, you yourself being an Irish colleen, the men of Ireland have a duty to their country. You must allow the man to decide for himself, so you must."

Kathleen was mortified. She looked again at Sean

264

who lowering his eyes made no response. So it was, for the second time in her life, she was appalled at the opinion of an Irish Catholic Priest. With tears in her eyes she handed the paper back to her nephew whom she had desperately wanted to help. "I'm sorry Sean," she choked on the words, "Goodbye now."

Hurrying out of the Chapel, she got into the car where Garth waited for her. The tears of sadness, anger and frustration stinging her eyes, "I never intended…" she sobbed, "Its all gone horribly wrong, he's going back to fight."

"This life is full of surprises darling," Garth attempted to console her, "it very rarely turns out as we expect. Come on, let's go home."

.

CHAPTER SIX.
AS THE YEARS ROLL ON

It was a hot day at the end of July when the party of four arrived at Seafield house. They had journeyed from Brindle Hall, Sussex, by chauffeured limousine to Fishguard, then by sea to Cork. In order to command an escort of British Army outriders from Cork to Bantry, Brigadier Rothmere had chosen to travel in Army uniform. Whether or not his action was a wise one, Kathleen and Garth were not too sure. However, the travellers arrived safely and were welcomed with joy. David had brought his fiancee Diana to meet his parents. She was a true English rose, with blonde hair and brown eyes. Kathleen knew instinctively that she was going to get along famously with her daughter in law to be.

On arrival, Pearl made an early request that Simon should stay for most of the month's vacation at Seafield, instead of alone at his rambling Kenmare mansion. Kathleen and Garth were happy to accede to her request. It was the following afternoon before her reason became apparent. Kathleen was upstairs in Pearl's room helping her to sort through her wardrobe. David and Diana were out riding, Garth and Simon were walking together around the gardens.

Looking down from the open window Kathleen remarked, "We ought to be outside with Daddy and Simon, it's such a lovely day."

"Perhaps we shouldn't disturb them," Pearl replied hastily as her normally pale complexion heightened.

"Why, what do you mean," Kathleen said sensing the tension. "Is there some secret?" she replied jokingly.

"Don't be silly Mother, how should I know?"

"I think you know more than I do," Kathleen probed. "Why are you so up tight?"

Pearl looked straight at her mother as she quickly answered, "Simon's asking Daddy for my hand, we're in love, we want to be married."

"Married – to Lord Simon – but he's – but you're –" Kathleen was speechless. In spite of the fact that she had suspected something untoward, she was not prepared for her daughter's revelation.

Pearl replied with deliberation, "You were going to say Mother, that Simon's too old, but he's not too old, he's only forty-six and I love him."

"But you're only nineteen, how can you be sure?"

"I am sure, he's a wonderful person, so kind, so loveable. I'll never marry anyone else Mother, I've loved him since the day we met on the road from Barley Cove, remember?"

"How could I ever forget," Kathleen murmured. "You were only a child."

"But I'm not a child now, I'll be twenty next year."

"We must see what your father says, do you think Simon will have asked him?"

"Yes, he said he was going to ask Daddy this afternoon, that's why I came up here. Just think of it, when we're married I'll be a Baroness, Lady Rothmere.

The wedding took place at the Parish Church of Brindle on July 21st 1921. It was a comparatively quiet family affair. Post war rationing was still in force, sumptuous food being difficult to obtain. To avoid any jealousy, the two oldest daughters of James and Elizabeth were chosen to be bridesmaids.

"I have so many nephews and nieces," Pearl declared, "I can't possibly have them all in the bridal party."

A reception for one hundred guests was held at the ancestral home of Brindle Hall.

James amused his Mother when he remarked, "If only the neighbours in Garden Street, Bury could see us now, they would be surprised. Just imagine the daughter of Kathleen Duffy, married to a Lord of the Realm, well I never!"

Pearl and Simon spent their honeymoon in the south of France. In spite of the twenty-seven year age difference, they were very much in love. Eleven months after the wedding, Kathleen became a grandmother for the eighteenth time. James had four sons and four daughters, Elizabeth seven daughters, and Rosie gave birth to two sons, the eldest now promising to become a famous dress designer.

Simon and Pearl named their son Edward Simon. Two years later they were blessed with a daughter whom they named Kathleen Rosalind, she became known as Kate for short.

"Do you realise, our grandson Edward will one day be Baron Rothmere?" Garth stated.

"Yes, I do indeed," Kathleen answered.

When Pearl became twenty-one, her Mother wrote a verse:

> *"You are Twenty-One*
> *And the leaves of life*
> *Have fallen gently for you,*
> *As the years roll on*
> *From Twenty-One*
> *May the gentle leaves blossom anew."*

Ten months after Pearl's wedding, Kathleen and Garth again had reason to journey to the south of England, this time to Hampshire. David's fiancee Diana had been killed in a riding accident.

After the funeral David told his parents, "No one will ever replace Diana, I will never marry."

On July 9th.1921, hopes had been high that peace would reign in Ireland. The dashing leader Michael Collins had signed a Peace Treaty with the British. The War of Independence came to an end, only to be replaced by Civil War between the two opposing elements of the Sinn Fein Party, those accepting the truce with Britain and those refusing to accept it.

The Armstrongs returned to life at 'The Gables', once again leaving Seafield House in the care of John and Sally O Brien, but this time taking Uncle Seamus, whose grief was profound, to Bury with them. He could pass his days helping in the garden.

It was July 6th.1922 when the *'Irish Independent'* newspaper gave a detailed description of the destruction.

Garth read some of the account recounted in *'The Times'* aloud to Kathleen, "just listen to this,"

1.30 p.m.- several portions of the burning building collapsed simultaneously and only skeleton walls remain. The fire begins to die down and the buildings on each side appear to have escaped catching alight.

2.30 p.m.- The Gresham Hotel was noticed to be in flames in the front ground floor. The fire spread rapidly to Sir J.Mackey's Seed Stores, and pushed along to the rear. The southerly breeze carrying the flames northwards across Findlater's Place, towards Parnell Street.

Kathleen interrupted, "Please don't read any more Darling, it's just too dreadful for words, I can't bear to think of that hotel destroyed, we'll never be able to go there again,"

Almost seven weeks later on August 22nd the I.R.A. leader, Michael Collins, was shot dead. Kathleen's nephew, Sean Finnerty, lived to see his beloved Ireland free from British rule, but his left leg, becoming gangrenous, needed to be amputated, after his return to the training ground at Kealkil.

The Irish Civil War ended in 1923 and on April 24th, Garth and Kathleen sailed out from Liverpool on the Mauretania on their long awaited trip to America. They were met at the New York dockside by their nephew Sergei who drove them south down to Portsmouth, Virginia. It was such a joy for the two sisters to be together again after almost nineteen years. They had so much to talk about, so much to tell each other. Kathleen and Garth were thrilled to meet their brother in law Alexander, for the first time ever. He had come to America at the age of twelve but still retained a Russian accent. Kathleen loved to listen to him.

The farmhouse was large, built of wood with a front porch verandah where they could sit enjoying the sunshine, looking out on a rolling vista of cornfields. The Zaltowski's had arranged to take a holiday with Kathleen and Garth at Fort Lauderdale, Florida.

The two couples drove down the interstate highway to stay for two weeks at a hotel overlooking the beach. The weather was hot but not unbearable, the food was delicious and the service second to none. They spent fourteen unforgettable days in this place named after Fort Lauder, the Scottish Castle situated south of Edinburgh. They despised the segregation and servitude of the black Americans.

"It's man's inhumanity to man rearing its ugly head again," Garth would remark.

Before returning home, sailing from New York, Sheelagh and Alexander agreed to visit England for Kathleen and Garth's silver wedding celebration in September 1925.

As time is wont to do when one becomes advanced in years, the next two years passed very quickly. Kathleen was almost sixty-one years old, a great grandmother to Elizabeth's first grandson, when the time came to celebrate the anniversary. Garth was merely a young fifty-nine years.

The party was held at the Derby Hall, Bury. They had looked forward to this day so much and what a wonderful time it turned out to be. Guests, including children and grandchildren, nieces and nephews, came from Ireland, America and many parts of England. Kathleen and Garth waltzed together, even more in love than they had been the night they danced in this hall at the turn of the century. Many guests needed to be accommodated at 'The Gables' and 'Arbour Lea', The Derby and The Boar's Head hotels. It was a great joy to take Sheelagh back to Ireland to visit Kilgarvan where she had not been for forty-two years. She wept at seeing the old country once again.

A further memorable time for celebration came on April 16th.1927, when it was possible for Kathleen and Garth to stay in one of the 120 apartments at the re-opening of the newly built Gresham Hotel, Dublin. The *'Irish Independent'* of April 18th 1927 gave a full report of the opening:

"The new Gresham Hotel, which was formally opened on Saturday, April 16th.1927, marks a very definite step in the restoration of the portion of O Connell Street destroyed in the troubles of 1922. The new building surpasses the Gresham of pre-1922 in every respect"

In future years, Kathleen and Garth were to spend many happy hours at their honeymoon hotel. The V.I.P. suites were said to rival even the Churchill suite at the Hotel de Paris, Monte Carlo. Kings, Princes, Presidents and many famous film stars would be future guests at The Gresham in Dublin.

At Garth's request, Lord Simon Rothmere was never told about the eviction causing so much devastation to Kathleen and her family. One day the idea came to Garth, he would ask his lordly son in law to sell him the land where Kathleen had been born. He would have a small holiday home built there and surprise Kathleen. Granted the land would eventually belong to their grandson Edward but he wanted it now, whilst Kathleen was still young enough to enjoy it.

In the event, Lord Simon would not hear of any money changing hands for the eighteen acres of land his father in law wished to possess in the village of Kilgarvan. He arranged for the legal exchange to be carried out by his Dublin Solicitors forthwith.

It was to Kathleen's undoubted joy and amazement in June 1934 that Garth instructed her to get into the passenger seat of her own Baby Austin car. "Why do we have to go in my car?" she queried. "What's wrong with the Rolls?"

"Nothing darling, we'll be driving on some narrow roads, your car is easier to manoeuvre."

It was a lovely sunny afternoon with very clear visibility.

"Where are we going," Kathleen was curious.

"We're going for a ride," Garth replied as he drove along the Bantry Bay coast road turning right along the road following the course of the Coomhola River. Then turning left they began to climb the steep and narrow mountain road.

After they had driven about two miles, climbing all the time, Kathleen asked, "Are you sure it's safe to drive over here?"

"Safer than a donkey and car perhaps?" he replied. "You've told me about this road so many times, I've been determined one day to explore it."

"But this is the road to Kilgarvan darling, where I came with Daddy and James."

"Yes I know it is, that's why we're going this way."

"Isn't it beautiful, I told you it was. It's even more fantastic than I remember it."

Garth was compelled to drive very slowly on the very narrow mountain road. Fortunately no other vehicles or horse and cart would normally venture along it.

Eventually dropping down toward Kilgarvan Garth said, "We'll go back along the main road, I'm not going to venture over that road again, but before we go back I have something to show you."

Kathleen laughed, "What can you possibly show me I haven't already seen in Kilgarvan."

"Oh you'd be surprised my dear," he joked, "Places do change you know, even Kilgarvan." Stopping the car, and pointing across the field to the left he said, "Isn't that where you used to live?"

"Oh look, there's a house, someone's built a house on our land."

"Yes it was your land darling," he said whilst unable to conceal the excitement of surprising his beloved. Taking a bunch of brand new keys from his pocket, he handed them to his wife. Leaning over to kiss her cheek he said, "And it's your house too darling, I hope you like it. Shall we walk up the driveway?"

Opening the car door Kathleen got out, "Not our house?" she said, "on our land, Garth, how did you do it?" The tears began to stream down her face.

"Here, I thought you might need this," he handed her his large white handkerchief, "Don't blow your nose on it," he laughed, "the house isn't furnished, that's your department."

"Garth, how can I ever thank you, it's so wonderful, the children will be able to come for holidays, they'll see where I used to live won't they?"

Turning to her husband she put her arms round his neck and the elderly couple embraced in the bright June sunshine. The bitter memories of the eviction were to be replaced by future happy, holiday times!

The happy couple continued to live a long and peaceful life at Seafield House and 'The Gables'. In 1938 Kathleen was surprised to read the news that the Georgian mansion, 'Alderley Park' the home of Lord Stanley of Alderley, had been destroyed by fire. The Italian style lodge gatehouse, where she had first lived as a young bride, was undamaged.

David Armstrong remained a bachelor. He devoted the best years of his life to running Armstrong's Mill with James and Cousin Thomas O Sullivan, until King Cotton no longer reigned supreme in Lancashire. The Mill was sold in 1939.

Kathleen and Garth drove to the cinema in Cork City in 1942 to see the much talked about film, 'Gone With the Wind' which they thoroughly enjoyed. It was the last excursion they ever had together. Death claimed Garth at the age of seventy-nine.

Having no will to live without her beloved one, Kathleen died three weeks later, the last words on her lips, "Thy will be done on earth."

The devoted couple were laid to rest beneath the green growth of shamrock, in the tiny graveyard, by the shore of Bantry Bay, where Kathleen had requested her brother so long ago, **"When I die James, will you bury me here?"**